Andre Norton

VICTORY
on
JANUS

FAWCETT CREST • NEW YORK

VICTORY ON JANUS

Published by Fawcett Crest Books, a unit of CBS Publications, the Consumer Publishing Division of CBS Inc., by arrangement with Harcourt Brace Jovanovich

ISBN: 0-449-24216-1

THIS BOOK CONTAINS THE COMPLETE TEXT OF THE ORIGINAL HARDCOVER EDITION.

Printed in the United States of America

First Fawcett Crest printing: January 1980

10   9   8   7   6   5   4   3   2

The girl's body had fallen between two rocks. Ayyar saw it first, tried to fend off Illylle, but she had already seen it and pushed past him. Her horror faded as she leaned closer. The hounds had shredded away the girl's throat, but there was no blood—only wires, broken bits of metal, and cogs.

Illylle drew a deep breath. "The stench of evil has not been washed away by the rain. This, too, is of the White Forest . . . the work of our Enemy."

And suddenly Ayyar began to realize that the false Iftin, who wore their shapes and defied detection, were only to be part of the incredible struggle for survival that lay before them. . . .

A WINTER SUN was sullen red over Janus. Its bleak rays lit up the Forest that was being destroyed. Flame bit, grinding machines tore life from soil-deep roots. Quivering branches clicked together a warning that reached into Iftcan-of-the-trees, the city that once had been.

And in the heart of a mighty tree, Iftsiga, the last of the Great Crowns that still leafed and had sap blood, the indwellers it sheltered stirred from the depths of hibernation.

Larsh! Out of memory nearly as old as Iftsiga itself came that name. Death by the beast men. Out, brothers, defend Iftcan with sword and heart! Face the Larsh—

Ayyar struggled wildly with the covering over him, forced open unwilling eyes. It was dark here in the core of the giant tree. The summer festoons of lorgas, the light-larvae, were missing. Like all else they slept, snug in the crevices of the sheltering bark. But it was no longer quiet. About him like a wall was a trembling, a throbbing. And though Ayyar could not truly remember having heard it before, he recognized the alarm of the Forest Citadel.

"Awake! Danger comes!" Every throb of that great pulse beat through him. But it was so hard to move. The lethargy that had gripped him and his kin in the fall, that had brought them to shelter and sleep, had not lifted gradually as nature intended. Ayyar was not yet ready to face the new life of spring. Painfully he crawled from his nest of mats.

"Jarvas? Rizak?" His voice was hoarse and rusty as he called to those sharing this chamber. The force of the warning grew stronger, urging him to—flight!

Flight—not battle— That from Iftsiga, the stronghold that even the ancient Enemy could not reduce? Had the great tree not been seeded in the legendary time of the Blue Leaf, been grown to shelter the race of Iftin in the day of the Green, and of the Gray of the last disaster, outlasting the wrath of the Larsh, preserved to help awaken the Iftin anew? This was Iftsiga, the Eternal—yet the warning was—

"Flee! Flee!"

Ayyar crept to the nearest wall of the tree, put his shaking hands on that living surface. Now it was warm beneath his cold flesh, as if its life arose to fever pitch.

"Jarvas?" He clawed his way up, swaying. There was movement in the other two bed places.

"The Larsh?" That question came from the gloom on his right.

"Not so. Remember, the day of the Larsh is past."

Once again his memory had to be welded—for he bore the memories of two different men, as did all those now within Iftsiga. In an earlier time, he had been Naill Renfro, an off-world labor slave. Ayyar's lips drew into a snarl in reaction to that memory. As Naill he had found a treasure within the woodland. And because he had dug it up, the dreaded Green Sick had struck him down.

From that terrible illness he had emerged as an Ift, green-skinned, hairless, forest-attuned, provided with the tattered memory of Ayyar, Captain of the Outer Guard in the last days of Iftcan. And as Ayyar-Naill he had found others like himself—Ashla of Himmer's garth or settlement, who became Illylle, one-time priestess of the Mir-

2

ror, Jarvas-Pate, Lokatath-Derek, Rizak-Munro, Kele-mark-Torry.

Over the South Sea were still others who had earlier undergone the same change. But they were such a very few, for not all off-worlders were to be drawn into the net of the buried treasures set by the first Iftin-kind at their dying; only those who had the right temperament. And none of the changelings were truly whole. In them was an uneasy balance; one past set against the other. So was he now sometimes Ayyar, sometimes Naill, though for longer periods now Naill slept and he could draw upon the knowledge of Ayyar.

"There is death abroad." Ayyar spoke now. "The warning—"

"True. And the time of sleep not yet done." Jarvas answered him. "But we must have the awakening draught—"

In the gloom Jarvas crawled on hands and knees to the opposite wall, his hands fumbling with what was set into the living fabric of the tree.

"Ah—Iftsiga denies us not!" His cry was one of wonder and hope.

Ayyar lurched across the chamber. Jarvas drank from the spout set in the wall, not waiting for a cup, but catching the sweet sap in his hands, sucking it avidly from his palms. Ayyar followed his example.

The chill in him vanished, warmth sped along his veins, spread through his body. He could move easily, and his mind cleared.

"What is it?" Rizak crept up to drink in turn.

"Death—death to Iftsiga!" Jarvas stood tall. "Listen!"

The murmur, the crackle of branch against branch, was

a struggle of the ancient tree to communicate with the Iftins—or the half-Iftins—now within it.

Jarvas swung around. "From the east it comes!"

To the east lay the clearings of the garths, the settlements that were black death blots in the Forest. There, too, were the buildings of the port where off-world spacers set down.

"Why—what?" Rizak turned, refreshed from his sap drink. "They do not clear land in winter, and this is not yet spring."

"We shall find the answer only by seeking it," Jarvas replied. "Iftsiga would not wake us, except in extremity. This is grave danger—"

"The others—" Ayyar went to the ladder which led both down and up in the center of the chamber, linking all levels of the tree tower.

"Jarvas? Ayyar?" A soft call came from below, even as he set foot on the ladder rungs. He looked down into a face turned up to his.

"Haste, oh, make haste!" Illylle's voice arose. "We must haste!" She moved before him, descending to yet another level where many small chests stood stacked against the walls.

There were the others, Kelemark and Lokatath, pulling at those boxes, moving in frantic haste to drag them to the ladder which led on down, deep into the earth and root chambers of Iftsiga.

"The seeds!" Illylle lifted one of the chests. "We must save the seeds!"

With her words a sharp urgency struck Ayyar also. Every one of those chests contained seed for the regrowth of the Iftin. In them were the treasure traps to draw new

4

changelings into their company. Should anything destroy
these chests their dream of a new nation would die. Yes,
above all, the seeds must be saved.

"Where?"

His night-oriented sight had grown keen since the sap-
drink, and he could read the sorrow on Illylle's face.

"Into the root chambers—"

Dreadful indeed must be the peril! To use the root
chambers meant that Iftsiga had no hope of survival. How
could Illylle be that sure—yet she was.

"The seeds—" She turned to summon Jarvas and
Rizak now on the ladder.

Jarvas nodded decisively. "The root chambers." He
did not ask, he ordered.

So they toiled, using their new-born strength, stripping
Iftsiga of the meaning it had held as the Citadel during
ages more than Ift or man could reckon, carrying those
precious chests, each with a sleeping memory and Ift
personality, to the farthest limit of the long roots and, in
doing so, killing the tree that had been the refuge and
shelter of their race. And ever, as they worked so
feverishly, the warnings heightened; the need for speed
enveloped them, so that they ran, pushed, carried as they
cleared one chamber, two, three, a fourth—

Then they were done, and Jarvas and Illylle, working
together, sealed the cramped ways through which they had
crawled and pushed their burdens, using the substance of
the tree, with earth and certain words to bind with power.

Then they came up into the entrance chamber from
which they could emerge upon a limb and let down a
ladder to the ground. There they gathered supplies to make
packs. Jarvas took command.

"Iftsiga dies; by what means we shall learn. But in its dying, may it also fight against those who destroy it. Thus—"

He and Illylle went, one to each wall, laying their hands against the tree's now shuddering surface, to speak almost as one:

"Let your spirit not depart gladly, Great One,
But harshly to those who come.
Of all the days, may this be the worst
For those who ill use you.
Die in battle; make of your branches swords,
Of your twigs needles to tear,
Of your sap poison to burn,
Of your trunk a crushing weight.
Die as you have lived, Ift-friend, Ift-protector,
That your seedlings may spring anew.
This be our promise, Iftsiga—
Your seed shall sprout with ours.
Ift-blood, sap-blood, shall be as one.
Ift to tree, tree to Ift!"

Around them the tree swayed; a sound came from the trunk and branch that was not a groan but rather the growl of beast aroused.

Then Jarvas gave his orders. "We must know the enemy, whence he comes, what he strives to do here. Scouts to east and north! And you, Sower of the Seed"—to Illylle he gave the old title—"to that which is our help, to the Mirror, that mayhap you can call upon what lies there to our aid—"

She shook her head slowly. "Once I did so, yes, but twice perhaps not. Illylle is not wholly Illylle. I have too many memories not rooted in Ift. But what I can do, I

6

shall. And"—she faced them—"brothers, let not death choose you. Ill-faced may be our stars, but still are we the new seeds, do not forget that!"

It was night, the time of the Iftin, as they came into the open. Around them was a flow of movement. Peecfrens slid swiftly along branches, leaping in bounds from one limb to another, their fur silver in the moonlight. Borfunds grunted and snorted below. Flying things sought the air. All the Forest dwellers were on the move. Most of them had roused from hibernation, but they were alert. None of them need Iftin fear. But other things, deadly enemies, might also be on the move.

"Hooo-ruurrru—"

It was a welcome cry that was also a querulous complaint. A large bird settled beside the Iftin, turning its tufted head to survey them sleepily, sullenly. The quarrin was an old hunting companion. Ayyar opened his mind to its thoughts.

"Break—tear—kill!" Red savagery answered him.

"Who?"

"Things that crawl! Hunt the false ones! Kill, kill, always kill!"

"Why—?"

The quarrin hissed, was gone on wide-spread wings.

"Things that crawl," Rizak repeated. "Earth-grubbers?" Out of his off-world past he made tentative identification.

Machines could alter the face of any planet, given the time and the determination of human will. But such machines were few on Janus. This world of trees had been pioneered by the Sky Lovers, a dour religious sect who worked with their hands and with the aid of animals, refusing to allow machines anywhere but at the port site. Earth-grubbers were not for Janus. Unless, since the Iftin had sought their winter sleep, some powerful change had been wrought in the world they wished to reclaim as their own.

"The port lies northeast," Kelemark said. "But why would they be using machines? The forces there keep within their own boundaries. And—in the winter—the Settlers would not be hunting 'monsters.' "

No, the Settlers on the garths would not stir after those they called "monsters" and who enticed hunters into the Forest.

"The garthmen would not use machines." Lokatath spoke positively. He had been one of them before the Green Sick change.

"Guessing will not provide us with the truth," Ayyar-Naill returned. He had been a soldier; his answer was action.

"Do not play your life too boldly," Illylle called after him.

He smiled at her. "I have been knocking on the door of death since I first walked this world. But I do not throw aside a sword when I go to face the kalcrok," he said, naming the most fearsome of the Forest enemies.

"Split up," Jarvas said as they moved through the frosted vegetation. "Then return to the Way to the Mirror. I think that is our safeguard."

They became a part of the Forest, each to find his own path north and east. Fewer animals passed now; some moving sluggishly as if their awaking from hibernation had been so recent they had not had a chance to drink sap.

Ayyar's nostrils expanded, cataloguing scents, wary

8

for the stink of kalcrok. There was the stench of man to beware of also—for man to an Iftin was an offense, carrying with him the smell of the death he dealt to Forest life—and perhaps they must now quest also for the odor of machines.

Kalcrok he did not scent. But man—yes—there was the taint of man on the air, to be easily trailed. He passed two of the Great Crowns, but these were bone-white, long since dead—probably from the time Larsh stormed Iftcan. Ayyar had been one of the defenders, but no small spark of memory remained past his first standing to arms. Had that first Ayyar "died" during that attack? They had no knowledge of how the personalities they now wore had been set within the treasure traps and then transferred by the Green Sick to off-world men and women. But Ayyar had been a city guard in the old days and now it would seem that Ayyar-Naill must play the same role.

The smell of man now mingled with an even worse stench as a pre-dawn wind puffed about him. It was the smell of burning, such as the garthmen did to clear their lands.

Dawn was near. Ayyar reached into an inner pocket of his green-brown-silver tunic. Kelemark, who had once been the medico known as Torry Ladion, had devised a daytime aid for light-dazzled Iftin eyes, goggles made of several layers of dried leaves. So equipped they could travel in all but the brightest sunlight.

That thick stench of burning could mask the odor of men. He must now depend upon sight. Around him the saplings, the brush, were leafless. Patches of blue-tinted snow lay in shadows. The air warmed as tendrils of smoke wove ribbons of mist from smoldering mats of blackened fibers. He looked through a shriveled screen into wide-spread desolation and again his lips were a-snarl.

When they had gone to sleep, the river had divided the remnants of Iftcan from the land of the garths. But now burnt paths stretched well back into the Forest. Each ran spear straight from a beamed ray. This was no garth work, but that of machines. Why? The officials at the port had no reason to clear land, in fact they were forbidden to.

Ayyar flitted along the edge of the ash-powdered strip, now and then covering nose and mouth with his hand as he passed some noisome pocket. The beaming had not been at random, but laid down with definite purpose. It was plainly meant as an assault against the whole of the Forest.

He now fronted open charred ground on which stood a machine, a dark box squatting sullenly on treads to take it across rough and broken ground. Farther off was an earth-grubber, its snout at present raised and motionless, but behind it lay soil, gouged and ravaged.

Dawn was very bright to Iftin eyes. Even with the goggles on Ayyar squinted. Beyond the machines was a hemisphere, as if the tortured soil had breathed forth a stained, dun-colored bubble. A camp!

Again this was no garthman's shelter, but the kind the port men brought with them. Ayyar called upon Naill memory as he searched for any official symbol that might identify the camp.

After the discovery of Janus the planet had been given to the Karbon Combine for exploitation, almost a hundred years ago. But they had done little with it. Then a galactic struggle, which had torn apart old alliances, devastated worlds, and made of Naill Renfro one of the homeless wanderers, had given the Sky Lovers a chance to buy out the Karbon interest, since the Combine had gone bankrupt. The war had given a death blow to many thrusts of space expansion and cut back for a time mankind's outward flow. Janus, with its wide, thickly forested continents, its narrow seas, its lack of any outstanding natural riches, had been easily relinquished to those who wanted it as a homeland.

Once it was assigned to the garthdwellers, off-world powers would have no reason to meddle with the planet. Their jurisdiction extended no further than the port. Yet now they were carrying on a systematic battle against the Forest.

There was no symbol on the bubble-tent, or on the other two smaller ones nearer the river. Ayyar settled himself to wait and watch. He knew the danger of over-confidence; yet he was sure that no man in that camp, or any garth of the tree-hating Settlers, could match an Ift in woodcraft. The dogs of the garths were to be feared, but here he did not smell dog.

The light grew stronger. He glanced back now and then at the Forest. The dead Great Crowns were bones. Around their huge trunks, roots spred out in high buttresses, taller by far than his head, dark caverns between their walls. In the old days one beat upon those, and the call would be repeated, so that in moments signals ran from one end of Iftcan to the other. But if one sounded such an alarm today, who was to answer? Unless troubled ghosts would gather, unable to defend their graves. Scraps of Ayyar memory stirred.

''Take into your hand a dead warrior's sword and beware, lest his spirit come to claim it—and you!''

Naill had such a sword. It lay smooth and straight

against him now, its hilt ready to his hand, its baldric across his shoulder. Naill had taken the sword, so he was Ayyar, to be claimed by Ayyar's battles.

There was movement at the nearer of the bubble shelters. A man came out. It was no garthman—he wore no brush of beard, nor their sad-dull, coarse clothing. He had on the uniform of port security. Then this *was* an official expedition. What *had* happened during Iftin slumber?

Ayyar measured by eye the distance to the machines, to the camp. The ground was far too clear to risk any advance on his part. And that physical and mental change that had so forcibly altered Naill into Ayyar had also planted deep in him a revulsion toward his former species. Even to plan close contact with them made him giddy with waves of sickness.

Yet the only means of learning the truth was to get within listening distance of those men. And once they manned the machines he would not dare to linger—there was too good a chance of being caught by the sweep of a beam ray.

More men came out of the sleeping quarters. Two wore guards' uniforms, the others the clothing of port workmen. But, Ayyar noted, they all went armed. Not with the stunners that were the usual planet side weapons—but with blasters, only issued on inhabited worlds under the most imperiled conditions! That was another reason to keep well out of range. Iftin swords were not equal to blasters.

The men went into another bubble—mess, probably. Then Ayyar heard the hum of a flitter. He froze under his change-color cloak. It was coming from the port and would set down not too far from his place of concealment.

Two men dropped from its cabin door. They walked, not to the camp, but to the beamer, one of them sighting along the dead paths its rays had cleared.

"—take us months to char this off. There is a whole continent to clear!"

He who did the sighting glanced over his shoulder. "We cannot wait for off-world help. You saw the Smatchz garth. And that was the third. As long as they have these forests for cover, we cannot track them."

"But *what* are they?"

The other shrugged. "Ask me after we catch one. As far as their *word* is concerned they are green devils. I"—he hesitated, running one hand along the ray tube almost caressingly—"was on Fenris and Lanthor during the war—and the Smatchz garth was worse than anything there. We face the hardest kind of war, hit and run attacks where the enemy has all the advantage. The only way to drive those green demons out is to blast away their cover!"

"Well, the sooner we get to it then. . . ."

They turned back to the camp. Ayyar watched them stop a little way from the shelters. There was a shimmer in the air; they stepped forward, once more the shimmer —but it was behind them. A force field! The camp was ringed by a force field! Which meant that those inside that barrier were guarded against some greatly feared danger.

Green demons from the forest? Ayyar glanced down at his own slender hand, at its green flesh. Could they have meant Iftin? No, that could not be. The only Iftin, except for those wintering across the South Sea, were those who had sheltered in Iftsiga. The "green demons" could not be Iftin—but then who or what?

II

FOR THE IFTINS there was an older, greater-to-be-feared Enemy than any from garth or port, THAT WHICH ABIDES. Of old the Larsh had been ITS army, issuing forth from the noisome Waste. Yet in that same grim desert stood an Ift refuge, the sanctuary of the Mirror of Thanth. Now under the sun, THAT'S weapon, Ayyar entered the time-worn road leading to the crater-cradle Mirror.

Could they summon again the Power of Thanth? Illylle and Jarvas had called up that force months ago, to battle by storm and flood the servants of THAT pinning the Enemy back into ITS own place. And the flood that had spilled over the rock lips of the Mirror has washed across part of the Waste, cleansing much of it from evil.

So much the Mirror had done for them. What more it might accomplish they did not know. Could it be used against off-world men and machines, bound by no natural law of Janus? To each planet its own mysteries, powers that were tools or weapons for its natives, but that had no meaning for invaders from other stars. To the Iftin, the Mirror and that which acted through it, were things of majesty and force. To others this might only be a lake of water in a basin of rock.

"Ayyar—"

He raised his head, for his eyes had been on the age-worn pavement under foot.

14

"Kelemark," he acknowledged. So he was not the first here.

As Ayyar, Kelemark wore cloak and pack and carried sword. But over his arm lay a length of cloth, stained and torn. From it came a smell that wrinkled Ayyar's nose.

It was a smell, not of man, nor the taint of machine —this was something else—insidious. So, having once filled his nostrils, the smell remained to poison each following breath. Yet otherwise that rag appeared a portion of Iftin cloak, for it was green-brown-silver, each color flowing into the other.

"What—?" Ayyar pointed to it.

"I found it caught on a thorn bush." Kelemark stretched out his arm. Suddenly the rag writhed, twisted as if it had life. With a startled exclamation Kelemark threw it from him. Now the odor was stronger, and they both moved back, standing instinctively on guard.

Ayyar's sword was out, though he did not remember drawing it. He held the blade, not with its point to an invisible foe, but gripping it just below the hilt, slanted skyward.

"Iftin sword, Iftin brand—
Light fails, Iftin stand.
Cool of dark, fire of noon—
Green of tree, evil's doom!

From his mixed memory came those words, as did the movements of his sword, back and forth, up and down. He was no Mirrormaster, nor Sower, nor Tender, nor Guardian—but a warrior. However, there were ancient safeguards against THAT as all men knew.

Now the sword he held blazed and dripped green fire, and those droplets ran along the ground to encircle the rag. Yet the fire did not destroy it; it only enwalled. He heard a cry from the stairway that led to the Mirror, the thud of running feet.

Illylle came in haste, and with her, Jarvas. But when they saw what lay upon the pavement, fire imprisoned, they halted.

"Who found this and where?" Jarvas asked.

"It was caught in a thorn bush near the burning," Kelemark answered. "I thought—I feared it was of ours. Then, when I picked it forth, I knew it was not, but that it was important."

Illylle dropped to her knees, staring at the rag. From her belt pouch she brought a white sliver of wood as long as her first finger. Though water had ofttimes washed this way, yet still were there pockets of sand, and one of these was nearby. She pointed the end of her sliver to that which lay within the ring of fire; then she touched that same end to the sand.

Her hold was loose, merely designed to keep the sliver erect. Now it moved, marking the sand. And the symbol that appeared there was a tree with three large leaves—Ift! But the sliver was not yet done, for it jerked between Illylle's supporting fingers, scoring out the leaves it had just drawn, altering them into angular bare branches.

Ayyar studied the marks. Those sharp branches, he had seen their like before.

"Ift—not—Ift—but of the Enemy!" Jarvas half whispered. "What is the meaning of this?"

He looked to Illylle who studied the drawing on the sand. She shook her head.

"This"—she pointed to the rag—"has the semblance

of Ift. Yet it is of the White Forest! I do not understand." She dropped the sliver and put her hand to her head. "So little can I remember! If we were of the true blood, more would be clear. But of this I am sure, what lies there is wholly evil and a weaving of deception."

Jarvas turned to the men. "What did you learn?"

Kelemark reported first. "They are on this side of the river, first burning and then grubbing. They are determined to erase the Forest—to kill it and its life."

"There is a camp of port men," Ayyar added. "And—" he repeated the conversation he had overheard.

"Green demons raiding garths!" Jarvas broke in. "But—*we* are the monsters their ignorance has feared for years. And we of Iftsiga are the only ones this side of the South Sea."

"There is one way to learn more—" Illylle arose. "I shall water-question at the Mirror. But"—she looked to Kelemark—"do you remain here, for until you are purified you may not approach Thanth."

She put no prohibition on Ayyar, so he followed as she and Jarvas climbed the stairway that led to the ledge above the silent, brooding lake in the crater cup, the repository or focus of a power they did not understand.

Once more Illylle went to her knees on the edge of that ledge, stretching out her arms over the water.

"Blessing upon the water which is of life," she said and then fell silent. She stooped to wet a finger tip, and this she raised to her lips that her words might give them the needed answer, her mind now open to the Mirror. When she spoke, she did not look at her companions but across the lake, and upon her was the aura of one who is a vessel of power.

"Ift is not Ift. Evil wears the semblance of right. One

17

defeat in battle does not end a war. The seed is endangered before the sowing—''

To Ayyar it made little sense. But he saw that Jarvas, perhaps by the power of interlocking thought the Mirrormasters once had, gained knowledge, his expression now being grimly dark. He put forth his hand to lay on Illylle's head. She blinked as an awareness of self flowed in.

"Come!" Jarvas brought them back to the walled road. Now Rizak and Lokatath were also there.

"Jarvas, there are Iftin—" Lokatath began.

"Not Iftin, true Iftin!" Illylle cried. "They may wear Iftin shapes, but they do the will of the White Forest, not the Green!"

Jarvas nodded. "It is so. THAT has not been defeated, only awakened. IT has set the off-worlders against us in this manner."

"They have overrun garths," Lokatath reported. "I hid in the river rocks and heard those at the camp speak of it. They have slain and destroyed, these false Iftin, in a manner to arouse garthmen and port against them, so that old differences are forgotten and all off-worlders unite to wipe out the Forest and any Iftin found there—without mercy."

"The Forest is very large," began Illylle. Then she looked to Jarvas. "Can they really do this thing?"

"There are few of them here now," he replied soberly. "But they must already have summoned off-planet help. Yes, they can do this, if such aid comes."

Ayyar's hand fell to his sword hilt. "If THAT uses them, as IT used the Larsh—"

"Yes," Jarvas agreed. "It was after my time that the Larsh became the weapons of THAT. My memory is of the Green Leaf, not the Gray. Now, it seems IT would use these off-worlders in the same fashion, perhaps to the same victorious end.''

''I wonder''—Ayyar put his thoughts into words—''does THAT always have to use others as tools? There was the space suit that herded Illylle and me into captivity—we never discovered what wore it. Was it not the same when THAT took you prisoner before us? Those wytes, ITS hounds, hunted us, and we felt the drawing of ITS power when we escaped to the Mirror. In Ayyar's day the Larsh were sent to pull down Iftcan. Now the off-worlders are provoked into serving ITS purposes. But never does THAT venture forth ITSELF. Why? What do you remember from the Oath of Kymon?''

''As to the nature of THAT?'' Kelemark asked. ''That is a thought, Jarvas. If IT is so strong, why—?''

''Kymon went into the White Forest and strove with THAT and forced upon IT the Oath, which held during the Blue Leaf and the Green, to be broken in the Gray.'' Illylle repeated well-known history.

''And the nature of THAT which he found in the White Forest?'' Ayyar persisted.

She shook her head. ''Jarvas?'' she appealed in turn.

''Nothing,'' he replied. ''IT uses mental control; we all know that. Beyond—'' He shrugged. ''Now, apparently, IT also has Iftin, or beings resembling Iftin, fighting for IT. Those Iftin we must seek.''

''Our noses should lead us.'' Rizak nodded to the rag.

''Meanwhile, the Forest dies,'' Illylle pointed out. ''What has been our hope? To raise up a new nation, then seek our freedom from an off-world colony under the law. If they continue to destroy our home, there will be no chance for us ever to treat with them.''

''She is right,'' Rizak agreed. ''We have to make them

understand what is really going on before they reach a point of no return for any of us!''

''And just how will you do this?'' challenged Lokatath.

''By capturing one of the false Iftin,'' Ayyar said, ''and proving the difference.''

They stared at him, and then Jarvas laughed shortly. ''Simple, yet perhaps the best solution. So now we go ahunting for the Enemy, and I think that means prowling along the river.''

''Can you foresee their trail there?'' Kelemark asked Illylle.

''Not in this. While they move, they are encased in their master's protection, and I have not the skill to break that. We must do this by eye, nose, and ear.''

It was decided to follow the shore south from the entrance to the Mirror, along the river. Night would favor them most, since Iftin senses were nocturnal and already the day was far sped. Thus, wrapped in cloaks, they lay against the road wall and slept.

Swiftly at dusk they sped along their chosen route. Winter-dried reeds, far higher than their heads, made a small woodland. But these beds they skirted. The change in temperature from day to night, as always, altered odors. Some were sharper; others faded. There were sounds; the scratching which was an earth-lizard dragging a river worm back and forth across gravel, the calls of hunters winged and four-footed. Once they crouched in silence, waiting while one of the great felines swung its muzzle under the water at the river's edge, champing jaws meanwhile, to wash out its mouth after feeding. And the fresh blood smell of that meal reached them.

But no unusual scent tainted the air. The land the Mirror

had cleansed was now behind them, and the darkness of the true Waste lay to their right. In the north the sky was bright.

"Now they beam at night." Lokatath stated the obvious.

"They grow impatient or more afraid," Kelemark replied.

Was Iftsiga already burning? Ayyar wondered. And what of the seed chests? Would their hiding place among the roots of the Citadel be deep enough to protect them from the earth-tearing snout of the grubber?

Water vapor clung to the river at this point. And here they picked up the trail they sought. Lokatath spat, and Ayyar tasted bitter moisture gathering in his own mouth. The stench from the rag had been bad, but this was infinitely worse. Drawn into one's nostrils, it seemed to fill one's lungs with a lingering, loathsome residue.

"Fresh?" Rizak commented.

"Yes, and leading over river to the garths."

Ice-rimmed logs and rocks, their surfaces just above the winter-shrunken stream, made a bridge of sorts. The Iftin used it.

"Ah—" The soft exclamation from Illylle drew Ayyar's attention. She was frowning, her head turning from right to left and then back again, as one who tried to discover some half-forgotten landmarks.

"What is it?"

"This way, does it not lead to Himmer's?"

West and south— Yes, not far from here he, newly Ift himself, had seen the transformation of Ashla Himmer into Illylle, had aided her through the worst of that discovery that she was now alien to her kind. Though she had not believed—not at first—that she was alien. She had insisted upon returning to her garth, to seek out the younger sister she cherished. Only when the repulsion each felt now for the other had been made plain had she been convinced that kin of Ashla were not of Illylle's. Yet perhaps now a faint stir of that old affection worked in her.

Over the river the trail did not run straight. It was almost as if that which they hunted had quested, like a hound seeking a quarry of its own. Then, far away, sounded the barking of garth dogs. From Himmer's? Ayyar could not be sure. But he hoped it lay more to the west.

Now the trail straightened, and they fell into a half run natural to Iftin. A woodland engulfed them though this was not the Forest. Yet it was good, like unto a drink of cool water in the day's heat, to have trees close about them—bare of leaf, winter-ravaged as those were.

This was a forest already emptied of many of its inhabitants for garth clearings had gnawed at it steadily to north and east. And the creatures that were wary and shy had long since departed. Not all, however. Some still holed up in tree or ground burrows. Now these slept through the dead season.

Strong was the scent and louder the clamor of the dogs. At least those sentinels must long ago have aroused their masters. Remembering the fate of other garths, they would be doubly alert. Armed with blasters, they should be able to turn back an attack.

The Iftin party must take care. It would do no good to be caught in some fight and mistaken for the Enemy. Ayyar caught Jarvas' sharp hand orders, dividing them into two parties, right and left. It was right Ayyar turned, Illylle beside him, Rizak a little behind.

They detoured about the clutching, dangerous branches

22

of a large thorn tree. Now the scent was not so strong. Ayyar sniffed another odor, the death that surrounded each garth where tree, bush, all green life died in ragged cuttings gouged out of the true beauty of Janus. And he knew again hatred for those who thus slew.

Was this Himmer's garth? He asked Illylle. She looked about her. But now she shook her head.

"This is too far east. Perhaps it is Tolferg's." But was she sure or only wished it so?

It seemed to Ayyar that the barking had lessened. Fewer hounds giving tongue? Now, flickering light among the trees—torches?

They slackened pace and kept to cover until they looked through a screen of withered brush, out over raw land where huge stumps stood, charred from the dogged burning of fires kept going for weeks, even months.

The light came from torches blazing on a stockade wall. Behind that was the garth building. Several of the torches had been pitched down to set fire to dried material heaped in the open, so that the stretch of cleared land was as light as the besieged could make it, though every half-burned stump provided a pool of shadow. With their hindquarters pressed against the now barred gate of the garth enclosure stood four hounds, showing their fangs to the night. They had not come to that stand easily. Wounds bled on their flanks and shoulders, and another dog lay struggling to win to its feet but unable to do so.

Between the edge of the wood and the gate lay at least six more of those vicious four-footed guards. It looked as if they had been loosed to buy time for their masters.

"To the right, beside the forked stump," Illylle whispered.

The black clot of stump had been fire-hollowed into an

unusual shape, its center portion burnt away, but the two outer rims rising in projections, giving the remaining stub the appearance of an animal head, ears up, alert to any sound.

Between those ears was movement, a rounded shadow arising for an instant. From the rear the skulker looked Ift, cloak spread out in the concealing sweep Ayyar used upon need. The head turned—Ift. Illylle's fingers tightened on Ayyar's arm. The counterfeit could not be detected, at least not here and now. Rizak whispered.

"Could THAT have captured some of the old true race, made them ITS servants?"

"Who knows? But this is of the Enemy." Of that Ayyar was sure. "How many?"

He searched the ground with hunter's eyes and used his nose to locate five more before him. Since they were certainly not all bunched here, perhaps double or triple that number might be abroad.

Illylle drew a sharp breath. "They wait—for what?"

A scream answered her, such a cry as only extreme fear and pain might tear from a human throat. Out of the brush to their right stumbled a weaving figure, rags of clothing still about it, but not enough to conceal that it was a woman. Shrieking, she staggered on between the hidden attackers who made no move to prevent her, heading for the garth gate. Ayyar saw the false Iftin, flitting along in her wake but making no move to pull her down.

"She is their key to the gate," Rizak said.

Would it have worked? Perhaps, had not the hounds moved. Two of them sprang, almost as one—not at the creeping shadows, but for the woman. Their fangs ended her screams as she was borne to the ground. Then the

24

hounds howled as ray beams from the stockade crisped them. Their masters must have believed them mad.

One of the false Iftin sprang into the open, caught an outflung arm of the woman, hurled the body back into the shadow of a stump where two of his fellows pounced upon it and dragged it away with them.

"Aloft—over there!" Rizak's head was up.

One of the port flitters was in the night sky, and from it lashes of fire beat the ground.

"Back!" Ayyar pulled at Illylle. They ran from the death that would spare nothing in the ignited woodland.

"Down river—south—" panted Rizak moments later. He was right. The rock and sand there would not burn; they might find shelter if they could reach it. As yet the rays struck only about the garth clearing—but they would work out from there.

In this much they were favored, the trees took long to ignite. It was only when the ray lash touched the lower growth that danger spread.

They heard sounds in the brush, the flight of other things. Then two figures burst into a glade on the left —false Iftin, one wearing the rags of a smouldering cloak about his shoulders, as if he felt no heat or pain from that burning garment. They were heading for the river, too.

Were those the only survivors among the attackers? Some must have been caught in the first lashing of the flitter, Ayyar was sure.

"We—can—not—make—it—" Rizak coughed through the smoke.

"To the right!" A momentary glimpse had suggested salvation to Ayyar.

One of the trees, almost the size of a Great Crown, had

fallen here ages past. Its roots pointed to the sky on one side of a deep pit. From that hole came a smell Ayyar knew of old, kalcrok. He had been web-captive in just such a burrow. But this scent was old. The burrow could not have been used lately. Perhaps the absence of large game, driven away from the garth, had led to its abandonment.

"In!" He followed his own order, pulled Illylle with him, to land on a mat of evil-smelling debris, Rizak sliding down behind.

What Ayyar sought lay directly before him, the entrance to the inner burrow. The webs about the walls were only tatters. This was safely deserted and could save them. He scrambled forward into the heart of the kalcrok nest hole.

III

IT WAS a tight fit as they wedged into that runway in the deep earth. Somewhere along was a side chamber wherein the once owner had had its nest. This should house them from the fury of the flames. When they lay together in that evil-smelling hole, Ayyar's heart still pounded heavily.

"Jarvas, Kelemark, Lokatath—" he heard Illylle whisper.

Yes, what of the others? Had they found the small measure of safety offered by the river lands? But Rizak was thinking ahead.

"Burnt-over, this land will be bare for any searching. If they loose hounds . . . ''

"These burrows have more than one door." Ayyar could speak from his fearsome earlier experience. "And they run straight. The other door will open nearer the river."

"Rizak, when will the brethren now over the South Sea return?" Illylle asked.

"We roused early. They should come with the true spring."

"To find the country arrayed against them."

"They do not come openly ever," he defended their fellow changelings, the ones who were moved by implanted instinct to invade the Forest, set the treasure traps and wait thereafter to find and aid the new Iftin who emerged from the Green Sick as their kindred.

"But neither have they yet faced such danger as this," Ayyar pointed out. "They may return to find no Forest and all off-worlders hunting them down. THAT plans well, striking in winter when we do not move."

"I cannot believe," Illylle's head lay on her arm, her mouth in these close quarters so near to his cheek that Ayyar felt the warmth of her breath with every word she spoke, "that the Mirror failed us! We saw the flooding and the storm and what struck the Waste. THAT could not have escaped—"

"But we do not know the nature of THAT," Ayyar interrupted. "It may be that danger arouses IT to greater strength and efforts, to the summoning of more servants and warriors. With the Larsh IT brought down Iftcan. Now with these off-worlders IT will hammer the remains

27

of that city into black ash. There is only one way to face IT—''

"Yes—deal with those at the port, see that they know the truth!''

Ayyar could feel the shiver run through Illylle. His own body reacted thus as well. To go among the unchanged, to speak to them face to face, to be so close—that was an ordeal that perhaps none of them could stand up to, physically or emotionally. If there were some other way, one that did not include a meeting—a communication, until that could be used at long distance.

It would seem that Rizak's thoughts marched with his for now the other asked Illylle:

"These garthmen, they mount coms to keep in touch with the port, do they not?''

"No, that is worldly.'' The former garth girl made swift answer. "Only at the port will you find such things.''

"Or perhaps in that camp,'' Ayyar amended.

Again Rizak picked up his thought. "Any camp would be well-guarded. They would expect attack in retaliation for the Forest spoilage.''

Ayyar's memory of the port was such a small one. He had landed there but had still been groggy from the deep frozen sleep of a labor transport. All he could recall was standing in the line of human wares while that bearded giant Kosberg looked them over critically to make his choice. Then he had helped to transfer bundles of bark from the carts of his new master to a loading platform. He had never seen Janus port again.

"You know the port?'' he asked Rizak.

"The port? No, I did not planet there. I crawled out of a lifeboat that downed in the Forest, sent from the space ship

28

Thorstone as she passed through this solar system. The plague had hit us, but we kept going, hunting help. When we reached here I was barely living. They threw us in lifeboats to get rid of us. I landed with a party of dead, but I lived. Then I found one of the treasures—and became Ift. So I do not know Janus port at all.''

"Lokatath was a garthman." Ayyar ran down the list. "But Kelemark, he was a medico there."

"But back in the days of the Karbon Combine," Rizak reminded him. "A lot can change in more than fifty years. And Jarvas was a First-in Scout before the port was established at all."

"But I was there for four hands of days," Illylle said. "And that was only a small tale of seasons ago. I know the port. Is it in your mind, Ayyar, to go there?"

"To go there for a com. If we can get even a travel-talker we are that much closer to communication."

"The port," Rizak repeated, "I do not know. But your thought of a com to talk to them is good. Only we must first get out of this burrow. Let us put our minds to that."

And he was right, for there was a time during which Ayyar feared they had chosen their grave rather than a refuge. They found breathing hard as the flames outside fed on oxygen, and they lapsed into a comatose condition near to what they had known during hibernation. But when they stirred again there was more air, though it carried the reek of smoke.

Illylle was coughing, and Ayyar felt the choking fumes biting his nose and throat. They had better move, unless it meant going into the fire. He rasped out as much and pushed into the passage.

"Listen!"

But he did not need Rizak's cry. It was raining beyond. He had not expected such a heavy downpour. Perhaps the season was later than they had thought. The floor of the burrow was wet with a seepage of water. It must be pooling in the old trap pit. Ayyar crawled on, the others following.

A smoking mass of half-consumed vegetation had fallen across the outlet. He thrust at it with his sword and made them an exit. Although it was now day, the clouds were so massed that they emerged into twilight and around them the storm beat icily. The ray beam mounted on the flitter had accounted for the underbrush and the crowns of the trees, but the great trunks, charred and blistered, yet stood. Among these they made their way to the river bank.

It was between two rocks at the improvised log and rock bridge that they came upon a body. A white arm outflung, the flaccid hand turned up as if to cup some of the flooding rain, was what Ayyar saw first. He turned quickly.

"No!" With one hand he tried to fend off Illylle, but she had already seen it and pushed past him to look down at what lay beyond.

Horror faded, she leaned closer as Ayyar and Rizak joined her. There was a human face, with no expression now, but rather a queer blankness that Ayyar did not associate with the peace of death. There could have been no peace, however, for the throat and the upper breast had been shredded away by the hounds, and that attack had uncovered metal, wires, and broken bits of cogs.

"Robot!" Naill memory supplied the proper word.

Rizak hunkered down, ran exploring fingers along the arm. "More—feel this!"

With distaste Ayyar followed his example. The

30

"flesh" was cold, rain wet. But its texture, to his inexpert touch, felt the same as if it had been part of a real body. Yet the rips in it were not bloody, and there was no denying that metal lay beneath.

"A made thing!" Illylle gave verdict. "But unless one knew—"

"Their key." Rizak nodded. "Send her in screaming and garth gates would open. Only this time, something went wrong. Those hounds knew, poor brutes, and died proving it. The false Iftin must have dragged her this far because she was important to their plans. Then, for some reason they had to abandon her. Which may be the worst mistake they have ever made!"

"How?" Illylle wanted to know.

"We needed some proof. Well, we may not have a false Ift, but we do have something here to make any off-worlder think. This is unlike any robot I ever saw, but it is a robot. Now, suppose we put her out in plain sight. In time they will send a snoop scouter over here, perhaps more than one. Let them find her and begin to wonder!"

He was right, Ayyar knew. Give the port authorities a mystery such as this, and they would be more amenable to belief in a difference between Ift and false Ift.

"Those false Iftin—are they as this?" Illylle wondered.

"Perhaps. But—who made this and where?"

Illylle leaned still farther over the battered robot, drawing deep breaths. "There is no need to ask, brother. The stench of evil has not been washed away by the rain. This, too, is of the White Forest."

"I do not see how it can be," Ayyar protested. What *did* he know of the Enemy? He had been once taken prisoner by a walking space suit of antique design which

31

had herded him and Illylle through the Crystal Forest to imprisonment at the depths of a chasm. But—this robot, it could only be the work of a high technology of a type of civilization he could not equate with Janus at all.

"Do you not see," Illylle demanded of him now, "we know so little of THAT. Remember the space ship that sat on the desert sands— Perhaps there are other ships lost in the Waste, things from which THAT may use at will!"

Possible of course. But there was no use wasting time in speculation now. Ayyar helped Rizak free the robot woman from between the rocks, stretch out the body face up in the open to be clearly seen. If Rizak was right concerning the coming of a scout snooper, this ought to be in port hands soon. Meanwhile, they must get back across the river and find the rest of their own party.

"Let us trust that they made it across." Rizak glanced back in the direction they had taken when they had reached the other bank of the river. "With this weather that dam-bridge will not last long."

"Where do we look for them? At the Mirror?"

"No." It was only a feeling, but the belief that it was right made Ayyar put force into his answer. "To the south."

The narrow sea lay south, and somehow its dune-hilled shore promised safety. To the port men the Forest would be the proper place to hunt their demon fugitives. Perhaps the others agreed with him, for they did not dispute.

Here where there were no trees, the brush and rocky outcrops must provide them with cover, and they kept to what was offered, listening always for any sound of a flitter. They had worked their way well downstream from the crossing when they heard a hum and lay flat among the stones. "Hovering," Rizak murmured. "I think they have sighted our lady."

"Ahh—"

To their night-oriented eyes that flash of flame was almost blinding. Those in the flitter were laying about with a beam, making sure that the body was not bait in a trap, or, if so, that the would-be trappers were taken care of before they landed.

"Move!"

With the flitter so occupied, they must put more space between themselves and it. Ayyar trotted around a shelf of rock to halt and look down. This gravel held no tracks, but just as the stink of the false Iftin was to be easily scented, so did his nostrils now inform him that those of the true blood had passed this way, and a very short time ago. Some of their party, if not all, had also won to this side of the river and were heading seaward.

When they were well away from the vicinity of the flitter, Ayyar whistled. To ears not trained in Iftin calls, the notes were a song of a river bird. And he continued to whistle so at intervals until he was answered. The replying trill took them into a maze of shrub, winter-thinned but still walled into thickets. And here, in a wide nest of marsh grasses and cut reeds, which had once been the lair of a finkang, they found Jarvas and Kelemark.

"There—someone is hurt!"

The third form in Ift clothing lay to one side, and Ayyar started forward. That could only be Lokatath. But why should he be tossed so—and there was something strange about his body— It took Ayyar a minute of sharp study to see that that strangeness was due to the fact that the supine form lacked half a skull!

Rizak strode forward to gaze down. "So we have another machine!" His mouth puckered wryly as if he wished to spit upon the body.

"Another one? Then you have also found one of these things?" Jarvas demanded.

"A woman—fashioned to resemble a garth dweller. She must have been used to open the gates, but the hounds finished her. Or did you not see?"

"We saw. What did you do with her?"

Rizak smiled. "We left her where she has already been found. To give the off-worlders something to think about." He went down on one knee to inspect the Iftin robot the closer. "Clever! Meeting this one face to face, I would say he was Ift. Until I saw this—" He jerked a thumb at the broken head and the mass of melted wires and other material it contained.

"No, you would not!" Illylle corrected him sharply. "This is evil! Your nose would tell you that."

"But off-worlders do not have such noses," Jarvas reminded her. "And the false Ift could seem true to those not of our kind. Clever indeed, with a devil's cleverness. In this fashion THAT has set a barrier between us and any garthman or off-worlder."

Rizak agreed. "But Ayyar suggests we try contact by com—"

"Com!" Kelemark swung around to look at the younger Ift. "And where will we find one of those?"

"At the port," Ayyar returned. "All we need is a handtalker—get one of those and—" He spoke to Jarvas. "You were a First-in Scout, you know the official codes. Suppose you broadcast, would they not hear you out? Really listen?"

"They might. If we had a com. But to pick one up at the

34

port—'' Jarvas stopped. His expression changed from one of irritation at stupidity to thoughtfulness.

"Where is Lokatath?" Illylle asked. "Did he—was he lost?"

Kelemark shook his head. "No. He has gone to the signal rocks on the coast. There must be a beacon set there to warn the brethren."

She smiled. "Wise, very wise. But we cannot look forward now to an early planting—and perhaps they will not come soon."

"That is it. We do not know how early we have been awakened. So we dare take no chance."

Jarvas seated himself cross-legged in the deserted nest and brushed aside the fabric of its stuff at one edge, clearing a small space of ground. On it he laid out small pebbles.

"This is the port—am I right, Kelemark?"

The former medico looked over his shoulder. "I have not seen it for many years—"

"But Illylle has," interrupted Ayyar. "She went there not many seasons ago for medical aid when her mother was dying. Illylle?"

"Yes." She sat down in turn to face Jarvas across the cleared space. "Here is where the ships land and of those there are never many. Once each tenth of a year a government cruiser comes in. Between times, at the harvest season—the traders."

"Do not forget," Rizak warned, "that by now they may have beamed a call for off-planet help."

"Concerning that we shall have to take our chances," returned Jarvas. "So—the ships planet to the west. What else?"

"Here"—she put down a larger stone—"is the building that houses the customs and the other government offices. Next is the hospital, then the barracks of the police, beyond—the quarters of those others who work there. Here are the sheds for the storing of the lattamus bark waiting to be shipped—that is all. Oh, yes, another building here to house and store the working machines.''

"That is farther north, and now it must be empty," commented Ayyar.

"North," Jarvas studied the plan. "They are blasting into Iftcan from this direction." A sweep of his hand indicated east. "And they patrol along the river. To the northwest is the untouched Waste and THAT'S stronghold. Also we are haunted by time."

"The garths must all be alerted." Illylle rested her chin upon an upheld fist, her elbow based on her knee. "Perhaps they have offered the safety of the port to any of the garthmen who care to come there."

"And would any?" asked Ayyar.

"I do not know. All their beliefs are against it, but perhaps in great extremity some would. Himmer's lies here—" She gestured to the north and east of their present camp.

They waited for her to continue, aware some purpose moved in her mind.

"Himmer's I know. Also, I know the animals there. Himmer has two phas broken to ride. They will come to the call—so mounted . . ."

"Too wild a chance." Jarvas denied her plan. "Every garth will be standing alert for attack—they would have hounds out."

"How did the garth that was attacked call the flitter?" Ayyar asked suddenly. "The flyer came in ready to blast—they must have been ready for trouble."

36

"Maybe the garths have coms now, because of this," mused Rizak.

"And if they have—" began Ayyar.

"No—trying to get to one of those, undetected, would be like walking bare-handed into a kalcrok web, expecting to talk that double mouth out of fanging one!" Kelemark protested.

"There is the scout flitter—and that—" Rizak nodded to the robot Ift. "Plant that out in the open as we did the other. Let them see it."

"They will take good care to flame lash all around before they ground, and everyone in the crew will be wearing a blaster," Kelemark pointed out.

But Illylle looked thoughtful. "Suppose we have a way to defeat such caution?"

"How?" Ayyar wanted to know.

"Sal bark—"

Old lore was what she called upon now, the Forest learning. Bark stripped from a small, red-brown tree with leaves so tiny that even in the full life of summer it never looked to be more than autumn-bare, pounded and fed into a fire, made a smoke which stupified and bewildered. It had been used to finish off kalcroks, when those monsters could be kept from retreating into the deep corridors of their dens.

"They will expect one trap, give them a different one—" she began when Ayyar picked up her idea and elaborated upon it.

"Pick a place that is open but that has brush around it at a little distance. They will fire that before they land. The sal bark will be in that brush. If we have any luck, we can then use the com of the flitter or the personal travel-talk of one of its crew."

"And the sal fumes, the fire, how do we ourselves walk through those?" Rizak asked dryly.

"We find a place close to the river," Kelemark chimed in. "One of us takes to the water and waits. The sal smoke will not last long—we shall not be able to find too much of the bark—if we are lucky enough to discover any."

Jarvas laughed shortly. "As rocket-happy a scheme as I have ever heard—but—"

"You are forgetting something. Are you now more men than Iftin?" Illylle frowned at them. "Men must depend upon what their two hands hold, their eyes see, their ears hear. There are other powers that can root in those senses and by belief grow beyond the visible and the touchable. I have lost much, but once I was a Chooser of Seed and a Sower, and from such planting there was growth beyond the normal. It was our gift and we used it well then, as we must do now!"

A little of the awe that had touched Ayyar at the Mirror of Thanth when this slim girl had called upon powers truly beyond mortal sight and sound again shadowed his mind. Illylle seemed so sure of what she said that her confidence carried over to the others.

The search for sal bark sent them out among the rocks, though not into the fringes of the Waste. For a thing of such virtue could not be found in that garden of all ill. Kelemark was right; any harvest would be a scanty one. Ayyar had perhaps two handfuls, taken from one small seedling, when he returned. Illylle herself had done best, for she had made a bag of part of her cloak, and it was a quarter filled with the aromatic twigs.

Jarvas vanished up river in search of a proper place to set out the bait and the rest worked with care, using one of their cloaks to keep off the rain which was now a drizzle, as they shredded each tiny piece of precious bark into one pile. When they had done, Illylle ran her hands back and forth through it, crooning in a whisper. Ayyar did not strive to distinguish her words, for this he knew was a growing chant. Not *the* chant, of course; that was too sacred for any such use, but still one to send virtue into their small pile of sal.

Rizak shared out supplies, mainly the flat nut-meat bread from the Iftsiga stores. The refreshing sap which had awakened them had sustained them for long, but now they must turn to real food.

"With the night our chance passes for now." Kelemark leaned back against a rock.

"There is always another sunset." Illylle shook bits of bark from her fingers.

Yes, thought Ayyar, there was always another sunset. Yet time did not linger for the good of any man—or for Ift—or for THAT which moved back there in the Waste, the thing they had gone into winter sleep believing muzzled, defeated— Defeated? It would seem that they had witnessed only a small opening skirmish in that spectacular meeting of powers when the Mirror had overflowed its basin, not a final battle. And THAT had resources beyond any they had dreamed.

The knowledge that had gone into the making of the false Ift—that was not born of the half mystical, other-worldly influence Ayyar thought pertained to the realm of THAT WHICH ABIDES. It was far closer akin to off-world technology.

What had Illylle said—other ships planeting mayhap, out in the Waste, their cargoes open for THAT'S use? The woman robot, yes, that could have come from such a ship. Not the Iftin, however. Those were of Janus. Someone or something had fashioned those to be used for this purpose—to set all Iftin apart as outlaws and the hunted. Was this off-world—not part of THAT at all? No—they knew the stench of old, and it clung to the false ones.

They must learn what their half memories continued to deny them—the nature of THAT WHICH ABIDES. If IT was not a power beyond description, like unto that which arose from the Mirror, then IT must be force of another kind. But they must *know!*

Ayyar turned his head, looking westward to the Waste. They had seen, other than the false Iftin attack, no sign of any movement out of there. The flying thing which had once spied upon him and Illylle, the walking space suit —none of those had appeared. This strip along the river was normal healthy ground. But—there was the White Forest, and the chasm, and somewhere the true lurking place of THAT.

Jarvas slid between two rocks, joining them after a whistle announced his coming.

"There is a good place not too far away. Also, the flitter continues to patrol. But we must wait until mid-morn—"

"Morning!" Rizak grunted. "Very well, we wait."

It was difficult to reverse the natural order of things, to sleep through the cool of early morn until dawn and wait for the deadening sun and the light of full day. But they had to adapt to man's time again if they would accomplish their purpose.

Ayyar took the last turn at guard, watching westward. Nothing stirred there. In the Forest there would have been life which he could understand, with which he felt kinship, which would bolster the spirit. There, there was nothing—save the feeling that storm gathered. Not a gale of wind and rain and massed clouds, but another kind. And they must be prepared to face it as best they could. From it there would be no shelter, no hiding place.

IV

GULLIES OF SAND, hardened by winter frost, ran between rocks as might rivers of water. And the water—Ayyar looked at it with little favor. There was ice in it. At least the rain had stopped and the clearing sky gave promise of a bright day—far too bright for Iftin tastes. In the dawn, still comforting to their eyes, they were setting their trap.

The robot body was placed to sprawl convincingly half across a rock. Its protective camouflage cloak was ripped away, the form could be plainly seen. Around it were winter-dried brush and reeds, and into this they wove their sal, putting the larger amount to the north from which the wind blew.

Jarvas made a last adjustment to the bait and stepped back. They had drawn lots for the one who must lie in the water to spring the trap, and Ayyar did not know whether to be glad or sorry that the banded stone had been his portion.

Now, stripped of cloak, pack, everything save his clothing and his sword, he lay at the water's edge, ready to take to the stream when and if they heard the coming of a scout flitter. So loosely woven a trap, yet it was the best they could devise.

Ayyar put out a hand and let the chill of the river flow across it as he cupped his palm and brought it up, spilling drops. Illylle was not the only one to remember old invocations. Once Ayyar of Ky-Kyc had held a curiously marked cup and poured its contents thus upon the earth and spoken such words as Naill-Ayyar whispered now:

"As thus I pour this water by my strength and will, so may my enemy be poured, to lie helpless and spent upon the earth!"

That prayer had not influenced fate and the Larsh, nor would it probably be any more effective against off-worlder, garthman, or THAT. But man—or Ift—needs must cling to some belief or hope in something greater than himself at such an hour.

He clipped the leaf goggles down over his eyes. They had been right in their fears; the day would be bright. And there was some taste of spring in the air, as if the heavy beat of rain had unlatched the prison door for another season.

Spring in Iftcan! Ayyar caught at scraps of memory dim and faded, yet his blood ran quicker, like the sap rising joyfully through the Great Crowns and all that grew in the Forest, as he remembered this small picture and that. Spring was for seeding, not for death. Yet death had been forced upon Ayyar once before and now faced him again. He had his hand and a sword in it—that was the way for Ift to ever front the Enemy!

There was a buzz—davez, his mind identified—very early for that insect to seek the river. He lay very still. If

42

one did not move, the stinging blood-sucker would not attack.

Then came a sound greater than any insect buzz—the flitter! He did not need Jarvas' warning whistle to send him into the water between a storm-battered tree and rocks. The hum grew louder. Now—surely they would sight the robot! And if the woman thing found earlier had aroused interest—

Yes! Ayyar sank beneath the water as the hiss of a flame beam lashed across the water-logged tree, swept the rocks, onto the brush screen now between him and the robot. The wind and the height of the riverbank should keep the sal fumes away from him, but it was a chancy thing.

With a whisper of displaced air, they were landing. Now he must angle around a rock and crouch again. Ayyar jerked and almost cried out—he had forgotten the davez, and the pain of the sting was sharp. He struck at his shoulder, flattening the insect feeding greedily, and then was ashamed at his lack of control. What if that movement had betrayed him to those in the flitter?

"Over there—cover me!"

The words in Basic sounded odd, as if in a foreign tongue once well known but just slightly remembered. Ayyar pulled himself between two rocks. Above, the smoke swirled. Would enough of it reach the men—one climbing out, the other still in the small cabin? Ayyar watched the off-worlder stride confidently to the robot and put out a hand to settle on its hunched shoulder. Then he coughed, shook his head vigorously, and fanned smoke away from his face. He tugged one-handedly at the false

Ift before, with a mutter of exasperation, he holstered his blaster and used a double grip to work loose the leg Jarvas and Kelemark had spent so much time wedging tight.

"Another robot," he called back over his shoulder. "It seems to be caught fast—" He staggered against the rock. Then he turned and took a step or two toward the flyer before he slumped to the ground.

"Rashon!" The hail from the flitter brought his head up, but he could only crawl, and before he reached the cabin door, he lay face down and still.

"Rashon!"

A hand holding a blaster swung into Ayyar's line of vision. Sal smoke had knocked out one of them, but his fellow had been in the cabin. Had enough of the fumes entered there? The off-worlder emerged crouching, his eyes darting from side to side, surveying the smoking brush wall. Hooking one hand in the fabric of his fellow's tunic, he tried to drag Rashon back to the cabin. But the fact that his comrade was a larger and heavier man made that difficult. However, he made a valiant try, refusing to put up his weapon.

Wind drove smoke about him. Ayyar heard a desperate burst of coughing. Then the would-be rescuer half fell, half flung himself at the cabin door, to fall across the entrance.

Ayyar whistled. They had no idea how long the narcotic effects of the smoke would last. Thus he must search at once for what was needed, and the others were prepared to pull him out if he too succumbed. With a wet-sleeved arm held across nostrils and mouth, Ayyar approached the flitter. It would seem that that last burst of smoke was the

44

end product of the burning sal, for Ayyar could smell nothing now but the brush afire.

He forced himself to the flitter, revulsion for the off-world machine weakening him. There was a com unit in there, right enough, but it was built in. Perhaps Jarvas could command his antipathy long enough to use the broadcaster for a single message. But on the other hand, either man might wear a travel-talk.

The shrinking in him was worse pain than any davez sting, but Ayyar dared not surrender to it. Putting out his quivering hands, he turned over the man lying in the cabin doorway. What he wanted was fastened to one outflung wrist. Shuddering, Ayyar fumbled with the seal-catch, jerked free the strap, and brought away the call disk. It was as though he held unmentionable foulness against his Ift flesh. So greatly had the change conditioned him against those who had once been his own kind that he could hardly continue to grasp that small round of metal, the strap still warm from the arm against which it had been locked.

But grimly holding on, he plunged down the riverbank to the place beyond the smoldering fire, where the others waited. He dropped the com on a rock, unable any longer to stand its touch; and then tramped away some paces to retch and retch again.

When, sweating and shivering, he returned, only Jarvas and the girl were there. Jarvas, beads of moisture gathering on his hairless head, was examining the com.

"Where are—?" Ayyar began hoarsely.

Illylle nodded to the now almost dead fire. "They send the off-worlders back to port. Rizak sets the automatic return. They will carry with them the false Ift."

45

"But why—?"

"He says"—she nodded to Jarvas who was still rapt in concentration over the com—"their safe return there shall prove our good will. They will now believe more in his message if they receive it."

They saw the flitter rise, swing about, head in the direction of the port. Then the other two Iftin came unsteadily to join them. Rizak sank down, his head thrown back, his eyes closed, his mouth hanging open a little, his chest heaving. To have entered the cabin and set the controls must have taken a strength of will such as Ayyar was sure he did not possess. Why had the change set in all of them such a terrible aversion to those who had once been blood, flesh, and bone kin to them? Jarvas had said it must be a safety measure provided by those master Iftin biologists—to keep the new race apart until they were in such numbers they could not be reabsorbed by their own kind. But the master biologists had not foreseen this present difficulty. How *could* Iftin deal with those who made them physically ill to approach, mentally disturbed? Perhaps all their communication could come only through such a device as Jarvas struggled now to make operative.

"Can it be used?" Illylle dared to ask at last.

Jarvas' face was drawn, wasted. He kept his place near the rock by manifest effort.

"We can only try," he mumbled. The cover of the com had been raised. Instead of speaking into its tiny mike, Jarvas held two twigs together just above its surface. Now he clicked those together in a pattern of sound that meant nothing to Ayyar.

Twice he looked up, his twigs silent, a lost, wondering

46

expression momentarily crossing his face, as if some supposedly well-rooted memory had failed him. Then he went on, less confidently, but with dogged purpose. It was in mid-click that he was interrupted by the com itself. The voice was thin, metallic:

"Vorcors! Vorcors! What are you doing?" There was a peremptory sharpness, a demand for the truth and that speedily.

Once more, and more slowly, Jarvas clicked.

"Vorcors! What in the name of the Seventh Serpent?" Then there was complete quiet, save for Jarvas' clicking out of a code once almost better known to him than the name of Pate Sissions, how long ago, how far away? And Pate Sissions was no Ift.

"They ought to be taping it," Kelemark remarked. "Once let them decode it—"

"If they can." Rizak's answer was a half whisper. He pointed to Jarvas. The clicking grew ever slower, the moments of puzzlement longer, closer together. It was as if the longer he strove to use his off-world memory, the more difficult it became.

At last he turned to them with a wry grimace. "That is my best, I am afraid. One more run through. And let us trust I did not do as poorly as I fear!"

He readied the twigs, but that metallic voice came from the com:

"You—whoever you are—we have a fix on you!"

Rizak glanced up and over his shoulder as if he feared to see a scout already hovering to descend.

"Why should they warn us?" Ayyar wondered.

"Perhaps," Illylle answered him, "because Jarvas is

not as inept as he fears. Perhaps already they have read or found someone who knows his code. Shall we wait to meet them?''

Jarvas shook his head. ''Not now, not until we know more. However—'' The twigs he had used for message sending he now put to another use. Wet and dipped in the ash of the burned bushes, they provided him with clumsy writing materials. And around the com on the rock he put some symbols, not in any off-world writing Ayyar knew but in one that must have potent meaning, or at least Jarvas believed so enough to take pains over the inscription.

They headed south, their cloaks and packs weighing on them. Ayyar had lost all the strength he had gained from drinking Iftsiga's sap. His head whirled giddily at intervals, and he wondered how long he could keep the pace Kelemark set. Somewhere before them was the sea, but still the Waste brooded on their right hand. And in it things stirred; he was as sure of that as if he could see them.

A small copse provided them a breathing space. Even so limited a stretch of woodland was refreshing. Ayyar rested on the dried leaves of other seasons, but he dared not close his eyes. Sleep was too close, weighting his eyelids, slowing his body.

''What will they do? Will they come?'' Illylle questioned.

''I do not know.'' Jarvas twisted a scrap of moss he had picked up absently. ''I do not doubt they had the fix. And they must believe in the code, or they would have attacked without warning. In a short time the flitter will come home with the crew safe, plus the robot. That should prove our good will. When they come, they will read what I wrote about the com. Even in a century, the scout recognition symbols cannot have altered too much. They may then send a message off-world, to trace one Pate Sissions.''

''But all that will take much time!'' protested Illylle.

''Yes. And time we may not have. But just now I see no better way. Do any of you?''

Even Illylle was forced to concede he was right. But Ayyar noted that she turned her head now and then, to stare out over the Waste. He wondered if she also had that sensation of a watcher there, biding time for a purpose that in the end would do them no good.

Though they listened, there was no sound on the com of any flitter homing. Ayyar could not deny his disappointment, though he knew that it was foolish to hope for such a quick reply. As Jarvas had pointed out—the port authorities must be checking and rechecking.

The Iftin did not go any farther than the edge of the dune land. And it was there that Lokatath came to them. A raw and bleeding scratch crossed one cheek, as if some branch had laid whip to him, and he breathed with the heavy gasps of one who had gone a distance at a speed he had to drive himself to hold.

''They muster!'' He pulled himself to a sliding stop by holding to a bush.

''The off-worlders?''

Lokatath shook his head in answer to Jarvas' question. ''Those—from there—'' He pointed with his chin to the west.

''The wytes are out coursing the Waste. And they hunt with the false Iftin—who move toward the river!''

''How many?''

Lokatath shrugged. "Who can tell? They weave in and out, and it would seem that the ground itself sometimes moves to hide them or to confuse—"

"As it can," agreed Illylle. "THAT has many strange powers. But why do they move in the day—?"

"Because time is our enemy; can you think of a better reason?" Rizak wanted to know. "THAT is aware that we are here somewhere, that we were unable to follow the brethren overseas last fall. So IT has launched this attack. Thus when our kin do return, they must land in the thick of it, perhaps to be burned down before they know the why or even that they have any enemies!"

"And what of our com message?" It was Ayyar following the old pattern of marshalling his thoughts aloud. "If those from the port find the false Iftin waiting there when they come, they will deem it a trap."

"Yes," Jarvas acknowledged. "Therefore—we must discover wherefore this horde moves and if they plan to leave the Waste." He balled his right hand into a fist and ground it into the palm of the left. "If only our memories were sharper! I had thought ITS servants did not venture beyond the Waste—yet the false Iftin crossed the river."

"Never forget the Larsh. They moved at THAT'S will beyond the barriers of the Oath. What seems to bind the master does not prevent the servant from carrying out orders," Illylle replied.

"One of my last clear Ayyar memories is that of slitting a wyte at the very foot of a Great Crown. Yet in an earlier day such would not even bay at the distant shadow of Iftcan," added Ayyar. "I say again, what of any who are drawn to the com? Trap of our setting it will not be, unless unwittingly, but trap it may well prove!"

"Therefore"—Jarvas got to his feet—"trap it must not be! If we lose this chance to tell them the truth, we might as well flee before the wind like leaves, with no hope of seeding. So—now we must spread ourselves. Illylle, you most of all have need to fear attention from THAT. What would IT not give to have even a memory-crippled Sower within ITS hold. Therefore—back to the seashore for you."

"And for the same reason"—she rose to front the standing Jarvas—"must you be careful, Jarvas. Oh, yes, you remember less of the Words and the Gift even than do I, but once you had them. And who knows whether THAT might not have ITS own ways to awaken more memory than you wish. Therefore, run not into a net."

He smiled, but grimly. "Perhaps I alone have other memories to convince those from the port of who and what we are. Therefore, I have no choice but to return to our ordained meeting and there do the best I can. Now—" He faced the rest of them. "Rizak will come with me. And Kelemark, do you go seaward with Illylle. For you twain"—he looked now to Ayyar and Loka-tath—"scouting—one north, one along the river. Decide which between you."

"And west?" Lokatath asked.

"West we shall leave, for now. To track the enemy on his own ground is a risk we are not yet driven to taking. It is more necessary to see what garthmen and port force are about."

They stripped off their packs but kept their cloaks for cover. Illylle and Kelemark, loaded with the supplies, started south, the rest, north.

"Smell it, brothers?" Lokatath's nostrils were wide, his head up, as he tested the air from the west.

"Yes, false Ift—and others—" Ayyar made identification.

"I will take cross river if you agree," Lokatath said. "That land is known to me." Out of the garths as he was, the choice was sensible.

So once more Ayyar trotted north. At first he would share the trail with Jarvas and Rizak. Then he would be on his own with perhaps the remains of Iftcan as his final goal.

The sun was high and bright. Even wearing the leaf goggles, they suffered. But they saw nothing move, save now and then a bird in the air, an animal or stream dweller going about its business. Burnt lengths of wood drifted down the current, bringing the rank death stench with them. Ayyar did not doubt that those destroying the Forest were still about that murderous business. And could the Iftin hope to prevail in any argument against the hatred and hysteria of the garthmen? Or the determination of those from the port?

"Flitter! Northeast—"

As one they took to such cover as the ground afforded at Rizak's warning. The hum they could hear, but it was a second or two before they saw the machine against the too-bright sky.

"Too late! We cannot get there before they ground—" Jarvas muttered.

"In more ways than one, too late!" Ayyar added. From the Waste came a shrill yapping that roughed his skin, brought hand to sword hilt, and blade half out of its sheath before he was conscious of that move. "The wytes are coursing."

Garthmen had their hounds, so did THAT. But the

wytes were not any hound such as honest flesh would own. Once before in this time he had faced them as they bayed at Illylle and him in the Enemy's seared land. They could be killed or sent to what they knew as death, but only one by one, whereas they hunted and slew as a pack.

"They close in—" he cried.

"Seeking— Ah, look you!" Rizak's cry was even louder. The flitter was larger than the scout they had grounded to gain a com. It was coming fast. But from somewhere deep in the heart of the Waste, there flashed a searing beam to meet it, envelop it with incandescence.

All three of the Iftin fell upon their knees, their hands to their eyes, blinded for a moment. Ayyar knew a stab of fear. Were they to be blinded in truth? Painful tears trickled from beneath the lids he kept tightly closed. All he could see was red, blood red, filling the world.

"Is it—is it gone?" Out of the red world he heard Rizak ask that. Against his will he opened his eyes. Red, more red. But through it dimly he could distinguish rock and brush. He was not blind!

The hum of the flitter he no longer heard. The machine must have flamed into nothingness in that ray. But now he was dragged to one side as a hand fell heavily on his shoulder and gripped him tightly.

"It—it is still flying—landing—!"

Blurred as his sight now was, Ayyar could see that Jarvas was right. There was the flitter, no longer concealed by a dazzle of light, descending as if normally piloted. Yet the hum of motor was gone. And now the shrilling of the wytes arose to a scream that hurt his ears, to add to the pain of his outraged eyes. That pain acted as a spur. He got to his feet and started to run, though he staggered from side to side, toward the place where the flitter would ground. Behind him he heard the others coming, at intervals during that awful baying.

Why he was so bound and what he would do there, Ayyar had no idea. But that he must do this, he knew. And he swayed out into the open as the flitter touched down, without thinking for the moment that he might well be running into the fire of blasters. Only, as some measure of sense came back to him, he stopped. There was no opening of the cabin door.

"Dead?" Rizak asked from his right.

"Perhaps." Jarvas advanced to the flyer, walking in an odd, stiff-legged fashion, his body rebelling against the orders of his mind.

But before he could set hand to the flitter, the cabin door slid back and a man crawled into the open on hands and knees, falling the few feet to the ground. Scrabbling for leverage, he then advanced, still on hands and knees and crept back to the side of the flyer where he pulled himself up. He wore the tunic of the port security police, and officer's star on the shoulder, and he stared straight before him as if he were as blind as Ayyar had been moments earlier.

A second man emerged in the same helpless fashion. This one was older, and he had a civilian's tunic. He sprawled forward, lying face down, moaning a little, providing a stumbling block for the third man, this young one in a pilot's uniform.

"In shock, I think." Rizak supplied one explanation. "Listen!"

A wyte bay, very loud and clear. To the hunters from

the Waste these off-worlders would prove easy prey. Jarvas clutched the arm of the pilot.

"Get them—we must take them away before—" he ordered in gasps.

To touch—to hold and support one of these men—he could not! Every atom in Ayyar screamed that. But he must! He had to! They could not be left for the wytes.

He stooped and caught at the outflung hand of the elder man, pulling at him. To his surprise the off-worlder arose, as if he needed only Ayyar's tug to bring him to obedience. He got to his feet and allowed the Ift to lead him back among the rocks where they had a small, a very small chance at defense. And as easily, the other two came with Jarvas and Rizak. But they continued to stare straight ahead, no change in their blank faces, as if they were now the robots.

Once among the rocks the Iftin set the off-worlders at the back of that small space and faced outward, their swords drawn and ready.

V

THEY HAD CHOSEN, to the best of their ability, that temporary fortress, and, it would seem, with luck they had chosen well. The off-worlders were backed by rocks, and nothing could come at them from that side, while—before the sword-armed Iftin—the passage was narrow. Not more than two of the wytes could storm them at a time.

There could be no pack maneuver there to drag them down. Only—perhaps servants of another species followed. Would it be this day that the true Iftin faced the false?

Ayyar listened until it seemed to him that his whole body was one giant ear. For a long moment now the wyte had not given tongue. He could hear the murmur of the river, other sounds all normal. Why were the Enemy running mute?

Then he drew a sharp breath. From here they could see the flitter. Something slim, white, narrow of head, long and bony of leg, pattered into the open and rounded the flyer to sniff at the open cabin door, thrusting its head and shoulders into the interior in search. The wyte withdrew to nose the ground over which the off-worlders had stumbled. Now it swung around to stare at the rocks and sighted the waiting Iftin. Its jaws opened; a thin, pale tongue showed. The creature flung back its head, voiced one of the shrill howls that hurt Iftin ears and rang inside Iftin minds.

So having summoned, it trotted forward to hunker down well beyond the range of any prudent sword. A movement beside Ayyar caught his eye. Rizak fumbled at the belt of the off-worlder he had guided. His hand moved jerkily, force of will tensing his body until his fingers closed about the butt of the blaster holstered there. With strained, clumsy movements, he brought that hand around, as though the light weapon in his grip was an almost intolerable weight. The barrel rested on a rock top, pointing at the wyte. Rizak fired.

Fire sped to dazzle and hurt their eyes, their goggles notwithstanding. There was no cry from the wyte—the beam had been too swift. It left death behind in a twisted thing resembling the gnarled roots of a long dead tree. Ayyar rubbed his smarting eyes, goggles pushed up. As he snapped them back into place he waited, tense, for some answer to the summons the wyte had voiced. Rizak had finished off the pack scout, but it was only one of many. And could blasters deal as well with robot Iftin?

"Riverside—to the south—" Jarvas ordered suddenly.

Ayyar was dismayed. To leave this shelter, small as it was, for the open was rank folly. But—perhaps to wait for untold odds could be stupid too.

"Come!" Jarvas spoke in Basic to the off-worlder of the police. He raised the other's limp arm, placed its hand upon his own shoulder. But now Ayyar saw the eyes in that slack face move, fasten on Jarvas. And surely there was dawning intelligence—awareness in them!

With each of them guiding one of the off-worlders, the Iftin went down slope to the ice-packed gravel of the water's edge.

"Look!" Ayyar whirled, knocking his charge back and down. But Rizak needed no warning. He sprayed the beam of the blaster, and the things that had moved in upon them from the south twisted in its flame. Wytes—three of them—running mute.

"What—what— Who—are—you?"

The voice speaking halting Basic startled Ayyar. He had come, even in that short time, to think of the off-worlders as semi-inanimate, without any claim to a share in this, mere burdens for the Iftin. Now he looked at the man he had knocked to the ground. He was older than the flyer and his face was no longer blank. He raised a hand, reaching for a weapon; Jarvas spoke first.

"Get on your feet, if you can. Here they come again!"

No warning bay from the wyte, nothing but a flicker of movement from among the rocks. Rizak cried out. In his forearm hung the quivering shaft of an arrow. He dropped the blaster, and in the same second Ayyar stooped to scoop it up. He rayed a green-clad figure standing among the rocks, but it did not fall, though the beam crisped away its clothing.

"The head!" Jarvas shouted. "Aim for the head!"

Aim? It was hard to hold this alien weapon at all. It shook and wavered. He rested the barrel on his forearm to steady it, shivering at its touch. But the second sweep of that beam went in across the head of the archer. The false Ift did not stagger, but it began to run back and forth with small jerky steps—until its erratic course brought it to the top of a small cliff and it crashed over and down, to be hidden from their sight. Another arrow clattered against the stone at Ayyar's shoulder. There was no going south into that.

"Back—upstream—"

The off-worlder who had spoken got to his feet and obeyed Jarvas' order as if he were one of them. He had his blaster out and accounted for the second silent rush of wytes as they flowed down upon the party. Ayyar's hand shook so he could not aim properly, only sent a beam spraying across the rocks.

Then, as suddenly as the attack had lipped toward them, it was finished. Nothing stirred among the rocks, and even that heaviness of spirit that had been a cloak about those who served THAT lifted from them, though whether this could be depended upon as a signal of the Enemy's retreat Ayyar could not be sure.

"Who are you?" Again came that demand from the off-worlder. His blaster was now covering the three of them.

"We are Iftin—of the Forest," Jarvas replied.

"More robots—" The pilot's hand struck the blaster from Ayyar's hold.

"Not so. Your robots are out there." Jarvas pointed to the west. "You have just seen them and their hounds in action. We left you one of them to let you know the truth—"

"As if we believe you—"

"Hanfors!" The third of the flitter crew—he of the police—cut in sharply. "Who signaled thus—" He repeated a stream of numerals.

"Two, seven, nine," Jarvas added. "Pate Sissions, First-in Scout."

"Where is he?" the pilot demanded.

"He is with us; he sent that message," Jarvas said. "We are not the robots, nor do we have any alliance with THAT which controls them. They are being used to create ill feeling between us and you off-worlders."

The man who had halted Hanfors' outburst lowered his blaster an inch or so. He looked to the oldest of their number inquiringly and the other spoke:

"You brought us down—to tell us this?"

"No. THAT brought you down, to be an easy kill for ITS servants."

"And just what is THAT?"

"I can give you no answer. Only IT is a power which has existed for ages, which has always stood as an enemy to my people, and which moves against us now through you."

"Through us?"

"You fire the Forest, grub out its roots—why?"

Hanfors snorted. "Why? To uncover the burrows of the vermin who raid the garths—you—you Iftin, if that is what you call yourselves."

"We Iftin have not raided you."

"We have these now, at any rate!" Hanfors spoke to the others. "We can take them in and get the real truth —with a snooper. I will set the flitter on ready; you bring them up—"

He holstered his blaster and ran up slope to the machine.

"Those swords," the older man said. "Suppose you drop them now."

Rizak supported his wounded arm with his other hand. There was a dark patch growing about the arrow shaft. Jarvas unbuckled his shoulder belt, dropped the sheathed blade on the ground as he asked:

"Will you let me see to his wound?"

"All right. But disarm him first!"

Rizak's sword followed Jarvas'. Then Jarvas laid hand on the protruding shaft.

"You!" The off-worlder pilot looked to Ayyar. "Put yours down, also."

But as Ayyar raised unwilling hands to put off his weapon, there was a call from the flitter. Hanfors came out of the cabin and down slope with greater speed than he had gone up.

"The controls are dead. We cannot raise her."

"Send in a call—" suggested the older man.

Hanfors was already shaking his head. "Everything is dead, no motor, no com—nothing—"

"Can you repair it?"

"Repair what?" Hanfors demanded. "There is nothing wrong that one can see."

"Nothing wrong except that it will not work," commented the third man. "If that is so, we are also off the port beam, and they will come looking for us."

"Just when, Steffney? And"—the older man glanced to where Jarvas was dealing with Rizak's wound, snapping the shaft to draw through the point—"we cannot believe that this is a particularly healthy spot in which to be grounded. I would suggest we start north. The clearing squad working on this side of the river must have put a com-find on us as we went over. They will be looking for us first. Also"—he tapped one finger against his blaster—"we have these. It would seem that the weapons mustered against us"—he looked pointedly at the swords, the broken arrow—"are less efficacious. And we now possess three hostages."

"Three prisoners. You, drop that sword!" Steffney ordered Ayyar. "We will not have too far to march, and it is all along the river, sir."

The older man looked upstream and then glanced at the remains of the wytes. As if he could really read his mind, Ayyar knew what the other was thinking. As they glided overhead, swinging well above the Forest, where men of his species were triumphantly wreaking their will, over the Waste that had no meaning for an off-worlder, this country held no fear. To be set afoot here, after a brush with strange enemies, that was another matter altogether. The Waste spread wide; the Forest was no longer just a nuisance to be swept from a man's path; man himself was reduced in size and power. To tramp north through a wilderness, guarding three prisoners, not sure of what might lurk behind or of anything else in the wild countryside, that was an undertaking this port official for one did not relish.

"This is not empty land. THAT and what and who serve IT are on the move." Jarvas must have read the same thoughts and was prepared to build upon them as an aid to some mutual understanding.

"We have you. They will not attack us—" Hanfors grinned.

"Will they not? And from whence came that arrow?" Ayyar asked. "Did our own comrades shoot at us? If so, to what purpose?"

The older man smiled slightly. "Do you know, those are questions to be answered. Of course, you may have been sent here to bring us down, stage a fake rescue, and so win our confidence."

"There is one answer. Look at the one he did shoot." Steffney interrupted. "If it is a robot—then why would he worry about blasting it? They could sacrifice a robot to make the story good. And that nick in the arm, that is nothing to howl about. You may be right, Inspector Brash!"

Jarvas shrugged. "There is no opening minds willfully closed. Only this I tell you, we are no hostage for anything out there. To them we are the enemy, and you cannot use us for shields."

"Maybe not. But we shall find other uses for you," Steffney declared. "Now let us be on our way—march!"

Ayyar reluctantly shed his sword, watched Hanfors gather up all three sheathed blades and sling their baldrics across one shoulder. At an impatient motion of the blaster in Steffney's hand they began to walk north along the river. Now and then a faint breath of burning wood came to them, marking the death of the Forest.

They had not gone out of sight of the flitter before Ayyar knew that the attention of THAT in the Waste was again turned upon them. But they heard no more baying of wytes nor saw any movement there. The off-worlders might not be scouts or woodsmen, but they went warily enough and did not relax caution.

Jarvas was nearest to the river, Rizak next to him, while Ayyar was the closest to their guards. Ayyar's mind began to play with the possibilities in that line up. Suppose he were to stumble, tangle with Steffney. Could Jarvas use that momentary confusion to get to the water? And would the river protect him from blaster fire? No, there was Hanfors moving up to the right, only a step or so behind Jarvas. Rizak must have been more badly hurt than they first guessed, for now and then he staggered, lurched over against Jarvas, though he made no complaint. If they only had a chance to plan—!

How far were they from the devastation about the Forest? It must be more than a day's journey away on foot. And with the coming of night the Iftin would have the advantage of clearer sight. But would THAT let them travel without another attack? IT was watching, and not far from here was the road to the Mirror—

No! As sharp as any order shouted aloud, that denial shot through his mind. One does not lead the enemy into the fastness of one's strength. The Mirror had served them against THAT, but it would not open its protection to them if they came with off-worlders. It was as if the revulsion they themselves felt against their one-time kin was multiplied a thousand times in protest.

It was sunset now, and the slow pace Jarvas, now supporting Rizak, held grew even slower, in spite of the urging of the off-worlders to hurry. Brash took the lead, but suddenly he paused and looked west.

"Hear that?"

Was it sound or something more subtle? Ayyar had that second or two of warning, perhaps because he had once faced its like. A shadow in the air, winged. One of THAT'S messengers. As it flapped lower, Brash shook his head violently, his hands to his ears. And behind, Ayyar heard Hanfors cry out.

He threw himself back, crashing against the pilot, bringing them both to earth. He tried to hold onto the other in spite of the revulsion that sapped his strength. Perhaps his head came in contact with one of the rocks, perhaps the other landed a blow. But a night that no Iftin eyes could pierce swallowed him up.

Waking came piecemeal. He was being dragged along, and he was sick, very sick! Did he cry out in protest or only think he so cried? In either case, his plaint did no good. He continued to be pulled forward. He fought against his sickness, trying to stabilize his private world so that he might learn what had happened.

At last he made a vast effort and opened his eyes. He hung between Hanfors and Steffney; before him moved Brash. About them was a weird interplay of light and shadow, which he could not understand but which made him giddy and light of head.

Jarvas? Rizak? He could not see them. Had they indeed escaped into the river? Or had blasters cut them down? He still marched along the river, but as his head cleared a little, Ayyar saw the difference in the off-worlders. Although they moved easily, they had an odd look. No longer did Brash glance to right or left, displaying the caution he had shown. Rather did he walk with disregard for the ground underfoot, with a straightforward stare, as if all that mattered was some waiting goal.

That last moment before the melee—Ayyar could remember it all now: the coming of the flying thing which was an extension of THAT'S eyes, as he had learned when Illylle and he had encountered it. And as it had then, so did it now strike a mental bolt, probing at the party of Iftin and off-worlders. With Ift it could not prevail, but with the men from the port? They moved as if under command—THAT'S!

There was no pause for rest. They might have been tireless robots as they kept to the steady pace. Ayyar did not struggle in their grasp. If was all he could do to control his aversion to that hold and keep his mind steady.

There was no howling of wytes but a sound alien to this side of the river, the rumbling clank of heavy machinery. And as if that had some particular meaning for those he traveled with, they halted, but to no spoken order, standing to face north whence that sound came. It grew sharper, stronger.

Some of it came from upstream, yes. But there were other sounds across the river, among which were faint cries, surely from human throats. Through the thin woodland there came the crackling of small trees and brush going down before the not-to-be-withstood force of a machine's advance. What pushed its nose through into the open was no flamer or grubber, as Ayyar had expected, but something that had no place in this wilderness, as if one of the space ships had fallen from its landing fins to creep reptile-like across the land.

This was a loader, combining in its body force enough to pull a heavy-laden truck, with the crane mast and other fittings to transfer those burdens into waiting cargo ships. The mast was now tilted askew, half ripped from its moorings, ragged banners of broken branches and winter dried vine caught up and wreathed around it. The same woodland debris was caught in every crevice of the machine as it ground forward, breaking through the edge ice along the river, advancing as if the force of the current, under which it shuddered and shook, meant nothing beside the necessity for crawling through that flood to reach the other shore.

It was pushed downstream by the current, yet it continued to fight doggedly to reach their bank, though now it traveled at an angle which, if the machine did finally manage to breast the full force of the river, would bring it out not far from them. Ayyar watched, hardly believing the truth of what his eyes reported. The blind determination of the loader was amazing. There was no driver in the small upper cabin which had been bashed and twisted, perhaps by the fall of some tree with which the machine had argued passage. It was as if the loader itself was imbued with brainless life!

The clamor from upstream on their own bank grew louder as the loader continued its fight for river passage. There, too, vegetation was being crushed. Finally they caught sight of the flamer, its nozzle covered with the same debris the loader bore, not belching flames but pointing with a slightly crooked finger obliquely toward the Waste.

Cleaned by the stream of most of its ragged covering, the loader's treads caught on some underwater sand bar and it splashed up the bank. All the time, the off-worlders with Ayyar stood, staring straight ahead. Whether they watched at all he could not be sure. But they showed no surprise or alarm at the coming of the machines.

The flamer clanked into the open, turned to point to the Waste, began a ponderous march westward. After it, ground-eating prongs erect, a third machine, the grubber, came into view from the forest clearing and turned in the same direction. The loader made heavy business of bringing up the rear.

From over the river the shouting that followed in the wake of the loader was loud. Blazing, waving torches showed there. Then Brash came to life, as did the two men supporting Ayyar, moving away from the stream, up slope in the wake of the three machines still grinding into the Waste. They did not turn their heads to look as the torches reached the water's edge, but Ayyar strove to do so.

He did not believe that the garthmen with their night limited sight could see the four men from that distance. The Settlers did no more than move up and down on the bank. There was a large party of them, and Ayyar saw the light shine on metal. Gleaming scythes, axes, and the long knives used in clearing brush could also be weapons in the hands of desperate and determined men.

Perhaps their party was sighted as they reached the top of the rise, passing in the rutted track left by the loader, for the shouting grew louder. But Ayyar, unable to turn in the merciless grip that held him prisoner, could no longer see what happened behind them.

However, now they were no longer alone, for, amidst the wreckage strewing the path that the machines had broken, came other men, walking with the same unseeing tread of his captors, staring before them. All wore port clothing and plainly were now controlled by some influence that did not claim him.

Ayyar stiffened, drove his booted feet as deeply as he could into the rutted track, strove to twist free from the grip that dragged him on. He might have been struggling alone to delay the loader. There was no loosing of that hold. They continued to compel him forward.

Was THAT summoning an army obedient to ITS will? Cries from the river! Ayyar could not see if the garthmen had conquered their hesitation or were also caught in THAT'S net. He could only fight for his own freedom as best he could, digging in his feet, struggling, useless though his resistance seemed to be.

Two of the company that had followed the clearing machines caught up with Ayyar's party. Neither group looked at their new companions nor gave any sign they knew the others existed. Both the newcomers wore uniforms of the police. They were armed with blasters, but those were holstered, as if here and now there was nothing to fear. And their calm march had a quelling effect on Ayyar, as if he were being borne along in a company of men who were both invincible and deathless.

They came to the edge of a gully into which the loader had plunged and was now making violent efforts to get up. Hanfors and Steffney turned sharply to the left, bearing

Ayyar with them. The other men headed for the stalled machine, put their shoulders to it, lending their strength to free it, though their efforts made no difference to the wallowing of the loader. Now came others, first port men, all blank of face, all going directly to the machine's aid. After them, four, five, of the bearded, dully clad garthmen, all wet with river water, dripping as if they had swum the flood.

Without a word exchanged between them and the men from the port, they joined in the task of striving to free the loader. Groaning, scraping with its treaders, the machine struggled. Then those treads caught—it heaved, gained a space, another, pulled over the top, leaving behind it men who had fallen and lay panting and spent but who struggled to their feet to walk blankly onward in its wake.

VI

BEHIND those who freed the machine came Ayyar, between his two guards, still at that mechanical, unvarying pace. They were now at the tail of the motley mob heading into the heart of the Waste. Ayyar saw to the north the shadowed rise of the mount that was the frame of the Mirror. But it might as well hang like a moon out in space for all it would serve him now.

The way was rough, the soil soft so that the machines crawled through it slowly, leaving deep ruts. This was where the Mirror flood had cleansed and swept free the land. But it was desert still, though the evil growth that had once formed leprous patches had withered into dried skeletons.

On and on. Now and again the flying thing that was the projection of THAT swooped over the straggling line of men and machines. If the wytes or false Iftin also roved this land they did not show themselves.

Ayyar no longer struggled. Better to conserve his energy for any chance fortune might bring. But his mind was clearer, more alert, and he studied both the land and the men about him carefully.

It must be near midnight. The moon looked queerly pale and far away. To off-world eyes the terrain must be very shadowed. But it would seem that the purpose that united his captors made them also impervious to day or night. Now and then a man did sprawl forward in the ruts, only to regain his feet and go on, with no sign that he was aware of his tumble.

Suppose one—or both—of his captors should so lose their balance? Could he guide them into any pitfall? Ayyar began to search the ground ahead for any promising hole or unevenness. Experiments taught him that he could not vary their progress route by much in spite of any struggle on his part. But perhaps only a handsbreadth right or left might serve his purpose.

Then came another halt; men tramped around the machine just ahead, as if alerted by some signal. Ayyar caught sight of the grubber in much the same difficulty in soft ground as the loader had been earlier. The strange army gathered about it, lending their strength to aid the trapped machine. Ayyar caught his breath in a gasp of horror.

One of those pushing it had fallen under the treads of the grubber. Not one of companions, even those nearest, made an effort to pull him out of danger. Instead, the machine lurched on and over him with crushing force. Then only did the men stand aside, their hands hanging idly by their sides, their faces blank, their eyes fixed on some point ahead invisible to Ayyar, while the grubber ground on. When the loader, too, had passed, they took up the march once again.

There had been no cry from the man who had so gone to his death. If the false Iftin were robots, then these were now even more alien for they had once been men and now were—what?

Ayyar's revulsion for the off-worlders increased a hundred-fold. Had the Larsh been so? He strove to make memory obey his will as he had so many times in the past. In this company it would seem that Naill was growing more clear, Ayyar less. He looked upon these men and machines as Naill would consider them.

Psycho-locked! That came out of Naill memory—and just what did it mean? There were drugs, it was rumored, to develop a mindless robot from a living body, so deadening brain and personality that the thing left had even to be ordered to eat, to carry out the other processes necessary to keep the body alive and serviceable to the master. But these men could not have been drugged, at least not those with him.

Left, right, left, right— Suddenly Ayyar realized that his feet were moving in time with all the others. This . . . was . . . right . . . this was meant—let go —be one—with them—with IT—

With Larsh, demanded another memory struggling in

his mind. Not one of the Iftin-kind; they did not share minds with Larsh!

Naill—Ayyar—he was torn between the two who were one in him. Naill who would be united with this plodding company, Ayyar who felt toward such companions only disgust and fear. To be Naill now was defeat. He must cling to Ayyar as a man in a spring-flooded river would cling to a floating log. He was Ayyar, Ayyar of Ky-Kyc, once Captain of the First Ring, who had dwelt in Iftcan. That city—Iftsiga—

Close to drowning, he clung to the thought of Iftsiga, its centuries'-withstanding strength, its healing, its sheltering. Iftsiga's sap had fed him only a few days ago. He was one with the Great Crowns, the Forest, not with these who would and did despoil that beauty.

As one who stumbles through smoke murk into clear air, so did Ayyar emerge, by strength of will, from Naill who would betray him into the hands of THAT. He dared delay no longer, for every moment of time he marched with this company locked him more securely to the purpose that animated them.

Deliberately he moved his feet to break step. He did not try again to weaken their hold upon his body, but once more he set to studying the ground ahead. He decided upon one of the dried skeleton bushes—for lack of anything better. Half of it had been driven into the soil by the track of the loader. But to the left of that rut projected a stub of the center stem that looked as if it might hook a man at shin level. Exerting pressure slowly, Ayyar began to move his captors inch by wearying inch into the position where the stub could trip Hanfors.

So small a thing on which to build any hope! But he had

not fought their grip for a while. They might have relaxed a little when they no longer had to brace themselves to defeat his pull.

So—just a little more— Ah, it looked as if he had planned better than he knew. Hanfors was walking in the depression of the left loader track, Steffney, on the other side, in the matching rut. This left Ayyar a little above them on the uncut ground in the middle, making their hold on him harder to maintain. He waited to see if they would adjust that to defeat his purpose, but they did not. Now if Hanfors would only trip on the broken bush— Ayyar made ready to take any advantage—

Three steps—two— Now!

The broken stub caught Hanfors on his shin. Fortune favored Ayyar, for the stub was stoutly enough bedded not to yield. The man staggered, tumbled forward, and at the same moment Ayyar jerked back with all his might.

He broke the hold the young pilot had on him. Steffney still kept his lock grip on the right, but Ayyar swung around, struck the other's undefended face as hard as he could. Steffney went down in turn, and Ayyar staggered back a step or two. Then he turned and ran, expecting any moment to hear them pounding after him. But perhaps the fall and the blow had slowed their reflexes, for after a few tense moments, he knew that they were not following.

Where away? Toward the river where the garthmen had gathered on the opposite shore? North to the Mirror? Or south to the sea? At least in the south were those of his own kind, and perhaps Jarvas and Rizak had escaped there also.

Ayyar had covered perhaps a third of the way back, angling southward, when movement before him sent him into cover. He tried to see or scent what waited there. Did the false Iftin and the wytes now patrol the shore? There was no baying.

"No!" He cried that aloud. Another company of marchers from the world beyond the Waste. Garthmen these were, carrying axes, any sharp-edged tool that could serve as a weapon. But they moved with the same thudding lock-step as had the earlier group. And with them —Iftin! False Iftin herding captives?

Then Ayyar caught sight of the face of the nearest guard—Jarvas! Was he caught by that compulsion? Had he reverted to Pate Sissions, and so was susceptible to whatever influence stirred all the rest of them? Beyond him was Lokatath who should have been scouting beyond the river. Jarvas was the nearer.

Ayyar skulked close to that line of marchers, crouched behind a tangle of dead and dried brush. Then he leaped, his hands closing on the taller Ift, bringing the other down under his weight on the ground. If Jarvas had been under the influence of THAT, it was now broken. He heaved under Ayyar, caught him in an immobilizing infighting hold that was of Pate's knowledge, not Jarvas'. Then their faces were near together, and Jarvas' slitted eyes widened.

He loosed his captive and sat up, Ayyar beside him. Coming at a swift stride was Lokatath. They were truly Iftin then, not controlled. Ayyar said as much in his joy, and Jarvas nodded.

"What compels them does not affect us—"

"Unless," corrected Lokatath, "we allow ourselves to remember that we were once as they. But what happens anyway? These—they were on the track of a raiding party—suddenly they became as you see them—marching as if to order, swimming the river with only the purpose of reaching this shore in their minds— What would THAT do?''

"Marshal an army, I think." Swiftly Ayyar told what he himself had witnessed.

"Machines, men—?" wondered Lokatath.

"IT has given up more subtle tactics such as the false Iftin and now IT moves to open warfare—" Jarvas got to his feet, stood looking after the marching garthmen. "IT is gathering all the servants and tools IT can garner—to prepare—"

"For what? To root out the Forest tree by tree?" Ayyar asked. "Already those from the port and the garths were doing that for IT. To fight us? We are but six on this side of the ocean. IT need not forge an axe to destroy a blade of grass. Why then?"

"Yes, why?" Jarvas gazed now not after the marchers, but north to that shadow of the Mirror's setting. "There is another power, another opponent IT would consider far more worthy of ITS full attention than us. Months ago that power struck, and perhaps that blow—or blows—was what aroused in turn this desperate need for retaliation. No, I do not think that these march against us, nor against the Forest any longer. Just as THAT once sent the Larsh to defeat Iftcan, so now IT will send what tools IT may gather to defeat the central point of all that opposes IT here—the Mirror of Thanth!''

Ayyar memory quailed from even considering such sacrilege. Always there had been the power invested in the Mirror or focused by it. And by that power had seed grown, Iftin-kind lived, Iftcan tossed great branches to greet seasons' winds throughout centuries of life. And, likewise by the will of THAT, had death and decay and desert crept, always threatening that life, ever held at bay. Now when they were so few, and THAT so strong because of the many IT could summon to ITS banner, there was a chance that the final overturn of all was before them. And even to think of that sent a man's brain close to the edge of madness.

Words out of the long past were on his tongue now. He had no sword any longer, but his hand went up as if it held such a blade—point out.

"This is Iftin answer then—any tribute will be bought at sword point."

He heard a high excited laugh from Lokatath. "Well said, brother! It is better to die fighting than to give over-lord's salute to THAT!"

"Better still," Jarvas cut in sternly, "to live and ask what our swords can do for Thanth. We go crippled into any battle, for we have not the powers nor the knowledge of those we replace, while THAT has all memories open to IT. But whatever we can do, we shall. And in this hour we must not be divided. Rizak is hiding by the river; his wound is not such that he cannot join with us. But Illylle, above all, we must have with us!"

"My journey that," claimed Lokatath. "Though"—he glanced at the sky—"day comes and it is THAT'S time. I will not risk too great speed."

"You must not!" Jarvas agreed. "It is in my mind that THAT will take no chances, even though the weight of advantage is now ITS. Forget not that the false Iftin still prowl, and the wytes. Also perhaps THAT pulls more Settlers. Run a broken course through this land of danger."

"Perhaps two of us—" began Ayyar.

"Not so! We must not separate too widely. For you and me and Rizak, the Mirror and the burden of waiting there."

They did not seek the river end of that road which led to the Mirror, but struck directly cross country, passing from the shriveled part of the Waste at a steady lope into that part where clean greenery had begun to find root, though this was now winter dried. The wall of the way, which grew taller the nearer one drew to the Mirror stair, was about shoulder high at the place they elected to cross it. Once that had been an effective barrier between the brooding menace of the Waste and the sanctuary of the road. For Ayyar, now, there was a difference on this side of that barrier. In the slot of the road he had had no sense of peace, nor of refuge, rather of withdrawal as if some hunter was hiding to watch and wait.

Jarvas made no move to approach the stairs that led to the Mirror, nor did they urge him to it. They were three, having brought in Rizak on their way. Over the arch which led to the steps glowed the symbols Ayyar had seen there months ago when a spark from his Iftin sword had turned some unseen key to bid them enter.

Then that symbol had been green; now it was darker in shade, and it pulsated as if behind it some energy flowed and ebbed or built by degrees. They watched it; but none spoke.

If their question had been, "What was THAT?" now it could also be, "What moves the Mirror or uses it to communicate at Iftin call?" Ayyar decided. And he knew the wariness of one who crouches in open ground between two hostile forces, so far beyond his own puny strength that he could not even guess at any bonds laid upon them.

Jarvas sat crosslegged in the road, his eyes fixed. Ayyar

guessed that he was now fighting for memory, to be all Jarvas, to know what that Jarvas who had been Mirrormaster had known. Mirrormaster? Not truly, no Ift could master that which reached through Thanth.

Rizak leaned against one of the wall stones, nursing his hurt arm across his chest, his eyes closed. But Ayyar—his restlessness was such that he prowled along the wall, first east and then west, looking out into the Waste. Dawn was coming fast and the heat of day was ITS own time. What was that in the graying sky?

No winged follower of THAT—rather a flitter from the base port flying straight out westward. Was THAT summoning all machines? Or did some foolish off-worlder come scouting here? The course would bring the flyer directly over the Mirror. Ayyar's hand half raised in an instinctive warn-off gesture. But even as he moved the flitter veered sharply, swooped as if control was momentarily lost, then rose again to make a sharp-angled flight to avoid the mount and its crater.

Once past the Mirror, the flyer followed the route of the vanished army. There were no other signs of life outside their refuge. But the rising sun sought out glittering spots here and there to the west—too far for Ayyar to make out their nature, but brilliant enough to hurt his eyes. So as he made his voluntary sentry-go, he watched only the space beyond the walls of the road.

How long it was before Jarvas stirred, glanced at his two companions as if he saw them, instead of looking into an inner well holding only thought, Ayyar did not know. The sun was well up and they were hungry. But their supplies as well as their weapons were gone. Ayyar was thinking of that loss when Jarvas asked a question:

"Anything out there?"

"No."

"Consolidation of forces." Rizak, whom Ayyar had believed asleep, spoke without opening his eyes. "And what do we do—march in to face what waits there?"

"If necessary, yes." And they could not dispute Jarvas' answer, for they knew it was true. There was no turning back now; perhaps there never had been a chance to since each of them in his own time had reached out his hand to take up that portion of the "treasure" that had made him a changeling. This was an old, old struggle for the Iftin-kind, and they were Iftin now.

"Sleep if you can," Jarvas said to Ayyar. "The watch is mine."

Though the sun glared, the road still held shadows along its walls, and they were shelter. Thankfully Ayyar lay in one such dusky pool, closed his eyes. Slumber came, though he had not thought it would.

Of what had he dreamed? Of something that might answer all their questions, that he was sure of when a hand shook him into reluctant wakefulness. But that answer was gone with the opening of his eyes to the refreshing dusk of evening. On the arch the symbol still burned, but steadily now, as if the gathered energy was complete. And there was such an atmosphere of expectancy that he looked about him, seeking to see what or who had been added to their company.

It was Rizak who had roused him. Of Jarvas there was no sign, but the other answered Ayyar's unvoiced question.

"He has gone—up there."

Ayyar stood to follow, but Rizak shook his head. "For us not yet."

Looking upon the symbol, Ayyar knew he spoke the truth. For them the summons had not yet sounded.

> "Blue the leaf, strong the tree,
> Deep the root, high the branch,
> Sweet the earth, lying free.
> Gather dark—"

With the words Ayyar's hands moved as one who wished to finger a curtain, draw it aside—

> "Gather dark, hold the night,
> Stars hang, the moon is bright.
> Blue the leaf, life returns.
> In the end, sword never fails—"

But that song was not true. Swords had failed once; they could again. And swords against blasters were no match at all. Naill thoughts troubled Ayyar's mind. From behind him came other words:

> "Blue the leaf, rise and grow,
> Deep strike old roots to reach.
> Star shine, moon glow—
> Ift seed—"

Rizak stopped. "It is gone," he added a moment later. "With so much else, all the wise words, the power songs. In bits and patches they come to mind and then they are naught. If we could sing together the tale of the sword of

Kymon, well might we guess the nature of THAT and how Kymon forced upon IT the restraining Oath. But we cannot.''

Why did they speculate now on wisdom that might or might not be hidden in an ancient hero tale, Ayyar wondered. Of course it could well be that Kymon had once walked this very path of Thanth. Or was he a legend who had never lived? No, old songs would not help them now, nor tatters of memory. Yet still in his mind rang the words that did have meaning for all Ift born or changeling made:

"Blue the leaf, life returns—"

For blue had been the leaf in the golden age when the city of Iftcan had been root-set and the Ift, masters of Janus.

The night was long as they watched and waited, knew hunger and thirst and must set aside as best they could such demands of their bodies. They watched the Waste where nothing stirred, and listened, always listened for anything that passed outside the road.

Even with dawn Jarvas did not return from the Mirror. But Ayyar found a depression in the rock where drops of dew gathered, and those they licked to dull their thirst. He remembered more and more the rich, life-restoring sweetness of the sap in Iftsiga's walls and wondered how much longer they could deny the needs of their bodies.

It was deep in the second night that they heard sounds from the east. Ayyar armed himself with a stone, the best weapon chance now granted him, only to drop it again at a familiar soft whistle. Three came along the road. By some good fortune Lokatath had bettered the time allowed for his mission. Illylle and Kelemark, each carrying a small pack, ran beside him, straight for those who waited in the glow of that purplish symbol and what lay behind it for good or ill.

VII

FOR THE FOURTH time in his life as a reborn Ift, Ayyar stood on that ledge overhanging the Mirror of Thanth. Each time the lake had been different—the first time when he and Illylle had come that way it had awed him, making him wish to creep quietly away, lest he disturb the meditation of something far greater than his imagination, human or Ift, could encompass. Then, the second time, when they had all fled to Thanth as they would to the last refuge left on a hostile world, it had been a cup of rising power, again awing them, yet with that which had sustained them through the fury that followed.

This time he might be looking down, not at a flood of water, silent, untroubled, fathomless, but rather into a mist that writhed and billowed and was, he was sure, a substance not of Janus nor any world his kind knew. And there was no welcome, no security, only restless tossing and—not fear, no—but an uneasiness, a tensing, as if before battle.

Even Illylle who had climbed here light of foot, as one who expected communication, halted self-consciously and stood at a loss with the rest. Jarvas had not turned his head to greet them as they advanced on the ledge. He stood there, statue still, his arms at his sides, his whole stance that of one who waited, and waited, and waited—

It was Illylle who moved first, joining Jarvas. Perhaps she did remember more, perhaps she was daring to improvise now because of their need. Both thoughts came to Ayyar as she raised her arms, held out her hands, palms up, as one who asks alms.

Words she chanted. Some he knew, others were of the Hidden Speech, sounds to evoke answers from powers beyond their ken.

Up from the Mirror came a mist, not a surging as it had been when the water overflowed. It formed a tongue to lick down the presumptuous, to wipe out those who would demand an answer. All fear Ayyar held in memory from both his lives was as nothing to what he knew now. For the fear one holds for an enemy is naught to the fear which comes when that which one believes to be a strong protector turns against one, and there is no refuge left.

Yet none of them broke and fled that ledge as the tongue of fear swept closer to them. And now Jarvas chanted also, as if Illylle's words had unlocked his own past priesthood.

The tongue did not lick them from the stone as Ayyar thought it might. It curled higher in the air, menaced—but it did not strike. And then Illylle moved her hands as one who sows seed, and the tongue began to swing in the same way, following her gestures. While from Ayyar fear passed, leaving only awe. They were accepted. In the midst of a great and abiding anger such as his kind could not measure, the force that found focus in Thanth recognized and accepted them.

The tongue of mist withdrew, and they were alone. But

a chill which was not of winter was about them. Shivering, Illylle spoke though she did not look to them, staring instead into the Mirror.

"I have said—we are ready. Now we must wait to see what task shall be laid upon us."

What is time? In the life of men a numbering of sunrises and sunsets, of days, years, seasons, plantings and reapings. Man makes time, dividing it into narrower and narrower portions as he needs it for living which becomes more and more complex in its demands. Naill Renfro was space born; thus time had not laid so tight a bond upon him as upon most other men. And when he had become Ayyar he had walked into a time that was reckoned by seasons, by growth and winter sleep. Now he was caught up in another time in which his body was nothing, in which he was only to wait. And how long was this time he could not afterwards have told, nor did he remember it clearly.

There came a moment when the mist below lay quiet, collapsed into water. But now the water was not a smooth, set mirror. Through it ran ripples of blue and green which thinned and paled into silver, and these formed lines and patterns which were not normal for any water, if the Mirror of Thanth was, or had ever been, mere water.

Illylle and Jarvas chanted together—the girl's lighter voice rising, the man's making a lower, stronger note, yet both fitting, one to the other. And again the words were not to be translated but were meant to be sounds in which the meaning lay only in the melody.

The silver lines moved back and forth, tracing fantastic pictures one could almost understand, but never entirely. Now the whole of the flood lapped higher about the walls of the crater, as it had on the day when it had spilled over to cleanse the wilderness about and to challenge THAT with storm and flood.

From it arose another tongue, this not of mist but of substance, lifting higher and higher into the air as it circled the wall, thinner and thinner, until it could have been a vine of the Forest. And into that writhing, curling vine of water poured all the silver, so that it was alight throughout its length, although the gleaming brilliance of it did not strike harshly on Iftin eyes.

It approached in its round the ledge on which the Iftin stood, and its tip was star bright, curling down over their heads. It quivered, swinging back and forth, lingered for a moment above each in turn, sometimes for only a second, sometimes longer. Twice did it so quest, and then it struck at Illylle. Down over her head and body ran the coruscating silver, beading shoulders, limbs—

Then it raised again, and once more swung out over the rest of their small company, seeking—seeking—

Ayyar started. He was the target this time. He did not feel the touch of the water as it chose him, rather a tingling through flesh and bone and blood, as if the silver flood had entered into him. Then that was gone, as was the tongue itself, fallen back into the Mirror.

And the turbulence of the Mirror died away so that they looked down into a calm surface. Ayyar knew that what had dwelt there for a space had now withdrawn into the place which was its own, and that a door between was closed.

But the reason for what had just passed was what he must know. He looked down at his arms, his shoulders, his body where that river of silver had run. He was warm, and the hunger, the thirst he had known, was gone. Instead he was alive as he had been after his draught of sap, filled with energy, with the need for action. But what action? In the answer to that lay the importance of all that had happened here.

Illylle turned away from the edge of the ledge and came to him.

"Thus has it been ordained. As it was with Kymon, the Oath Giver, so is it now with us. We go to where THAT abides, that we may be the vessels through which what lies in Thanth may loose wrath upon the Enemy."

And the choice had not been his at all, was Ayyar's first thought. No, that was not the truth either. By coming here he had indeed offered himself for battle. Now he could not protest when he had been accepted. But why? He was no Mirrormaster; he was only a warrior who had once fought in a lost cause against this same Enemy. But—Kymon also had been a warrior—if Kymon ever truly *was*, inside the wrapping of legend and hero worship. And there was no denying that the choice had been made.

He turned to Illylle. "We go now—?"

"Now."

"Take this." Kelemark drew off his baldric, pushed it and the sheathed sword it supported into Ayyar's hands. It would seem the others accepted the fact of their out-faring.

Jarvas drew his cloak closer about his shoulders. "What can be done here is done. We must not linger."

"Then where?" asked Illylle.

"To the bay at the shore, if fortune allows us to win there. If the brethren come overseas we shall meet them." He paused and looked for a time-stretching moment into her eyes and then into Ayyar's.

"I know not what you face, save that it is peril indeed.

And one which none can share with you, no matter how much they wish it. What good fortune may come from willing and from our desires shall march to your right and left, but whether that can arm or defend you''—he shrugged. ''Can any man tell? This has been laid upon you to do—the best with it—and you!''

They crossed into the Waste where the road walls were waist high. Day sky was above but there were clouds; by so much did the weather favor them. But—where were they to go? Venture without plan into THAT'S stronghold?

''Where we go, that I can guess,'' Ayyar said. ''But what we do there, that is another thing.''

''We shall know that also when the hour is come,'' she replied.

Her confidence grated against his doubt. ''To run blindly into THAT'S hold is to perhaps throw away every defense we have.''

Illylle looked at him over her shoulder. ''Defense? Is it 'once a warrior, always a warrior,' Captain of the First Ring of Iftcan that was? There may be other ways of fighting than with blade—''

''Yes,'' he told her grimly, ''with blaster and flamer! Have you forgotten what army has drawn ahead of us into this land? You say we are weapons in ourselves, carrying in us some potent force to meet that which the Enemy can muster. But it is in my mind that we must do as the song says Kymon did, win directly to THAT, face to face. And in so doing we must pass any defenses IT has set. Do you not remember how it was when that space suit took us so easily prisoner? And that may be the least of the dangers now ranged against us.''

''So, what then is your answer? We have no time to

creep and lurk, seeking out some unknown safe path—"

"Can we not? I say we have to or be finished before we are fairly begun. This is no Forest hunt, this is in a land the Enemy has made. There is one way—" He had been thinking, fast, clearly, more clearly, it seemed, than he had for some time.

"And what way is that?" she demanded. Already she had pulled well ahead of him on into the Waste, her impatience a goad.

"Does not the Enemy have the false Iftin? Are they not to the eye even as we?"

He had caught her attention. She looked back at him, a frown on her face.

"The false Iftin—but how—?"

"They are sent out to raid from whatever camp THAT keeps. They come and go—if we can track a returning pack, join it as stragglers—"

"They do not live as we, cannot THAT detect the difference?"

"We must take our chances. But they are no more, and they may be less than the perils we may encounter going blindly. There is no reason not to try this."

"And where will you find them?"

"They have been raiding across the river. Lokatath was with those who pursued them, garthmen caught in turn by the compelling of THAT. Therefore, if we strike south-west we may cross their trail."

Her frown deepened. "It is not good to waste time for something so uncertain."

"For us all the future is uncertain. But, in this, accept warrior wisdom, Sower of the Seed. One does not run blindly into a kalcrok's den because of a need for haste.

And to my mind it is better to enter into THAT'S city by *our* will, rather than ITS, if that may be.''

She yielded to his arguments, but reluctantly, and they went south, still also to the west. The day remained overcast, clouds serving them by so much. Ayyar remembered those glittering points he had sighted from the road, but they came upon nothing that could have given off those flashes. Finally they crossed the deep-rutted tracks which were the trail of THAT'S captives.

Ayyar watched the sky, fearing to sight one of the flying servants. But so far they appeared to move through a deserted land. At last he asked:

"Do you know what we must do when, or if, we reach THAT?"

"This only do I know, that we are in the service of the Mirror. It is my hope that when we reach that last moment we shall be moved in a pattern that will serve for good.''

Tradition granted Kymon more knowledge of his battle. If he had been merely a tool to carry one force to face another, legend did not say it. But legends were the shadows, not the mirrors of truth. And it might well have been that the hero of the White Forest had walked even as they, uncertain and unenlightened.

Ayyar's nostrils took in a new scent. Ah, in so much he had guessed rightly. False Iftin had passed. With wytes or alone? The answer to that might make a wide difference to any would-be trailer.

"They—" Illylle's voice was a half-whisper. Ayyar nodded, signalled her to silence.

A little more to the west—yes, the scent grew stronger, almost a thick reek! But which way had they gone —eastward-traveling raiders would not serve their purpose. He slid cautiously around a rocky outcrop, saw narrow boot prints in the soil—west! Again he signed to Illylle and looked ahead with a scout's eye.

Here the Waste was cut by gullies, with curiously shaped stone outcrops on guard along their rims or at their mouths. It would seem that time and weather erosion alone could not have sculptured those grotesque boulders, that some purposeful hand had pointed up the suggestion of a demonic face or beast. This was a land that had nothing in common with the Forest. It might have been on another planet altogether.

The soil underfoot was not quite sand, but it was barren of plants save for where, here and there, some bunch of long dead roots protruded from the side of a small rise in a way that made them seem to be clutching, misshapen tentacles. And here and there, uncovered by the wind, were patches of ground very hard and dark, so encrusted that a stone falling upon them gave forth a metallic ring. Ayyar was reminded of the scars left by rocket blast on spacer fields. But these patches were too small, too scattered, to be the marks of some ancient port, whatever strange activity they stood monument to.

A red thing with a scaled body surveyed them with bubble eyes set high on its narrow head and then skittered away between two stones. Ayyar watched it go suspiciously. He feared that all life here could in some way report to the ruler of the Waste, make known the passing of any who were not servants of THAT. But on the other hand birds, beasts and scaled things had shared the Forest yet been apart from Iftcan and those who dwelt there.

"It is a wild thing only." Illylle must have guessed his thought.

"How can you be so sure?"

"Do not those who serve THAT give off the shadow of their master? Though it is well to suspect all within this land. I wonder—"

"Concerning what?"

"What do you propose to do when we see this quarry we now trail? False Iftin certainly will not accept us. And they will—"

Ayyar swept her back, holding her half imprisoned against the gully side with his body as he listened, sniffed the air. The reek of false Iftin was suddenly so nose-filling as to make him gag. They must be very close to those they sought, and he had better have a quick and efficacious answer to the question Illylle proposed. She squirmed around to face in the same direction, her body rigid against his. Then she spoke in the thinnest of whispers:

"Just beyond that projection—"

The wall of the gully thrust out here in a sharp promontory. Behind that was an excellent site for an ambush. Ayyar searched the face of the wall against which they stood. One of the bunches of dried roots stuck out there within grasping distance; with such aid he might be able to climb above. He pointed to the crest and Illylle's eyes narrowed as she measured the distance in turn. It all depended upon his ability to make that climb undetected. To spread himself against the wall as a clear target was not good to think about.

Illylle drew her sword. She gestured for Ayyar to stay where he was, but she need not have made that warning signal for surprise kept him still. Along the blade of the Iftin weapon, seemingly coming from the hand curled about its hilt, ran a series of sparkling ripples, silver as the questing finger of Thanth. Now the girl swung the weapon back and forth, its tip up-pointed. She did not turn her eyes from the sword, but her lips shaped a word:

"Go!"

Ayyar jumped and his hand closed about the roots. They held against the pull of his weight. Then his other hand dug deep into the soil, and he climbed. Belly down he crawled along the rim. Illylle leaned forward. Now and then her sword dropped its shimmering point, and to his eyes it appeared that she had to make a great effort to force it up again. What she did he could not guess, but at least he had won to this advantage without being a target for attack.

Now he could see the other side of the buttress. Green, hairless head, tall pointed ears, Iftin cloak outspread—and in its hands no sword—but a barreled object not unlike a blaster. And with, Ayyar did not in the least doubt, perhaps the same force as that off-world weapon.

The creature's head was held high, though it was not searching with its eyes the rim of the cut. Instead that head was shaking slowly from side to side, even as Illylle wove her blade. And its eyes stared blankly at the stone against which it crouched.

Ayyar freed his own sword, though what effect that might have against the metal under the robot's concealing "flesh" he did not know. Only, the moment the hilt was in his hand, the silver ripple he had seen on Illylle's blade dripped from his own fingers. Not memory, but some command deep within launched him into action. He raised the sword so that its point was aimed at the false Ift's head. Ripples spread down and down until it would seem that what made them must drip onto that green covered skull below. And with the ripples there was a drawing within him, a feeling that some inner strength of his own went surging along that conducting blade.

The false Ift jerked, raised high upon its toes, and then fell forward, its limbs loose. On the ground it continued to jerk at intervals but it made no move to rise. Ayyar slammed his sword back into the sheath, a little afraid of the weakening ebb.

In a last spasm the Ift raised a little from the ground, fell heavily back. Ayyar slid down not too far from it. When it no longer moved, he approached it cautiously. The barreled weapon had been released from its grip during that last convulsion and he stooped, would have picked it up, when Illylle's order came.

"No!"

She came slowly, one hand against the gully wall to support her. Now she added:

"You bear within you one power. Dare you deny that after this? You cannot take to yourself the weapon of another!"

There was something in what she said. He picked up a stone and brought it down on the weapon, smashing it to bits. It broke brittlely which he had not foreseen. He then looked to the false Ift, bringing a larger rock to batter the head of that inert creature. The substance of which the skull was formed split. Inside were fused wires, slagged metal. Ayyar squatted on his heels to study the wreckage. Energy, some type of energy, had dripped from the sword in his hand to accomplish this! Yet with that stored within him he had felt no ill, suffered nothing.

"Do you not yet understand?" Illylle demanded. "You are the vessel to carry a force. But it must not be wasted. Now where do we go from here?"

"The same road—with care."

"It would seem we are going to be favored—unless they can sniff us out in turn. Look you above."

Those clouds that had kept the sun from troubling them were massing ever darker. Whether the turbulence coming was born from some machinations of the Mirror or not, they did not know, but that it promised them a concealing cloak was plain.

For a space they traveled the upper ridges of the gullies, crawling serpentwise when they would have been plain against the sky. If other false Iftin or their master had any knowledge of the finish of the one they had accounted for, they did not show it. But Ayyar was willing to proceed upon the assumption that that might be true.

Above the third valley they so avoided, they came upon the first sign that other protection against Iftin had been set up in the Waste. Only the dimming of the storm clouds saved them. Once they had been led captive through the White Forest—where trees of crystal mimicked the rich growth of true life—a dazzling reflection of the true world. Here was raised a pillar of that same crystal, mounted on a headland—to blind Iftin eyes with sun-reflected brilliance. Ayyar warily circled around it, being thus forced to lower levels. The chill of the storm was changing scents. He was not sure they could depend any longer upon their noses for warning.

Then the fury of the breaking storm drove them to any cover they could quickly find. Darkness Ift could face, but not such tearing winds, such buffeting of hail, such numbing sleet.

Together they crouched in a crevice, their cloaks drawn up so they might pull the corners over their heads, hiding their eyes as lightning leaped across a wild and riven sky. And to the wrath of the storm there seemed no end. Whether it was loosed by one power or the other, it had about it that which Ayyar deemed unnatural.

Illylle stirred. Her lips were very close to his ear, but he could hardly hear her words as she said:

"This will hide all trails—"

She was right. Perhaps when they could go on they must simply head west and—

She started; her arm dug into his side. But Ayyar had seen it also, illumined by a flash of lightning.

It had not been there when they had taken refuge, that he could swear to. Yet now it stood on the western wall as if as fixed as the crystal pillar.

Man—no. Nor Ift. But it had four limbs and it stood erect upon two of them. Memory stirred within him. Once he had known or seen its like. Where—and when?

VIII

IT CONTINUED to stand there, facing east, if such a thing had a face to turn east, west, any direction. Danger might lie in awaking Naill memory consciously, but Ayyar was forced to that in order to learn the nature of the Enemy. He told Illylle his plan and what might come of it.

"But that—I have Ashla's memory, and nothing such as that walks through it!"

"Garth memories do not know off-world well," he pointed out. "For years I was in the Dipple on Korwar. Prison though that was, still we had contact with half the galaxy. Korwar is a pleasure planet, save for those condemned to be planetless and so to live within the waste heap of the Dipple. Now and then I had a day's labor at the port and we saw there many strange things. And this—this moves deep in my memory. What we can learn now, anything we may learn, must be to our advantage. But if awaking Naill brings me into a trap set for off-worlders, then do you be ready for it—"

She smiled. "I do not truly believe that one who has been washed in the substance of Thanth can be so taken. But, I shall be ready—for what, Ayyar? To thrust a sword through you?"

He gazed at her with full soberness. "If I were to become such as those who marched through here—then, yes, I would welcome such death at the hands of a friend."

Illylle's smile vanished. "You do not jest. Do you wish to have me swear?"

"There is no need. Only, if I strive to move from here, then do what you must to stop me, at any cost."

He fixed his gaze upon that thing. There appeared no division between head and body, if head and body were terms which could be applied to a rectangular box supported on two stilt legs, two arms or like appendages dangling by its side. It was difficult for even his night-oriented eyes to see it clearly for the storm distorted it. A box on legs. Now that he studied it, he could also make out a series of small sparks of light set in a row across that section comparable to the breast. Also, he was very sure, it was metal, or metal encased. And he had seen its like. Where, when?

Naill Renfro—deliberately he set about recalling Naill Renfro— What were Naill's first memories, so deeply buried that they must be mined with effort bit by bit?

His father's ship—he made himself visualize it, cabin and corridor, his own small cubicle which was the only true home he had ever known. Captain Duan Renfro, Free Trader, and Malani, the wife he had brought from a warm, smiling planet of shallow seas, many islands, endless, gentle summer. The worlds they had visited—then the end with their spacer caught in a battle that was none of their war—Malani and Naill in the escape boat—picked up and brought to Korwar—and the endless gray life-in-death of the Dipple, the dumping place for those displaced by the war with no worlds to return to.

The ship—resolutely Naill-Ayyar turned memory back to the ship, combing it by recall. Nothing like that thing above had been in the ship. Then, on some world where they had gone trading. But that was hopeless. His faded mental pictures of those were past disentangling now. So—the Dipple was all that was left.

Not in the collection of barracks itself—then in the city—or the port. He settled for the port. There had been wide landing aprons on which set down fleets of very differing spacers—traders bringing luxuries from a thousand worlds, passenger liners, private yachts of rulers and the wealthy. They reeled through his mind until— He caught upon one of these fragmentary memories, strove to pin it down. Yes!

A long bank of computers—he had seen that in the heart

of a liner. The ship had been put in quarantine because of a new illness detected aboard. But laborers from the Dipple, hungry for the work, had been sent through a blocked-off passage to bring out some highly important sealed cargo. He had looked into the computer room as he passed, and just such a robot had stood there. It was a service type, meant to deal with computer repair—more than that he did not know.

What was it doing here? The best thing to do would be to follow it—for it must return soon. He was needed—it was most necessary to join the others. What was he doing here in the storm and rain when he was needed, greatly needed? He must be going—

"Ayyar!" A hold on him kept him from rising, from going as he should go. Angrily he strove to break that grip. He was Naill Renfro and he had that which he must do—now!

Look, the robot was turning—leaving— Unless he followed he would be lost! He would never find the others, be one with them as he should be!

"Ayyar!"

Desperately he pulled against the hold. Then something flashed before his eyes, its brightness blinding, searing. Now he was in the dark where there was no Naill —nothing—

"Ayyar!" Very faint and far away that calling. Why should he answer it? To make any effort was too much to demand of him.

"Ayyar!"

The calling would not let him be, pursued him, herded him up, out once more into the world. Very reluctantly he opened his eyes to look into a green-skinned face, into slanting eyes that held concern. Malani? No, Illylle! Slowly, painfully his mind matched a name to that face.

That was Illylle and he was Ayyar—Ayyar of the Iftin. And they were in a shelter between the rocks of the Enemy's Waste while about them the storm raged and from above—

He struggled to sit up though the girl's hands on his shoulders pinned him back with all the strength she could muster.

"It is all right. I am Ayyar—"

She must have read the truth in his eyes for she released him so that he could move, look to where the robot had rested. It was gone and he was not surprised. Had it been spying upon them? What *was* its function in the Enemy's service, for that it belonged in the ranks of THAT he did not doubt.

"It went—that way." Illylle pointed west. "Do you know now—what it is?"

"Very little. I saw its like once—long ago and on another planet—in the computer cabin of a liner. It is some form of service robot, though its real function I do not know."

"But what does it here?"

"Be sure, nothing to our advantage."

As Naill he had thought to use the thing as a guide. As Ayyar he must also do that, and the prospect of such a journey was not easy to think about.

"Come!" At least the storm was slackening, and he felt they dared not lose track of the robot.

They scrambled out of the crevice, winding their cloaks

99

about their heads and shoulders. Rivers ran down the gullies, but the robot kept to the heights, moving as if it were programmed for some independent activity.

Perhaps more than one spacer had in the past landed in the Waste to be used by THAT. They had found one on their first escape, an older type of trader like those Naill had known. But what if there had been more complex vessels, even a liner?

There was a crackle in the air, a blinding burst of light. Illylle cried out, stumbled against her companion. Ayyar rubbed his eyes, striving to wipe away blindness, unable to go on in a black world. Through his body ran again a hot tingling such as he had felt when the tongue from the Mirror had touched him.

Half blind, Ayyar supported the girl, peering about him. There was continued brightness from behind; he dared not turn to face it. Some instinct for preservation sent him staggering to a rock outcrop, dragging Illylle with him.

"What was it? I am blind! Blind!" Her assurance was gone; she clung to him with both hands, her shivering body pressed close to his for comfort.

"That may be temporary," he told her. "Close your eyes, wait. I do not know what it was, but there is now a bright light behind us. If we go forward we must keep to cover."

"Blind I cannot go," Illylle said. "If you can see you must leave me—you must!"

"I, too, cannot see—very much," which was not altogether a lie. This weakness of their Iftin bodies might defeat them yet. "We must wait, hope it will pass."

They sat with fear during that waiting, Illylle's hold on

his arm tight and painful. She said nothing after her outburst, and he did not dare to ask if she had any glimmer of returning sight. His own was clearing, but very slowly. And over such broken ground they dared not venture, not when they must go with two kinds of caution, against a misstep, and in fear of being sighted by some guard of the Enemy.

The storm cleared. Whether it was still night or day Ayyar could not have told. But around the rock against which they crouched still streamed the light from the east, making a fan that was shadowed by break of gully, rise of rock. Seeing that, Ayyar knew that his sight had cleared. He spoke softly to Illylle:

"What can you see now?"

Her eyes had been closed. Now she opened them, blinked, and her fingers dug into his flesh. "Some—a little—but all is blurred. Ayyar, what if—?"

"If you can see some, then it is clearing," he hastened to assure her, hoping he spoke the truth. "Do you see enough for us to go on?"

If Illylle's sight cleared no more, then he must find a better hiding place for them both and soon. Who knew what might roam this land? A cave, a place in some gully where one man with a sword could bar the entrance—that was what they needed. Yet he dared not go to seek it. They must stay together.

"Guide me." She spoke with determination, her will plainly in control. "Guide me and let us go."

So began the worst of their journey, taken with many pauses as from the shadow of each bit of cover Ayyar studied the way ahead for the quickest and easiest route to another. Long since, he had surrendered his hope of tracing the robot. Their only direction was west, and they took it in a weaving pattern, zigzag.

"Any better?" he asked at what might be their tenth halt.

"Only a little, a very little."

He hoped she spoke the truth, was not saying that for his encouragement. So far, he had found them no place for a refuge. They rounded a wall of rock and Ayyar saw glitter ahead. It was not as brilliant as the beam at their back, but it warned. He put on his leaf goggles, helped Illylle to don hers. That reduced the glitter, but Illylle stumbled even more.

"What can it be?" she asked.

"There is one thing—the White Forest."

The crystal trees, certainly those would pick up light from the east, produce just such points of glitter. And the White Forest, if it did not guard the heart of THAT'S domain, must lie very close to it. Could they penetrate the Forest without a guide? They had come out of it once because the alignment of the branches, always straight-angled from the prism trunks, had given them a check upon their direction. But into it they had gone as prisoners guided by the walking space suit.

"There is the wood—" Illylle said longingly.

Yes, the wood, that spot of green life that lay in the Enemy's own country, that had kept alive the Iftin captives. But that lay at the bottom of a chasm and down the stairway which led to it— Ayyar knew that they could never descend that steep way now.

"Come—"

He led her on. The glitter became more intense, but still there was something odd about it. The trees Ayyar remembered had stood tall and straight. This light lay close to ground level. And when their painful crawl brought them still closer, he saw what did face them—a truly insurmountable barrier. For those tall trees were now broken shards, splintered and riven, covering the ground in heaps to cut to rags anything venturing in among their ruins. So must the fury of the Mirror have wrought when it had unleashed that storm months ago. And THAT had either not been able to, or had not wished to, repair the wreckage.

"All broken—" Illylle looked at what lay before them. "We—there is no way through that!"

"None." So much they had lost when the robot outdistanced them. There was nothing left for them to do but cast along the edge of the shattered Forest seeking some refuge. Let the sun rise, strike those pieces—they could not face such reflected light, even if their lives depended upon it. Which well they might.

North or south? North lay the Mirror and the way they had once fled this place. South was unknown land. And was THAT watching? South Ayyar turned now, guiding Illylle, searching for any hint of refuge. They could not hope for clouds and storm a second day.

"Ayyar!" The girl's head was up; she was sniffing.

But what scented the air was not the stench of false Iftin, nor of any of the creatures of THAT. It was cool and clean, and it spoke of real growth and life. But here—in this desert—?

"That way!" She swung her head to the left. "Oh, hurry! Hurry!"

But before them lay the murderous shards of crystal, and Ayyar held her back. He was not sure he could pick a free path through without knowing how far they must travel, nor what lay beyond.

"This way is dangerous—" he began.

"That it is not!" She returned emphatically. "We must find—"

To take that way demanded such an agony of concentration from Ayyar that he held to his strength of purpose only by great effort. Illylle came behind him, heeding his words as to where to set her feet. Time and time again he had to set aside, with infinite care against slitting his hands, a jagged splinter too large to avoid. Yet to encourage them always was that scent of free earth and growing things.

"Growing things?" wondered one part of Ayyar's mind. This was winter; there should be no green here —anywhere. Another trap of THAT with bait no Ift could resist once he had journeyed through the Waste? No, that was one thing which THAT could not produce by ITS will—a counterfeit of true life real enough to deceive the Forest dwellers.

There was a lightening of the sky, or was it intensified radiance from the east? In either case it turned the crystal into a fire about them. Illylle's hold upon him tightened again, and Ayyar knew without any voiced complaint that her eyes suffered from the glare. How much longer—?

The shards vanished, pulverized in two beaten tracks, ground down to pave a roadway. Ayyar was tempted to turn into that road, to follow it. But the scent lay ahead. He looked up and down that road. On it nothing moved —yet—

"On!" Illylle pulled at him. "Let us go—"

They crossed that open space and then passed, while

Ayyar closed the way behind them with chunks of crystal. Wytes hunted by scent, but other patrolling sentries here might only scout by eye. Luckily, on this side of the beaten road the wreckage of the Forest was thinner.

Then there was a dip in the ground, and they looked down into greenery. Illylle loosened her grip on Ayyar —held out her hands.

"Tell me true," she whispered, "oh, tell me true—are those trees?"

They were not Forest giants. In fact they were far removed from the growth of Iftcan. But that they were trees and bore leaves in winter, he could not deny, though why they grew in the midst of territory which belonged to THAT, he could not guess.

Illylle turned her head. Her leaf goggles effectively masked her eyes and the greater portion of her face, but her mouth smiled as he had not seen it do in days.

"Do you not understand? THAT could not grow ITS own works without the force of true growth somewhere to draw upon. There must always be a seed, even if what is drawn out of it is unnatural. This is the seed from which the Enemy's White Forest grew, the energy on which it fed when it was small. But because that was false, it died when the Wrath of Thanth touched it. But the true seed was nourished, not slain in that hour. Nor, having once used it so, could THAT destroy it."

Where she got that knowledge Ayyar did not know, nor even if it was true, though he knew that she believed it so. However, there was no denying this refuge of green in the midst of a desert of death, and they needed it as a man dying of hunger and thirst needs food and drink. So, with only the remnants of caution acting as a brake upon their need and their eagerness, they went down to be swallowed up in the shade of leaf and bough. Illylle dropped, to lie upon her back, her arms outspread, her fingers digging deep into the rich earth as if they were now rootlets to sustain and feed her.

Food—drink— Ayyar leaned his back against a tree trunk, and nothing he could now remember had ever felt as good as the toughness of that rough bark. He had known the need for neither since he had left the Mirror, nor did he now. The scent, the sounds, the feel of the wood were enough to renew his strength, his confidence—

"That road"—he began thinking aloud—"that must be the way the off-worlders and the machines passed. But any Ift on it—unless a false one—"

"Ahhhh—" She sighed. "Here it is difficult to think. One must give oneself up to feeling, just to being—"

Ayyar was tempted even as she, but that inheritance from the Ayyar who had been Captain of the First Ring, a warrior in a desperate lost war, was his conscience now. They could believe welcome of this wood, surrender themselves to its healing, and be lost to the mission that had brought them here. No, somehow the road must provide them— Ayyar's thoughts hesitated, changed direction. This was a safe place in which he could leave Illylle! He did not know how far her eyes had recovered, but he suspected that now he must act without any responsibility for another. If he scouted along the road, he must do it alone, fortified by the belief that she was safe.

How to tell her? She was moving, bracing herself up on her arms. Some of the contentment was gone from her face, a shadow veiled the brightness.

"How well can you see?"

She sat upright; her hands came slowly, plainly unwillingly, to the leaf goggles. She took them off, turned her head from left to right, her lower lip caught childishly between her teeth.

"It is dim, still dim."

"Then you shall stay here for the present—"

"But we were both chosen to carry—"

"I do not say," he compromised, "that in the end we shall not both go. But first I must scout the road ahead—"

"In the day? Even my poor eyes can mark that." She pointed to a sun finger creeping into their green nest. "With the broken Forest to make the glare a hundredfold worse?"

"Be sure I will not move in folly. I would but see the road and if aught travels it by day. If I find the sun too great a torment, I shall return."

He put on his goggles and reclimbed the hill from the clean green into the hard glare of the Waste. The sun was up above the horizon, but as yet it did not pierce too keenly into the places where he crept, careful of every move, lest he cut hand, foot, or body on the jagged bits of the ruined trees.

He heard crunching sounds and pushed forward, lying in a small space between two piles of rubble. And he had been not a moment too soon in his coming, for there was travel on the road. Ayyar was past surprise at anything he saw here. Also this newcomer he knew of old. A space suit, its face plate fogged so that none knew what was within, or if anything was, stumped stolidly along headed east.

Ayyar lay very still. Once before, that thing or its twin had found and taken them captive, using the off-world weapons clamped to its belt. Was it coming to round them up a second time? He waited fatalistically to see it turn aside from the road, come clumping to his hiding place. So sure was he that this would happen that he blinked after it in disbelief as it continued along the track.

Then to his amazement, a second such apparition appeared. Space suit? He thought so. But the proportions of this had never been designed to fit a form of humanoid build. It was short, squat, abnormally broad across the shoulders, and it possessed four walking appendages, but no arms at all, unless the coiled tubing about its middle section represented those. The whole helmet must once have been a clear bubble, but, like the face plate of the other suit, it was now misted to hide what might be inside.

With the same unvarying stride it followed behind its companion eastward.

Although Ayyar lay there until the reflection from the crystals warned him of the danger of remaining in the open, he saw no sign of any human from the port or the garths, nor any of the false Iftin. But he counted four more of the ambulating space suits. Two were old style from ships of human occupancy. There had been another of the four-legged type and one of still another sort. This moved on small tracks, as might a machine. An ovoid body poised above that means of progress. Small openings like miniature portholes ringed it around, but all those were closed. From the top projected two antennae which might once have been limber and moving, but which now hung limp, bobbing against the outer shell of the ovoid.

All of this weird company headed east, two at a time, with an interval between each pair. Ayyar suspected that they were on patrol, but whether this was a regular form of sentry-go, he did not know. With this the full sum of his information, he returned to the restful green of the refuge and reported what he had seen to Illylle. She listened eagerly.

"These strange suits, you have not seen their like before?"

Ayyar laughed. "Even when I was Naill Renfro I did not know all there was to be known about the space lanes. The human suits are old, of a type long since discarded. It may be that the alien ones are the same."

"And those in them?"

Ayyar hesitated. "Somehow I cannot think that they hold life—as we know it."

"That is my thought also. Listen." She put her hand over his on the ground. "In the space of time I have been here alone—there has come a message for me. Not in words, no, nor even in clear thoughts. But this is a place of power, and we carry the fruits of power within us. I believe now that if we open our minds we may learn more of what has been striving to reach me—"

"THAT?" He was alert, remembering only too well what happened when Naill memory opened the doors to suggestion.

She shook her head vigorously. "Never THAT! Not here. But we were sent as tools and perhaps that which has entered into us will now work to open Illylle memory, Ayyar memory, when we have so great a need for more and more of those."

He was still wary, yet her earnestness influenced him, and at last he agreed to try.

IX

THEY LAY on ground, which was not the seared covering of the Waste, but dark and rich, welcoming to seed. And as Illylle had done earlier, they dug their fingers deep into that soil as if striving to root themselves, to be a part of what grew here. Ayyar still feared to open his mind. To do so was to loose a door through which THAT might attack. Still, in this green place, it was hard to think that could be so.

Iftsiga—none of the saplings growing here were of the stock of the Great Crowns. No, if what Illylle thought was true and this was the germ from which THAT derived power to grow the White Forest, then none of that seed would root here. But in that other Forest place, deep in the stronghold of THAT where they had been prisoner, they had found one of the old stock.

Iftsiga, Iftcan—the home Forest—his mind kept returning to the green there. Spring, and the rise of renewing sap—the awakening of Iftin bodies. Summer, with the long beautiful nights for hunting, for living. Fall, with the last securing of the Crowns, the coming of the need for sleep. Winter, when one's body was cradled safe within one of the Great Crowns, one's mind traveling—traveling through dreams.

Where had dreams led during the bodies' slumber? Memories—so faint they were only wisps, which, when he strove to catch them, melted. Winter—winter slumber, one learned then—much—much—

Such as—

One of those wisps of memory became solid. He could read it as if he watched a story tape. Yes, one could learn so. As thirstily as he had drunk Iftsiga's sap, so did Ayyar now hold to that memory. This and this—but could they do it? He was no Mirrormaster. What power had he to call upon?

Through the maze of dream memory, his body answered that doubting thought with a warm surge of life, a demanding of something within him for freedom of action. Ayyar opened his eyes upon the here and now, the green roof of boughs over his head. The need for action still spurred him. Beside him Illylle stirred, gazed into his face.

"Now we know," she said softly. "Now we know—"

"One of the space suits—" His mind was already weighing possibilities.

She frowned. "They are alien. Can they hold what we must send?"

"Where will we find a better key now? I do not think there is another. We can only try that first—"

"You shall be the one to go."

He accepted that readily. Ayyar the warrior, not Illylle the priestess. His life force could accommodate the energy that would burn her out if she strove to use the tool they must put hand to—her degradation would be so much the greater. Yet also with him, through him, would go that part of Illylle that the wave from Thanth had bestowed, so their double share of that energy would march to confront THAT.

As yet he was not sure just how that could be done. Only his own part was clear in his mind from that strange communication with the dreams of the far past. Now—for one of the space suits—a humanoid one.

Would they return from their patrol soon? And how could he capture one? The false Ift had been destroyed by the energy transmitted in sword touch. Could one of the marching suits be so deactivated? And dared he waste power so?

"The power—" He turned to Illylle. "If I must use some of it to capture a suit, will I then be the weaker?"

"For a space, yes. Were we not both so when we took the Ift? But it renews its flow again. I do not think that we would have been sent on such a mission without that assurance."

"And you?"

"When the time comes that I must give all I hold of Thanth's touch unto you, then I shall be as one asleep. So we must search out a bed wherein I may rest until you return for my awakening." She spoke with such serene confidence that he wondered. For to him it did not seem that even victory would bring about his return. Yet he did not voice that doubt.

"We do not have much time," she continued. "If the suits do not return, then we must hunt another key—"

To spy upon the road meant going once more into the sun and glare, but he had no choice. Ayyar hoped the goggles would shield his eyes enough so he could see, when the time for action came. How did one bring down a walking space suit? With a lump of the crystal? No, in the sun he could not be sure of his aim or even if such a blow

would topple it. And what if the suit was occupied?
By—*what?*

He could only let inspiration guide him at the proper
moment, Ayyar decided. Illylle said no more, but she
watched him climb from the pool of green into the desert
of the Waste. He wriggled back to the spot where he had
lain before and covered his eyes. Listen—his ears must do
duty until the very last moment, and the suits had made
noise enough before.

The heat of the sun was a burden on him, pressing his
body to earth. From moment to moment he feared he could
not stand it, that he *must* return to that slit filled with green
or die. Still he listened and fought his misery of body and
the nagging thought that this was useless, that only failure
waited him.

His ears did not betray him. There came a steady
crunch-crunch. Shading his eyes Ayyar looked to the east.
One of the roll-footed suits was returning, and after it,
several feet to the rear, a once human covering.

Wait—if they came back in the same order as they had
gone, he wanted the last in line—the one that had led
before. To take that might not alert the rest of the squad.

Number three was coming, one of the four-legged
trampers. Again a human, then a four-legged— Ayyar
waited, sword drawn and ready. One after another they
rolled or stamped by. Now! This was the last if the count
remained the same.

He crouched for a leap. The space suit was passing
—now!

Ayyar gained the rutted road in one bound. His sword
swung up and out so that its tip touched the helmet on the

space suit. There were sparks and the suit halted while its unheeding companions marched or rolled on.

The Ift waited for any sign that they knew of the loss of their rear guard, or for a hostile move from the suit. But the rest continued on and the suit was statue still. When the others were out of sight in a road dip, Ayyar sheathed his sword and caught the suit by the shoulder. At his touch it fell, startling him into a sidewise leap in wary defense. As it lay still in the road he returned to drag it back to their green hideaway.

To touch the metal made him sick, and he doubted whether he could ever force himself to do what must be done. But he could see no other way. The inert suit fell from his hands at the rim of the valley and rolled down, breaking branches as it bounced and flopped from side to side. Heavy as it was, he thought it did not cloak any body.

Ayyar came to where it lay and straightened it out on the ground. Although it was archaic in style, much older and more clumsy than those of the Renfro ship, the general shape was the same, and he was able to master the old sealing locks.

The fogged helmet came off. From the hollow within issued a small puff of vapor. Ayyar dropped the helmet as he choked and coughed. It was a sharp, metallic smell, combined with acrid, nose tickling ozone.

Plainly the suit did not cover any living, or once living, thing. Seeing that, a little of the lurking nightmare, which had always been in his mind since he had seen the first of these a year ago, vanished.

Ayyar set the helmet to one side and opened the rest of the protective covering. In that portion where the chest of the original wearer would have been there was a small box suspended by wire—almost, Ayyar thought a bit wildly, as if the suit had been equipped with a mechanical heart.

This was scorched and blackened and from it came small trails of smoke. Not wanting to touch it, Ayyar used broken branches to lever and break the wires, wrench it free. Still holding the box between branches, he hurled it out of the valley.

For the rest the suit was empty. Illylle pulled handfuls of leaves from bushes and saplings, selecting certain ones. With pads of these in her hands she came to the emptied suit and held them out to Ayyar.

"Rub these on the inside," she suggested. "They will cleanse it, perhaps make it easier to wear."

The leaves she had chosen were aromatic, good to smell. And he obeyed her with a will, making sure the whole interior was so treated. The mass left green stains on the lining, but he could no longer smell the taint of off-world when he had finished.

He guessed that the suit would fit him well enough, though he was more slender than its one-time owner. To walk planet side in its bulky weight was another matter, it would make him slow and clumsy. He only hoped that that awkwardness would not betray him to those or THAT which had set the unmanned suit on patrol.

Now—what about sight? The face plate of the helmet was fogged and he could not go blindly. Picking up the helmet Ayyar used leaves to rub the eye space. And, to his satisfaction was able to clean away some of the mist. He would have limited sight, but no worse, he believed, than through the goggles at midday.

No longer dared he delay. He turned to Illylle.

"It is ready now."

"Then, before you put it on—come—"

She led him back through the wood to the opposite wall of the narrow valley. "There—" She pointed.

"There" was a hollow recess in the wall. And at hand was a pile of stones, newly gathered, to judge by the broken moss and earth stains on them.

"When we are done with what we must do, then wall me up so that I may sleep undisturbed until you come to wake me."

"And if I do not—?" It was time to say that.

"We did not ever believe that this was a light task, laid upon us for pleasure or our profit. We do what must be done, that the Seed be not destroyed, and that that which raised us from the dust of centuries to walk again be served. Is that not so?"

He bowed his head, for this was truth. "That is so."

"Then"—she drew a deep breath—"give me your hands—and wait."

His hands in hers, Illylle stood with her back to the wall of the valley, singing—not loudly, rather as a murmur. And the words were not for him, but for a loosing, a surrender, a resignation of her will and strength.

Along her head, her shoulders, her body, into her arms, came a silvery flowing, as what the touch of Thanth had placed in her she now passed to him. From her hands into his came that tingling, spreading on into his body. So did they stand until the last of the ripples was gone from her. Now her eyes were closed, her face pale and haggard, and she swayed, falling forward against him.

Ayyar took up her light body; it felt very fragile in his arms. Gently he laid her in the hollow, wrapping both their cloaks about her. Swiftly then he built up the wall of stones, wiping away all the signs of disturbance that he could, lest they guide some hostile eyes to the sleeper.

Having done thus, Ayyar went back to the suit and began to clothe himself in it. Illylle had been right—the scent of the leaves with which he had scrubbed the interior made him able to stand wearing it, though it still took all his courage to fasten down the helmet, encasing him so snugly in the Enemy's covering.

To move so hindered was hard for his Ift body, used to the loose and supple clothing of the forest hunter. He took up his sword and managed to fasten the scabbard to the waist belt. He trusted that this might be thought a trophy of some victory and not a reason for suspicion. This done, he climbed awkwardly out of the valley and tramped to the road. He would lag far behind the rest of the patrol, but there was nothing he could do to remedy that.

It was good to reach the better footing of the broken track, for walking in the suit was a tiring process. Luckily he was able to see enough to avoid the pitfalls of the ruts.

The road descended in a series of dips as if it ran down a giant staircase of wide ledges. And on either side, the shards of the shattered White Forest covered the ground. Ayyar began to watch for the great chasm that had been the end of their journey on that former occasion.

But the trail he followed, when it did come to the edge of that break, turned south and ran along the rim. Mists curling below hid from his eyes the strange place of crystal walls through which he and Illylle had once sought a path, or anything else that might lie in those depths.

Now the path descended again, at a gentle incline to the left of the wall of the chasm, which rose higher and higher as a barrier. And along it were patches of that same crystal that had formed the trees of the White Forest—these protruding as if they were like unto the shelf fungi one saw in the Forest.

On one of these lay something dark, and Ayyar moved closer. A man from the garths by his bush of beard, his clothing—though that was rent into tattered rags—rested there. He was curled upon himself, his head turned away, and Ayyar thought that he was dead. He halted by the quiet stranger to look over the way that still lay ahead. There was a valley—wide. And from its floor were raised mounds which differed sharply in color from the red-yellow of the sandy soil on which they were based. They were black, a dull, lusterless black. And they had been shaped by design, not nature, in sharply geometric forms. From this place he could see them in part. From the sky above they must be very plain indeed. The labor that had gone into their making must have been enormous.

Among those mounds things moved, perhaps the men from the port and the garths, or other space suits animated by the will of THAT, but they seemed to do so aimlessly and without purpose. Machines did likewise. He saw the grubber rumble along a mound foot, dwarfed by that rise of earth.

What this place was or its use, he did not know, unless it was merely a keepsafe for the servants of THAT until they were wanted. Perhaps as one among many he would not be detected. But he must find a way to THAT, wherever IT might dwell, and to that he had no clue at all. If it meant searching through all the Waste and every wonder in it, then that he must do. He went on down into the place of mounds.

If this could be so clearly sighted from aloft, he wondered as he trudged along, why had none of the early explorers of Janus mentioned it? Why had it not shown up on any of the survey visa-tapes made before the planet was open to settlement? Such signs of a native intelligence would have kept the planet off the first auction held by Survey when the Combine had acquired rights here almost a hundred years ago. The trees of Iftcan could easily have remained a secret to explorers, as they had, but surely not this!

The closer Ayyar came to the plain of the mounds, the more he wondered at them. As far as he could detect, they were not buildings—but solid piles of earth. The burial places of some long vanished race? Iftin memory peopled Janus with naught besides their own kind, THAT, and the Larsh. And the Larsh were beast-men, only just emerging from the animal in the final days of Iftcan. Though perhaps the Larsh had a thousand years or more after their final victory to rise in civilization under the domination of THAT. Maybe these monuments were raised in honor of their ancestors or the power that had led them against the Forest.

Loose sand rose about the boots of the suit as he came out into the valley floor. His pace was now a shuffling crawl for it was labor to plow through this. Ayyar stopped short as a man approached. The other wore the tunic of one of the port security police, and in his tanned face his eyes were set, staring dully ahead as he walked, shifting and skidding in the sand unceasingly, as if he were a mechanical toy set to go and then forgotten, to walk so until he ran down into death.

All the others Ayyar could sight near enough to see clearly were like this man. They twisted and turned, went this way and that, with no reason, merely keeping on their feet and moving. He looked about for the animated space suits, but there were none about. Nor in this sand were there any tracks he could follow. Perhaps to circle the walls of the valley— In that way he could keep out of the path of the restless walkers.

Those walls were perpendicular, and on their surfaces the protruding crystals formed irregular splotches. Twice as Ayyar went on his slow survey of the wall, he sighted other men lying still, usually fallen face forward, arms outstretched as if they had collapsed, never to stir again. And both times these were garthmen, not from the port. Ever back and forth, into the shadows of the mounds and out again, walked those others without rest. And the machines crawled and rolled in the same aimless fashion.

Ayyar plodded on, the suit heavy on him, every movement demanding more and more effort. But he feared to stop among that ever-moving company, lest that halt alert any watcher. Only fatigue drove him at last to that danger and he rested, back against the wall, studying what he could see of the valley.

The sun marked afternoon. Ayyar longed for the coming of night. Nowhere in that crowd did he note any false Iftin. Perhaps both they and the space suits had their own place. Doggedly he began to march again.

There was something odd upon the top of a mound he now neared. He strove to raise his head within the lock of the helmet, straining to see better. That was a flitter resting there. At least it did not buzz about as did the rest.

Change came suddenly. Had he not paused from sheer fatigue, Ayyar would have had no warning at all. So close that he might have reached out a hand to lay on his shoulder, a garthman stalked stiff-legged. Now he halted, one foot still readied for the next step. For a moment he stood thus, then toppled to the ground. And he was not the only one. They were all going down, falling where they stood, some skidding forward as momentum carried them along. Ayyar was now the only one on his feet on the plain where activity had ceased in an instant.

He sensed what— A searching thought? Questing for him? Or just for anything foreign to the valley? Apprehension made him do the only thing he could, dampen his thoughts, blank out Ayyar as best he could. Perhaps normally he could not have accomplished that; perhaps it was due to the virtue that had flowed out of the Mirror that he was saved. He was conscious of a hovering, seeking thing, as if he could actually see some great hand, with crooked fingers ready to grab, high over his head.

Moments passed; the shadows of the mounds spread larger and darker, swallowing up many of those who lay upon the sand. Still that thought sought, hunted— And never dared Ayyar believe that truly he could escape that hunt.

Then, as swiftly as it had come, it was gone. Yet none of the captives rose again or moved, and the plain was deathly still. Dared he go on? Or would the very fact that he moved reveal him? He could not look in another direction without turning his whole body. Must he play statue here for perhaps hours? But with the night, surely with the night, he might draw the dark about him as a cloak and dare to walk again!

Ayyar did not have to wait for the night. From between two mounds came a couple of space suits, one human, one of the four-legged type. They halted now and then by some of the supine figures, though as far as Ayyar could see they did nothing else but stand so. Finally the humanoid figure stooped and picked up one of the limp men, held him on his feet, until the rope-like appendages of the other suit flicked forth and steadied him. Together they marched toward the end of the valley, holding the helpless body between them. And, daringly, Ayyar plowed through the sand to follow.

The man they carried wore a uniform tunic with officer's insignia on the collar. Perhaps THAT had drawn all the port personnel to IT, had the off-world force in its entirety here. The two space suits turned to the left, putting one of the smaller mounds between them and Ayyar. He kept on along the wall of the valley, striving to hurry a little to catch up with them when they came to the end of that mound. Only when he reached that spot, no space suits with prisoners were to be seen!

Ayyar waited, but they did not appear. Now he ventured away from the wall, shuffled through the sand to the side of the mound and edged along that, thinking that when the others came into sight he would fall in behind them. Still they did not come.

The mound ended, and he turned its point and looked back along the other side to where the others must be, fearing that they might have taken off in another direction while the pile of earth had been between them.

There was nothing there—nothing at all! The suits and their prisoner might have been wholly illusion. With the mound wall now on his left, Ayyar started down the side that had been the path of those others. Several of the garthmen and two from the port lay prone in the sand with no signs of life. But Ayyar thought he could make out, some distance away, a dragging path, grooving the sand, perhaps cut by the feet and legs of a man half carried, half pulled.

He came to the end of that identation, for end it was, midpoint of the mound wall. Either they had flown from here or simply disappeared. For loss of anything better to search, Ayyar lifted his arm in the stiff sleeve of the space suit and thumped a mittened hand against the earth of the mound. A clod was dislodged and fell, showing plainly against the lighter sand. Now he saw other such clods about the end of the trail.

Had they climbed? Swinging around to face the side of the mound, he inched along, squinting through the dim face plate at the earth. Only such a close inspection showed him the hollow, nearly at eye level. He raised his hand and set it into that.

Under his feet the sand stirred. He was moving down! Already he was knee deep, his hand pulled from that hole, sand pouring in about him as he sank. Waist deep, and now the sand was stopped. There was a ridge rising above to hold back that dry flood. Under the sand on which he stood was solid footing, and that platform, whatever it was, was descending smoothly as if through a shaft.

There was no way to escape. In the clumsy suit he could not hope to climb out quickly enough. He was as much of a prisoner now as the man he had seen dragged to this place.

X

He was not really in a shaft, Ayyar decided, for he could see no walls. And the sense of insecurity that that discovery gave him kept him very still on what he hoped was the center of the platform. It was dark here, even for Iftin eyes. And he could not lift his head, imprisoned in the helmet, to see the outer world above.

At last the carrier touched bottom, but for a long moment Ayyar made no move, almost hoping it would ascend. When it did not, he slid his right foot forward carefully, not raising his boot from the flooring. Sand from the surface grated under his weight, then his foot met another level, the floor of this burrow.

Ayyar took a chance, freed the helmet catch so he could push that back to hang between his shoulders. His head was free, his sight no longer dimmed by the plate. Now he could strain back, see that oblong of light above. It looked very far away, and now, though he flung the weight of his body to stop it, the platform, showering sand from its surface, began to rise.

His weight made no difference. Ayyar rolled off the unrailed surface. He stumbled back to avoid the flood of sand and bleakly watched the platform go. However, he could see a little more now that he was not prisoned in the helmet. He looked about swiftly before the source of light above was sealed by the platform.

Walls faced him fore and aft, within touching distance

were he to extend his arms. Right and left was darkness. Which way should he go to trail those who had preceded him? Two choices—with no clue to influence him one way or the other. He became aware of a kind of humming in the walls. This place had life, and awareness that was surely not the emission of any human or Ift mind.

Above, the opening closed, leaving him in the dark, but that blackness did not last. To human eyes, Ayyar decided, it might still be totally lacking in light, but he picked up a throbbing along the walls. If darkness had shades, then he saw one passing over another, blacker. Energy—could one see energy? He breathed in. The air carried faint, strange odors. But—yes, his guide—the scent of man! Could he depend upon his nose to track the off-worlder and his captors?

Ayyar started down the left-hand path, sniffing. That odor held, though it grew no stronger. Under his boots sand crunched and shifted. Within a few feet he traveled on smooth surface with now and then a ringing sound, in spite of his efforts to move quietly. The shadow pattern on the wall did not change. If he had set off any alarms by venturing into this place he had no warning of that.

There were no breaks in the walls. Looking back a short time later, Ayyar could not be sure where he had entered. If this was a trap, then he was surely and firmly taken. He was conscious that not only his nose, his ears, and his eyes were on guard, but also that inside him some other unnameable sense now did sentry-go, waiting for what he could not put into words. It too quested, waiting for —what?

On and on—only his nose continued to tell him that he was not on a false trail. Walking was easier with no sand to impede. And a compulsion grew to hurry as fast as those weights on his feet would let him. Ayyar fought that, determined to use a hunter's, a scout's caution.

He had begun to think the passage had no end when he saw the faint gleam beyond. Finally he came to a round plug door, intended to seal off the passage, but now swinging ajar. It was familiar enough to give him pause. This was the kind of barrier one found guarding an air lock on a spacer. Ayyar carefully put out his hand. It gave easily to his slight pull. He flattened himself as well as he could against the wall of the passage while he sent the door flying open against the opposite wall.

Light—thin, grayish, but still light. He waited alertly. This was far too much like a trap. Man or machine or whatever prowled these ways could be in ambush there. But they could not disguise what betrayed them to his nose, and he sniffed.

Acrid fumes—faint—linked unto that which had arisen from this suit when he first opened it. And other things, among them still the smell of man. But none strong enough to warn.

Ayyar stepped over the raised threshold, looked about him warily. To Iftin eyes this light was good. He stood in a space that was perhaps as large as Iftsiga's spreading girth. The bole of that Giant Crown had not been perfectly round, but this area was. Into it fed three other passages, or so he guessed by the doors he saw. There was, in addition, a curling stairway, hardly more than a ladder, made to rise about a wide center pillar. This too was familiar, of space ship design. Ayyar moved to the foot of that ladder, raised his head high, sniffing. Then he bent forward awkwardly to smell the steps.

The scent was there. But he eyed that rise dubiously.

Unhampered by his suit, he would have had no fears about the climb. Within this casing, such movement was another matter. But to shuck the suit might be far more dangerous. It might even be deadly dangerous to continue to go helmetless here. Only the need for sight made him dare it.

As he had foreseen, the climb was difficult, and he had to pull himself up and along by grasping both rails. The ladder was metal, a smooth surface on which his boots, unless planted very carefully, were inclined to slip. Space suits were equipped with magnetic plates in the soles to counter just such perils, but on his suit they were no longer in service.

He traveled through another tube now, this rising straight up instead of running horizontally as had the first. Again there were no breaks in the walls, no landings giving on any level. Ayyar continued to climb, pausing every few steps to listen, sniff, await a warning from his inner alert.

The light grew brighter as he advanced, near that of a moonlit night in the upper world. Ayyar marveled at the walls; there were no signs of plate seams. The whole great tube might have been cast in a single piece. There was a chill here, an alien feel that triggered his old revulsion. Yet he was sure that the technology Naill Renfro had once known had nothing in common with these burrows.

There was an end to the ladder stair at long last. He came into a second round area from which again ran hallways. But none of these were doored by locks. Here he made the daunting discovery that he could no longer depend upon his nose for guide. Too many odors, all foul by Iftin standards, fought one another. He could take any one of those passages and not be sure that it led him aright. Which way—?

"Try—"

Ayyar half crouched, his hand on the sword hilt which was to him the natural weapon. Then he knew that word had not been spoken in his ear as it had seemed for one wild instant, but rather had formed in his mind.

THAT?

"Try—sword—" Again, and very faint, a shadow picture only, of a thin face, an Iftin face—the eyes closed in slumber—or something deeper than slumber—the cheeks a little sunken—Illylle! Not quite as he had seen her last, but still—Illylle.

He did not cry her name aloud, but he strove to make it carry along his reaching thought of her to bring him assurance that it was she who had sought him thus.

"Try—the—sword—" The lips of that shadow face in his mind did move.

Ayyar drew the sword, swung to face the nearest hall. He did not know what he expected, but there was nothing—just the sword pointing. Slowly he turned to the next, again nothing. But at the third—ahhh—

Not the green light that had once dripped from it, no, this was a spark only, flashing and gone again in an instant. Warning—or guide? He must believe the latter.

He passed at his suit-dictated shuffle into that passage, the sword, pointing now to the floor, giving him no further sign. This was not a round tube. The ceiling was higher. And now and then he saw scratches on the walls as if large, moving objects had forced their way along with some difficulty.

"Illylle?" Once more he mind-called.

"Watch—sword—" No longer her face, just those words, and with them a sense of danger, as if this communication could awaken some peril. So he broke contact.

Yet he was heartened; he no longer walked so alone in this place.

The hum in the walls was stronger. He could feel also a kind of pulsation in the air. The stink of machines, a strong stench that gave him the impression of age, of long entrenchment in this place, was heavy. There was the outline of a door in the wall to his left and above it a shuttered slit. He paused to look within.

Vast dusky things he could not identify—machines, he guessed. And from there the hum was a muted roar—not truly of sound, but of vibration. It was hard to equate this place with the White Forest, with THAT as he had thought of IT—a power beyond such toys of men, as was the Mirror of Thanth, and what reached through it, far beyond the knowledge of the Iftin who had followed another path of life altogether.

What was THAT? He was beginning to revise his ideas. Or was all this merely used by the servants here? Who had built all this—and why?

After Ayyar left the place of machines, there were no more doors. But shortly he passed between two crystal plates set facing each other. And his sword sparked.

Suspicion was triggered. He swung to the right, touched sword point to that sparkling panel. A touch only, not hard enough to mar it, or so he had thought. But from the point of that Iftin-forged blade, cracks spread in a web. The block became dull in an instant. At once Ayyar turned and served the other panel in the same fashion. If that had been some warning or control, as he suspected, then it would not operate again. But had the warning of his coming already flashed ahead? Perhaps he had thus offered a challenge to what dwelt here.

He watched for more of the panels, intent upon breaking them before they could relay his advance. There were two more such.

Perhaps he gained too much self-confidence by his small successes. He was not prepared for what followed when he paused to rest by that last panel. Suddenly he found himself walking, or rather the suit was walking, carrying him with it. In spite of his struggles, his attempts to throw himself out of stride, even to the floor, it continued to carry him ahead.

By concentrating all his will on a single bit of action, Ayyar was able to force the hand holding his sword to return that weapon to its sheath. He was afraid that whatever now controlled the suit might drop or throw away that blade—upon which he centered all his hopes of ever coming out of this place alive. He had thought that the "heart" he had removed from the suit had been its control. But it would seem that the covering in which he was now a prisoner was still sensitive to outside command. It even moved more quickly, with greater ease than he had been able to use. Ayyar was being transported, as much a helpless captive as that off-worlder he had seen brought into this maze.

The suit bore him steadily past other doors, with only a short chance to look inside. More machines—but these smaller—and always totally unfamiliar. Now, here was another of the curving stairs and the suit confidently climbed.

Illylle, he longed to reach to her. Not that she could give him any answer to this last disaster, but because he needed, oh, how greatly, some contact with reality. What was here was not life as he knew it, rather something opposed to his species for all the ages.

Yet he dared not give his spirit that bolstering. How he knew that, he was not certain, only that it was as true as any oath laid upon him. His hands lay helpless within the gloves, reaching for fresh holds to draw him up each step his unwilling feet took. Up and up—where?

When he came out of that second stairway, he was not alone any longer. One of the ovoid space suits rolled along. Ayyar waited for recognition, for the thing to make some move toward him. Not until it had passed, was several paces away, did Ayyar realize that it had not been sent to deal with him. But his suit thrust him along in its wake.

His inner sense was a warrior waiting battle, the kind of battle which is the last stand against the assault of the enemy. Ayyar snarled. About him was a choking stench. His fear was cloaked and armed with anger. Already he knew that it was all of THAT.

Ahead another space suit came out of a door, moved diagonally down the corridor. Ayyar gasped as he caught sight of what that metal monster carried. For slung across its shoulder, arms and heads swaying lifelessly back and forth, was the unclothed green body of an Ift!

Illylle! How had they—?

He could not hasten the pace of the suit to catch up with that other and its burden before it had entered another door. But as he passed that opening in turn, Ayyar turned his head far enough in the unyielding collar of the suit to look within. The green body lay on a table there, face up—not Illylle!

Not any one from their own small band. Then he saw that slit at throat level, the metal arms rising up and out of the table slab to work—false Ift!

Ayyar witnessed no more for his suit went past, on down that hall which gave on many rooms, the contents of which he saw but did not understand until as last he came to one which the suit entered. Ayyar shut his eyes against dazzling light. He felt the suit move at its controlled march, then turn around, take two steps back, come to a halt. Cautiously Ayyar tried to move. He could wriggle a little within that shell, but that was all. To raise his arm was impossible. He was a locked-in prisoner as ably kept as if he lay chained in a cell.

Through slit-open eyelids he tried to see what lay about him. The light came from a series of reflecting surfaces, but luckily the spot on which the suit had elected to take root was not facing any of those. By turning his head Ayyar saw he was one in a line of robots and suits. Next to him was one of the ovoids on rollers, beyond that a repair robot such as he had seen at ports, but of a slightly different pattern, and fourthly another humanoid space suit. There were still others, but he could not see them clearly.

The line of mirrors or reflecting surfaces was on the opposite wall to the right. And facing the midpoint of that line was a tilt-top table, now moved from the horizontal to the vertical. Strapped on that table was the off-worlder from the sandy valley. His eyes were open, staring into the surface of the mirror in which he was reflected in every detail. But he was not struggling against the bonds that held him, and Ayyar was not even sure he was alive. He could see no reassuring rise and fall of his chest.

There was only one table fixed so, only one man. But in the mirror to that captive's right, there was another reflection! It was as bright and clear as if the one who was so pictured still faced it. Garthman—bushy beard, untrimmed hair, dun colored clothing—

Only no man himself!

Ayyar's suit began to move, pacing out from the wall. From that line a second humanoid suit followed. Was he to stand before the mirrors? He had to close his eyes; the glare was punishing. Yet there did not seem to be any great amount of light elsewhere in the room.

His arms were raised by the suit, the gloved fingers flexing and curling. They grasped small projections, turned them, and his own fingers felt the pressure of the grip. Ayyar stole a look beneath near-closed eyelids. The suit that held him prisoner and the other humanoid one were freeing from the wall the mirror that bore the reflection of the garthman.

The panel was a head taller than the suits and none too easy to unclasp. They worked slowly until they could pull it from the frame, swing it horizontal between them. On the surface, the representation of the garthman did not move. It could have been a tri-dee picture of Naill Renfro's knowledge. The suits persevered until they could carry it between them. Then they turned and walked from the room, paying no attention to the off-worlder on the table.

The other suit was in the lead and strode back down the corridor up which Ayyar had come only minutes earlier. Not too far away it turned into another chamber where were a series of tables. Two were occupied. On one lay an Ift body, but only in part. The hands were still blobs of jelly-like substance, the head shaped but still featureless, the tall, pointed ears only flaps.

It rested on a mirror surface such as the one the two suits

carried between them. And on that smooth, sleek table, showing only in part, Ayyar caught a glimpse of a picture, as if the reflection were a pattern to induce the growing of the thing resting on it.

On the second table was a mass of quivering jelly spread out to hide whatever pattern lay below it and over that lights played in swift, sharp flashes or a steady glow, each touching but one portion at a time.

All that was Ayyar, the Ift, shrank and rebelled against what lay in this chamber. His sickness of mind, body, and soul was so great that he could have spewed forth even his identity if that were possible. The stench of THAT here was more than he could bear, and afterwards he thought that he had lost consciousness for a space.

The gloves were moving, and so perforce his hands, snapping up catches about the rim of an empty table. Thus the mirror they had brought was immobilized. When their task was completed, the suits walked away, returning to the place of the mirror to take their stand again in the line of waiting servitors. Ayyar's head cleared a little, away from that foul place of unnatural growth. He swallowed the sourness in his mouth by will. For the moment at least, he mastered his unsteady stomach. He must free himself from the suit—but how?

He had come to believe during this excursion that whoever, or whatever, moved the suit either did not know he inhabited it or thought him so securely a captive that it did not care about his presence. If the first guess was the truth, then he might have a way to force escape, though afterwards he would have to continue in these burrows without the small protection the suit might afford.

But—to get out—?

The energy in his body, channeled into the sword, had incapacitated the suit the first time. But the sword was in the sheath at his belt, and he could not raise his hand to free it. His hand— Ayyar strove to turn his wrist within the glove. Since their return the glove had hung limp. The fingers did not answer to the pressure of his as they once had, but by using all the strength he could muster, Ayyar was able to move the hand a little until the fingers brushed the hilt of the sword.

So far—but no farther. The sword had to rest against his bare flesh before the energy would drain into it. His bare flesh—

Ayyar stopped struggling with those stiff fingers. The sword had conducted the energy—but did he need that? He had that energy within him. For moments he fiercely willed to release that power through any part of him that touched the suit. But with no result.

The suit came to life as it had before. This time, as it stepped from line, a four-footed space suit accompanied it. They headed for the table where the off-worlder faced his replica on the mirror. And once more Ayyar closed his eyes against the glare. They loosed the clamps which held the silent captive. Ayyar made a great effort. And because the movement he planned was in tune and not in opposition with the suit's ordered duty, he achieved his purpose. The Ift sword hilt caught in one of those clamps and was drawn from its scabbard as the suit moved away.

Now—his one lone chance! The suit leaned forward to loose the clamps about the off-worlder's ankles. Ayyar threw himself forward, over-balancing the shell that held him so it crashed to the floor. He turned his head, and his lips felt the coolness of the sword hilt. His teeth closed about it with a frantic grip. Already the suit was moving ponderously to regain its feet. And, as it came up, the sword swung back, with all the skill Ayyar could summon, to touch against its breast.

This—this was it! As he had striven to aim that energy along his hand and into the blade, now he attempted to send it forth from his mouth. And there were silver ripples answering, flowing down to the suit. Would it work?

The other suit was going about the business of freeing the prisoner from the table. But his had stopped. Tentatively Ayyar raised his hand and was able to take the sword hilt from his mouth. He was free from the will that had used the suit for a servant. But how long would that precious freedom last? Once before he had thought the suit his, only to be trapped in it. He began to loosen the seals.

Finally he stepped forth, and the suit, now an empty case, lay on the floor. While he had so labored, the four-footed suit had put off the final bonds of the captive and had taken up the limp body to bear it toward the door, leaving behind the mirror vividly imprinted with the reflection.

Ayyar caught up his sword, freed the baldric from the suit and hurried after, down the corridor but now in the opposite direction. Should he short-circuit that suit, strive to free the man? But the off-worlder had not moved; his eyes still stared as his head rested on the suit's back. To all appearances he was dead.

The suit entered another chamber, and Ayyar paused on the threshold, staring at what stood within. Row after row of tall cylinders—to his right clear and empty. But others were filled to the brim with a murky, pink fluid, then capped with heavy domes of dull red metal. In that liquid were half-seen solid cores. The suit he had followed approached one of the empty cylinders. One of its waist tentacles snapped out, pressed a stud in the base of the upright column. The huge container swung out and down. Into the waiting receptacle the suit slid its burden. Once filled, the container returned to its original position. A cap was lowered from overhead and, from a pipe in its crest, liquid trickled down to rise about the body.

Ayyar shrank to one side. The space suit had turned, was coming back to the door.

XI

COULD OR DID it see him? He had no chance against an attack with only a sword for defense. Then his mind steadied. If the suit was inhabited he might have to fear it, but if it were empty the sword energy ought to render it helpless. His confidence flooded back. But prudently he stepped to the left, out of its direct path.

It did not pause or show any interest in him, but stamped on into the corridor, leaving Ayyar free to explore the room. All the cylinders with liquid in them were so murky that he could only see shadowy forms floating within. But the number was astounding for the chamber was very large and the filled containers stood like a forest of evil trees. There were surely more here than the numbers of false Iftin they had seen, unless those formed a real army. But these—if the patterns for the false Iftin were bottled here—who were they? Changelings caught in the net of

THAT? Or—Ayyar's heart beat faster—were they from the old days, captives taken by the Larsh? And if so —could they be restored to life again?

As he returned, he glanced at the container that had so recently been given an occupant. The red liquid flowed now about the chin of the motionless off-worlder, lapping against his lips. In him was no sign of life.

Where was THAT which controlled all this? Ayyar had seen nothing moving except the suits. Should he seek a higher level or a lower? And where did these burrows lie—under the mounds or the rock walls of the valley cliffs?

He turned left as he came out, heading into the un-known, watching for any wall plates. There was a pair farther on, and this time he did not shatter them. Rather, he went to floor level, wriggling past on his belly, rising only when he was well beyond their frames.

Some time past, Ayyar had stopped depending upon his nose, for the mingling of what were, for him, stenches, blocked his ability to select any to follow. But now he did smell something, and it was like the clean blade of a knife cutting a foul kalcrock web.

For an Ift, you could not disguise the smell of growing things. He needed that as he had needed it in the valley where he had left Illylle. So he followed that scent ea-gerly, yet not so headlong that he failed to take note of his going and of any pitfall that might lie ahead.

No stairs—but a sloping downward of the passage, and ever the scent of true life. But—this was winter—and what he drew into wide nostrils was the odor of spring! Caution dampened his first excitement. It would seem that in THAT'S domain even the seasons could be controlled.

He crawled past two more of the wall crystals and then was out in the open. From a point below rose the heady fragrance of what might have been the Forest of Iftcan itself!

The light was silver moon radiance. Ayyar sighed with relief and pleasure as it refreshed his tired eyes, just as the scents restored his body. Slowly he relaxed, was content.

Content? Deep in his mind the alert sounded. This was not Iftcan—this lay in the hollow of THAT'S hold! Be not fooled by an outer husk—any more than by the false Iftin. Had he not seen how one thing might be fashioned to resemble another?

Still, what lay below beckoned him past any self-control. This was of his knowledge, his natural home. He began to descend a narrow path, so steep that he needed full attention for his footing. There were trees below, a dense growth of them, their crowns making a green floor for the eyes. And Ayyar's questioning nostrils picked up no evil scent.

He dropped from the path and moss rose about his ankles, made a cushion for his feet. Among that thick growth he saw here and there the night-closed bud of the tottlee, its blue so pale it was a small ghost of its daytime self. And here and there, by the foot of the wall, stood tall bargor lilies, light green with the darker spots fading into the leaves. Odd—these seemed to have no detectable scent while the night-blooming bargor of Iftcan could perfume the air for a wide area. So small a thing—

Ayyar stood staring at the lilies. Then he reached down, touched a finger to one of those velvet petals. It was alive—real. Yet where was the scent? A small thing, but one that broke through his unity with what grew about him. Now he studied what else was rooted there. The moss, yes, that was real.

And there was a sal bush. The moisture in its thin leaves exuded at night to form luminous drops, tiny water jewels. One by one, Ayyar catalogued the plants, saplings, flowers, strove to find them wanting in some particular. Only the lilies—

No! The fragrance of bargors, cloyingly sweet, rose about him in an instant, as if someone had released it from a hidden fountain within the lily clumps. Released? Ayyar licked his lips. He thought of the scentless lilies, found them unnatural and so was led to examine more closely the place wherein he walked, and here was the scent coming as if by order—only too late to allay suspicion.

He pulled one of the drop-hung leaves, crumpled it in his hand. It gave forth the proper aromatic odor, felt completely normal. But now he did not believe in it or in this whole woodland. This was a trap of sorts.

Ayyar returned to the path down which he had come, fearing this place that had seemed to promise what he needed most. The wall along which that narrow footway had descended was bare. What had seemed solid rock under his feet had vanished as if it had never been. So THAT must know he was here. But at least he was warned and alerted—by so small a thing as a scentless flower.

He looked to the ground and the trees. Those were not tall though he might walk under their lowest branches with good head room to spare. But to one knowing the Great Forest, this was a wood shrunken into a miniature. To off-world eyes the gloom under the massed leaves would have been close to total darkness, but to an Ift this was not unusual. He picked out the gleaming grains lying in clusters along trunk and branch—fjot eggs filled with the inner light that would also grace those delicate insect bodies that would issue from the tissue shells.

Where he now stood was the only open space. There was no way to skirt the wood by going along the valley wall on either side, and any retreat to the burrows was closed. His way must be forward unless he proposed to remain in the moss-carpeted pocket forever. He had his Iftin senses and his sword—and a very clever trap to penetrate. With a shrug for all folly, including his own, Ayyar walked under the first tree.

For all his careful examination, he could see no discrepancies between this wood and those natural to Janus. Almost, he began to suspect his own discovery concerning the lilies. He threaded his way between trees and came to another opening, a glade where there was a small pool, molten silver in the moonlight—moonlight!

Ayyar stared up to the patch of open sky. Yes, there was the moon. But—he shivered. Just as the lilies had been a warning, so did that moon appear not quite right. Though what was missing or had been added, he could not have sworn to. The water of the pool invited, lured him with the promise of a deep draught of clear, cold water. But that which had sustained him since he had been touched by Thanth dulled that lure, made it easy for him to put aside thirst.

On a rock by the pool rim a skeleton leg equipped with a hooked claw shot out, dipped into the water, arose grasping a struggling, finned creature, and disappeared again. A fishertonk—normal again in this place and hour. Ayyar listened to all the sounds. He identified hunters, both furred and feathered, all save one—no quarrin sounded its mournful night cry here.

Quarrin and Ift, long partners in the Great Forest—not as servant and master, but as equals of different, but intelligent species. And he had heard no quarrin call. Was he watched, traced through this wood? Would they now produce a quarrin as they had the lily fragrance when he had noted its absence? But though he stood and listened, that mournful "hooo-ruurru" did not sound.

He skirted the pool, reentered the wood, trying to fathom its purpose. So far he had not been menaced by any danger, and there were some native to the Forest that could reasonably have been used here to imperil him had "they" wished to do so. Who or what lay behind all this—and also why? In the burrows, machines did THAT'S bidding. Here the Forest grew in miniature, Ayyar firmly believed, to THAT'S will. Illylle must have been wrong to believe it could not do so. He stiffened, leaped instinctively to set his back against a tree trunk. Fragrance had come from lilies when he had noted its lack, but this was not any perfume; it was that rankness that matched with false Iftin.

Could it be that those robots must be nourished by a wood of illusion as if they had that much kinship with the ones they imitated? He waited. There was no sound of footfall, but the smell was stronger and he was sure that the creature came his way. A bush trembled as a rounded arm swept aside a branch, and she stepped into the open beyond one of the buttressed roots of the tree where he stood.

Out of memory she was, not like Illylle who had worn hunter's dress and been a comrade under the dark cloud of danger. This was an Ift maiden such as once had been at the Choosing in the courts of the springtime. And she wore the flower robe of that day, living blossoms spilling their perfume as she moved. Her face was oval, her slanted eyes dark, and there was all the beauty of her race in her. She gazed at Ayyar, she smiled and beckoned with the old, old gestures of the Choosing. Memory worked in him, and an old excitement his present changeling self had never known awoke, drew him away from the tree, his hand out to meet hers without his willing.

"False—"

A whisper in his mind, a face to match the whisper, though much faded now.

"False—" So thin and far away a warning, while before him swayed the maiden, her feet moving in the first steps of the Choosing dance, her hands reaching, reaching, but now her smile a little uncertain, almost hurt—

"Vallylle, I am Vallylle—I am yours, strong warrior—" The flower robe rustled; its perfume was so thick that Ayyar found it hard to breathe. Yes, once there had been a Vallylle, and he had searched for her at the Choosing. This was not false—it was true, true! Ayyar memory said it was true.

"False!" The whisper deep in his mind was despairing, urgent.

"Come!" She was imperious now in her call to him. "Vallylle does not wait for any warrior—many wait for her!"

Neither was that false, nor any boast, memory told him. There were many who would give much, very much indeed, to dance the Choosing with Vallylle. To hesitate now—

She reached again for his hand. He was not conscious that he had taken another step to meet her.

"False!" His hand jerked. It was for an instant as it had been when the suit controlled him, not he the suit.

The suit—the maze of the burrows, the place of mirrors! And—Ayyar blinked awake—the stench of false Ift! His hand went to his sword, drew that weapon. Before him the girl ceased to smile; fear made a stark mask of her face; beauty fled from the whip of terror. She shrank away, her hands raised as if to beg for life. If she was some creature of THAT, she played her role well. Ayyar hesitated. False Ift, yes, of that he was certain. Still he could not raise his arm, strike the blow to cut her down. They had chosen well which opponent to send against him.

"You are mad!" she cried out. "Mad!"

For the first time Ayyar spoke. "I am not mad, but you are made—made for THAT WHICH ABIDES, or by IT." Still he held the sword, knowing that prudence dictated "Kill," but unable to swing the blade. He watched her slip around the tree trunk, run from him, knowing bleakly that so perhaps he had not bought life, but his own failure and death.

All was quiet; yet the hum of the usual night noises underlaid that quiet. Like the scentless lilies, that was a small, revealing mistake, for in the real Forest the sound of their voices, Vallylle's flight, would have brought true silence for a short space. Almost, he was tempted to try the energy power of the sword on the tree at his back, upon all that grew about him, save that to waste the force was rank folly.

If there were any watchers in that wood, Ayyar sighted none of them as he moved on with hunter's skill.

No more Vallylles came to woo him, but he was increasingly conscious of the fact that he was under observation. Turn, twist, look about him as he would, he could sight none of those invisible watchers, or watcher, which he was sure followed. So keen did that feeling of being observed come to be that at last he went no farther, but once more put his back to a tree and stood waiting.

He longed to shout down the aisles of trees: "Come out!" But he curbed his fears enough to remain silent.

A vine caught his eye, and he studied the loops along a limb over his head. It curled also about the trunk, anchored by tendrils to the branches. In so much it resembled any parasite one could sight in some parts of the Forest. If it did not die, then, in time, its weight would bring down the limbs and trunk that so easily supported it now.

Only a vine—yet there was something about its leaves—

Small beads of moisture gathered there and along its stem; or maybe, as with the sal, it exuded sap at night. Ayyar raised his head to sniff. There was a faint odor, yes, and strange.

Those shining drops grew larger. They gleamed phosphorescently. He could see them even where the moonlight did not touch. Several drops ran together, formed a larger one that fell from the vine to the ground. Then Ayyar drew a deep breath. Where that drop had fallen, a tiny curl of vapor arose. Had he not been so intent he would have missed it.

More and more drops—larger. The hiss of their fall was like the sprinkle of rain. Ayyar muffled a sharp cry. Fire licked at the back of his hand. He saw the oily globule there. Even a flick of the wrist did not dislodge it, and the fire ate into his flesh with a pain so intense he could not believe it came from just that one small bead of moisture.

He was about to wipe his hand on his thigh and then hesitated. What if that drop of liquid agony soaked into his clothing? Instead he went to one knee, smeared the back of his hand against the earth, only to straighten with a cry as another spatter struck his shoulder. Rain—a rain of fire! There was not only one vine. The tree under which he stood supported another. There were more, festooned about him, all sprinkling their poisonous moisture. Ayyar ran. For moments he feared there was no end to that tangle of vine. Then, breathless, he gained the middle of another glade, stood under the open sky, free from that terror for a moment.

Once more he knelt, grabbing up handfuls of leaves and earth with his left hand, holding his sword with the right, smearing that mess wherever he could reach. Red sores remained when he wiped away the moisture.

Move two for THAT, he thought grimly. He might not understand the motives behind the moves, but that they were part of the other's game he was sure. Mankind had played many games across the roads of space, taken boards and counters, and the knowledge of moves and mates in their minds, gambling fortunes at times on skill and luck. Now he was playing a game, with life as the stakes, perhaps more than his life alone. And the game itself, its rules, if rules it had, were not known to him.

If he had any pieces to play, he knew not how to move them or against whom. What *would* be the next move? And from what direction? Ayyar crouched in the soft forest mold, hand on sword, looking round him as might a hunted animal.

Always the hum of a wood that was normal—its hidden inhabitants going about their business. About their business—

Ayyar turned so quickly in the soft earth he had stirred up to use as plasters for his hurts that he skidded and lost his balance. And it was that which saved him. For the sticky line that flicked out at the place where his head had been an instant earlier fell to the ground without touching him. This—this Ayyar knew. He squirmed away, his sword ready. Kalcrok! Not denned up and waiting for what might plunge into its noisome hole, but, far more dangerous, wandering loose during one of its periods between such in-den life.

He heard the snorting gibber of the creature, but there was no warning smell. Another of those sticky ropes dropped, this time across the point of his sword. The blade flashed and the line shriveled into ash. He had forgotten the power the sword could unleash. He pivoted, searching in the shadows for some movement that would betray the nightmare, only to see nothing at all. But it was against the nature of any kalcrok to give up so easily.

Only, he could not judge what inhabited this wood by what he knew of the normal life of Janus. He could try to withdraw under the trees where the branches would be protection against the web ropes. Yet on just such branches could the beast crouch in waiting—

Ayyar balanced one danger against the other. There was a third way perhaps. He set the sword blade firmly between his teeth and ran for a tree in which he saw no loop of poison vine. His hands caught on a low branch, and he used old skills to draw his body up among the leaves.

Now, along this limb, and the next, then jump for the

next tree, always making sure that no poison vine coiled there. Listen for any rustling behind, a sound of a horror scuttling along his trail—

The next tree, and the next—Ayyar was not even sure in what direction he headed. Always he must make sure that no danger lurked along his aerial path. Oddly enough, his passage flushed no birds, none of the small tree-dwelling creatures, the sounds of which he could still hear about him. Sounds—but not those who made them. How much of this wood was illusion? His burns pained him, the one on his shoulder making him awkward in his swings from tree to tree. He continued to feel no thirst, nor hunger, nor had he yet tired. But how long that would continue, Ayyar did not know.

He saw now that the ground under the trees was sloping gently downward as if the wood sank to some center core. And this made it more difficult to take the tree road. Dared he try ground level again? He squatted on a limb, sniffing and listening. There were growths of fern-like leaves, rank and tall, below in scattered patches. Like the vines, he found them new, thus suspect. Their fronds were tightly curled, the heads like balls, and their color quite dark, a dull green veined with black.

Ayyar broke free a branch, lay belly down on the limb, and poked at the ball head of the tallest fern. There was a soft pop, and it vanished in a small cloud of black dust. Ayyar grimaced. By so much was he warned to keep to the trees while he could, until the ground under them held life that at least looked familiar.

Perhaps if he climbed higher he could see more of what lay ahead. If the land was sinking he ought so to be able to scout ahead.

The fourth tree had what he wanted, a fairly easy way to climb and an old broken limb, lacking branches, from which he could see. Below, the ground sank even more sharply though it was still tree-covered. He gazed out on a moonlit floor of tree tops, much like the view from the passage mouth before he entered this wood.

Moonlit? How long had he been wandering here? Time had no measurement. But the moon, or what served for a moon in this nightmare, held the same position overhead. Perhaps no day ever broke here, no sun rose. This might be a weird sector intended for Iftin life alone, yet not the Iftin he knew.

Something caught the rays of the moon, held them, drew them, until they made a glory in outline—

Iftsiga! No, of course that could not be Iftsiga standing there, towering far above the rest of the wood. But there was no mistaking one of the Great Crowns! Here in the heart of THAT'S holdings was what any Ift would seek for salvation and life.

The shimmer of moon on those green and silver leaves—Ayyar could almost believe he heard their welcoming flutter from where he sat perched in this lesser, this inferior, tree. A Great Crown here!

It looked so close, yet the distance between him and it was not a short one. And what traps might lie between, he could not imagine. Yet that he must cross that expanse Ayyar did not doubt or question.

Could he keep to his path if he descended to the ground where the tops of lesser trees would veil it from his sight? He continued to study that distant tree, striving to pick out some landmark below to serve at ground level.

Finally he started on, keeping above the floor of the

wood, continuing to move in the branches. But, in the end, to find limbs sturdy enough to support his weight he was driven lower and lower, until at last the trees about him were hardly better than tall and thickly leaved brush, and he was on the ground once again.

Ayyar rubbed his burned hand back and forth against the breast of his tunic. The brush was thick. To force a path through it would be hard. He was afraid to use the sword to slash for fear that some of the virtue would depart from it. He had to burrow and twist and use his own strength from now on.

For some time he fought so. Then he came through that barrier into smaller, weaker growth. It was as if the roots of the Great Crown ahead had taken the full nourishment of this ground, leaving only support for small, weak things. Still this vegetation was tall so that only once in awhile did he see his goal, the tree. And the shimmer of moonlight around it appeared now and then to distort that straight trunk, warp or veil it. Ayyar believed that he did not front an illusion but reality, his inner warning was stilled at last.

Still the ground sloped toward the tree. Ayyar could see it fully now—tall, silver, alive as Iftsiga, as the trees of Iftcan had once been in the height of that city's glory. It was a promise, a hope to fill his mind and all the world, so that he knew only it.

Ayyar pushed on, unaware of the sharp whip of branches about his body, of the times he was shaken by falls. Kalcrok and poison vine might lie in his path now; he would no longer see them. Nor did he see the chasm that opened before his feet. With his head still up so that his eyes could feast on the tree, he plunged forward into darkness.

XII

AYYAR WAS SEATED in a confusing place of fog. There was a game board before him plainly marked with circles, in some of which stood playing pieces, like chessmen, wrought into shapes he knew. There was a miniature Larsh, its hairy face up-turned, as if the tiny, glinting eyes set therein could actually see him. And there were a garthman, an off-worlder in port uniform, and small machines. All faced him from the opposite side of the board in an array that, he knew without being told, meant attack. On his side of the playing space were pieces that did not differ so widely from the other. Iftin were there, flanked by trees like the Great Crowns.

In him was the knowledge that there was no retiring from this game. Yet he did not understand its complexities, and win he must. Only if he learned its meaning before a final defeat was there a chance for him.

A Larsh figure strode forward on its own tiny feet. Quickly, into the place it had just vacated, trundled one of the ovoid space suits in miniature. Somewhere off the board, out of Ayyar's sight, there was confident satisfaction.

That stung Ayyar into reply. He put out his hand and placed a green warrior to face the Larsh. Unlike the beast man, his piece had no semblance of life. It was a small doll in his fingers. As he put it down in a circle, there was a flash on the board and between the figures arose a barrier, mirror bright. On that mirror appeared the reflection of his

Ift, holding so for a long moment. Then the green manikin was gone. The mirror slipped down into the surface of the board. But in the ranks of the army facing him was now a green Ift.

Again that sense of satisfaction flowed toward Ayyar. Yet he could see no opposing player across the board.

What did that move mean? Had it marked the original victory of the Larsh over Ift? The using of the mirror, the transfer of his piece to the ranks of the Enemy—were those echoes of what had once happened?

Memory stirred. How had he come here? Where was *here?* There had been a wood surrounding a tree, and he had been seeking that leaf-crowned beacon. Then—nothing! His eyes were on the board, the figures there. But his thoughts were elsewhere, striving to make some sense out of what had happened. Movement on the board—he must be alert, warned his inner sentinel. This was no time to seek answers but to attend to what lay here.

But who was he to play such a game? He was Ayyar, one of many who carried swords in defense of Iftcan, no dreamer of prophetic dreams, no Mirrormaster. Who was he to—to speak for—

"Thanth," whispered a faint voice within his mind, "the power of Thanth, borne hither in your body and in mine—"

"Illylle!" His seeking thought called upon her. "What must I do, Illylle?"

"That which you see to do. But seeing is twofold, Ayyar—inner sight, outer sight. Be not deceived."

Outer sight—the board, the players on it? Inner sight—be not deceived—deceived? He was confused, and confusion was a weapon in the hand of the Enemy.

Board—there was really no board, no thin line of green pieces lined up to face a force thrice their number. He would deny all illusion. Ayyar put out his forefinger, set it on the semblance of a playing board, and willed—

Light spread out from his touch, sweeping across the rows of pieces. Then the board and the figures were naught, and he faced empty space.

The space was filled—with white things that rose out of the ground. He lay on his side looking at a rock wall that was studded with crystals, glistening in frosty light, until he raised his hand to cover his dazzled eyes. His body ached, was stiff, so that any small movement was painful. But he sat up, peered about. There was sand under him, the red, powdery stuff that had paved the valley of the mounds. He put out his other hand, and it fell upon chill metal, his fingers fumbling with the hilt of a sword. He snatched it up as a man in a river would seize upon a log to keep himself afloat.

Inner sight—outer sight? This was outer sight. Ayyar put his head back and gazed up. There was a rim to this ravine and over it dangled a torn branch. He had fallen here in his race to reach the tree. Thought of that jolted him into full consciousness. Only let him reach the tree and he would be renewed, able to face aught THAT sent against him! But the game board in the misty place—what had been the meaning of it? An arrogant promise that whatever went up against IT was absorbed into ITS own forces as the mirror had switched the Ift piece? The mirror—that was the heart of THAT'S mystery, but one he could not solve.

Now—the tree waited.

Ayyar hobbled to the wall, strove to climb it. He could

manage with the aid of the jutting crystals to gain part of the way; then an overhang closed the last few feet to him. Find a better place— He limped along the bottom of the cut. As he went the walls grew higher, steeper. Discouraged, he returned, went in the other direction, only to have the walls narrow over his head until they touched to make a dark cave.

Back again—if he could not climb the far side, then perhaps the one down which he had come would offer footing. Ayyar made the attempt only to have the loose earth slip, half burying him in a slide of dust. There was no way up over the wall, only a path in the cut. And at last he gave in and turned down that open way.

It was not only guarded by steadily heightening walls, but it also began to slope downward and more to the right. By that much was Ayyar heartened for the tree stood in that direction. Then, looking up, he saw those mighty branches, far, far above, between him and the sky. He had entered the shadow of the tree.

More and more to the right that way turned, denser and denser the shadow of the tree. The old lore of Iftcan—that a tree's shadow had power to harm— Yet here, in the heart of THAT'S domain, this tree stood—

Ayyar paused now and then, just to gaze up into that canopy, to savor the good feeling of being once more, even by so little, in the presence of a Great Crown. Then the knowledge came slowly to him that this was not as Iftsiga, not what his heart longed for.

Not one of those leaves above stirred. They kept ever the same. He waited for the feel of life, of the out-flowing with which one of the Great Crowns would welcome Ift. Instead there was silence—nothingness.

He knew the dead towers of Iftcan, standing bone white and terrible, heart-rending with the sense of loss they awoke in all passing. That was death as the Great Crowns knew it. And now he would have welcomed that.

For this emptiness was not the death of what had once been life—it was a nothingness of that which had never lived at all! At the same moment that his Iftin sense told him that, Ayyar realized that those banks towering far above his head on either hand were no longer earth but the buttress roots of the tree. He was coming to its very foot.

To his eyes those buttress roots were no different from any he had seen in Iftcan. This might be Iftsiga he now approached, save that that lived and this did not. Like Vallylle, it was false, a mirror-image of the truth, but as hard and lifeless as the surface that reflected it.

Was it both bait and trap to draw any Ift who sighted it as it had drawn him? In Ayyar's hold the sword hilt warmed, from its tip the silver spark flashed. This was the road he was intended to march; there was no turning back.

The root walls were so high they cut off most of the light as he neared the trunk of the tree. And he was not quite sure when he did pass within it. There was such a feeling of loneliness, of being cut off from all his kind—perhaps for evermore—that closed about him as he went into the dark, that he sent forth a silent call born of fear and foreboding:

"Illylle!"

He had not really expected an answer, yet when none came he was chilled, feeling like one who enters a prison and hears behind him bolts lock, knowing that for him there will be no going forth again. But he could not turn back; he was under command as when the suit had carried him into the burrows. Only this was not by THAT'S ordering. It came from the energy stored within him.

Ayyar passed through the outer wall of the trunk into a space where a thin red light issued from the ground under his feet. It was as if he walked over live coals on a dying fire. Thus he came face to face with Ift again. This time it was not one like Vallylle, meant to allure, to entice. Rather it had a worn face, scarred with a great slash that had healed badly, that of a man and a warrior who had fought—to little purpose by the bitter lines about his mouth. And in his hands he held not a sword, but the shaft of a banner that hung limp, torn and stained from a pole ending in splinters.

Memory awoke in Ayyar.

"Hanfors—"

His whisper of that name was a thin sound. He whom Ayyar had once known and followed into battle did not move but stood statue still. And beyond him was another and another, all warriors who had led Iftin forces in glory and defeat. Some Ayyar knew, for they were from the last days when he, too, had had Larsh blood on his blade. But others were earlier, and yet earlier—

Then a small doubt crept into his mind. Hanfors had led them in defeat, yes. And there was Vanok, also of the last days, and Selmak. But others—they were of the Green Leaf when THAT was still Oath-bound, and they had known the glory, not the end of their race. Therefore, if this was meant to be a triumph of THAT, it was not one that spoke the truth. And that small discovery was important, though as yet Ayyar did not know why.

Whether he fronted statues or the remains of living Ift set up to so glorify their conquerors, he could not tell, nor did he care to learn by closer examination. Then he saw on the other side a second line of figures, and these were armed—first with sword and spear to match the Iftin, then with other weapons. But those nearest to where he stood were Larsh. Slowly Ayyar walked on, peering at them in wonderment, for they changed. The beast men became different; they stood straighter and taller, their shaggy body hair thinned and disappeared, until he stood at last between those two who were the last in both lines. The Ift wore a type of clothing Ayyar had never seen, yet still he was wholly Ift—while that one to the right was no longer Larsh at all. And the clothing on its slender body was—it must be—a space suit! In its hands was clasped a weapon vaguely akin to an off-world blaster!

But the order in which those figures stood— The Iftin line plainly ran forward in time since Hanfors was first by the entrance. But the Larsh sequence was reversed, showing the slow evolution from the very primitive to a civilization high enough to aim for the stars.

How long then—how long since the Iftin had vanished from Janus? How many centuries had passed for the Larsh to climb and then in turn disappear? To think about that vast roll of time frightened Ayyar. For changeling that he was, the last frantic answer by the Iftin to the stamping out of their species, he carried the form and part of the memories of a man who had marched with Hanfors when the Larsh were part beast. And to cut such a great span of time into years, seasons— His head spun, and he pushed such speculation aside in haste.

So the Larsh under THAT'S guidance had at last tried for the stars? But then what had happened to them, brought an end to their civilization, wiped all traces of it from Janus, so effectively that no signs of it remained? While the trees of Iftcan, or some of them, had lived to guard the Iftin seed? It would seem, for all the self-confidence of THAT, this very chamber proved the superiority of Ift knowledge. The Larsh had come and gone, but Iftin once more walked the Forest.

For how long? So small a company of changelings—a handful here, and few more overseas. No nation, less even than one Company used to muster at the First Ring. And with THAT now ready to play ITS game against them —what chance had they, in spite of all the craft and skill which had brought them to life?

Ayyar did not want to look again at the lines of Ift and Larsh. Only that tantalizing thought remained, that the latter marked one failure of THAT—the Larsh were gone. Could it be that now THAT wove its own magic to bring them to life again in its present captives?

There was another doorway, another chamber. Again the red light glowed, and in it were machines, strange things, meant, he thought to fly, others to pass over the ground. They stood there, thick dust on their surfaces and piled about them—the dust of time so great that no mind might truly contemplate it. These had been born of Larsh brains, made by Larsh hands, and now they were as dead as those who had conceived them.

But he was pulled from his survey of the machines. In his hand the sword turned, pointed to the floor, and from that position he could not move. Instead it grew heavier, dragging his hand, his arm, his body downward as the tip dug into the flooring. There was a crackling; light sped out in a star-burst from the meeting of point and ground.

Where that crackling had centered the ground began to sink. It was another platform such as he had found in the valley of the mounds. It moved slowly, creakingly, not with the swift sureness of that other.

Down, he balanced carefully on the unsteady plate. Above, not too far away was the open floor and the red glow. Around him though, it was dusky. There was a jar as the platform grounded. A trickle of earth shifted from above. Ayyar stepped off, and his boots were now on smooth surfacing. He must be back in the burrows or diggings like them.

As he moved to the left, his sword glowed and from the hilt, up his body, warmth spread. The platform did not rise to seal the opening as had that other. This time a possible retreat was not closed to him. The sparkle of the blade was not green or silver as he had seen it before, but yellow, and the energy did not drain from it, but, Ayyar was sure, now ran the other way, from it into him.

He went along the passage, guided, he was certain, by the will which had sent him into THAT'S domain in the first place. And he went with rising confidence.

The passage ran straight with no doors along its walls. And the force continued to feed back into his body, making him ever more alert and alive. Yet Ayyar was certain this was no power native to that which reached through Thanth but rather something here that it could draw upon to recharge him.

He came to one of the lock doors, and this was firmly set, past any effort of his to move it until he touched the sword to it. The answer was a blinding light; so he shielded his eyes. And he smelled an acrid, stifling puff of air blown into his face. When he dared look again the door was ringed with a glowing line of molten metal, and at a nudge from his shoulder it fell forward.

Bright as the sword torch was, here its gleam was swallowed up in the vast space into which he came. Close to him he could see upright, slender rods of metal and, resting between them, row on row, packed closely together, yet with smaller rods keeping them from touching one another, were mirrors. They were covered with a cloud of dust. And, as he brushed it aside with an exploring finger on the nearest, underneath was a second opaque film. But it was dry and brittle, flaking off in great ragged pieces.

Ayyar held the sword torch closer. The mirror lay upon its side in the lock hold. But still he saw clearly the reflection of a face thereon—staring wide-eyed, as the off-worlder had looked at the gleaming sheet that had sucked his image into itself. Not Ift nor Larsh, but, he thought, what the Larsh had evolved into. It was a woman with ivory skin and massed yellow hair. He drew upon Naill memory. In the port on Korwar races of a thousand worlds came and went—some of them human, some of other species. Yet this face was unlike any he had seen before. And so mirrored with those staring eyes—it was as if he gazed upon a living thing who might at any moment speak to him.

The Green Sick, which had made of him a changeling, had also bred revulsion against humankind into him, now newly Ift. But what he felt at this moment, looking into those unblinking eyes, was hatred. Why? What harm could this mirrored reflection do him or his kind?

Unless—cold spread through him—from this mirror

could be reborn the semblance of the creature so portrayed. Was this what had happened to the Larsh—they had been reduced to mirrors and kept in storage? But if so—why did THAT now seek new mirrors on which to build servants, as he had witnessed? Here—he swung the sword light—were racks upon racks of mirrors beyond his counting, an army waiting, perhaps a whole nation.

Ayyar passed on down one aisle, but there were other aisles to his right, his left. How many he could not see, but all of them were filled with racks. Twice more he stopped to cleanse a mirror from dust and film. Once a man of the other race stared at him, but the second time he was startled to face a furred head, a sharp snout, unmistakably another species altogether, and one he would have named animal.

Then Ayyar noted that that rack had a red tube end while others were clear without coloring. Now he watched the tubes as he passed until he saw a rack marked with blue. Once more he cleaned a part of the nearest surface, and for the second time a weird face, if one might name it face, was revealed. This mirror was smaller, less than half the size of those that had pictured the people, and the creature on it was white and hairless with a pointed muzzle, small round ears. Its jaws were a little apart, showing fangs—

Wyte! No, not exactly like the hounds he knew, but enough wyte to once have been of common stock. Perhaps the wytes, too, had changed through the centuries, those sleeping here being of a later development. But THAT still used wytes to course the Waste, and those were like unto the ancient breed Ayyar had known in the days of Iftcan. Then what was this which was wyte and yet not wholly wyte—? He did not understand.

He was a long time walking the aisles in the dust and silence of what could truly be termed a place of the dead. Yet there was other than clean death here; something which to his spirit stank as the stench of the false Iftin fretted his nostrils.

Ayyar quickened pace until he was running through the drifts of fine dust, past rack on rack of the mirrors. Still there appeared to be no end to this storehouse. The glow of the energy which the sword still seemed to attract to it filled him. Almost he expected to see small sparks appear at his finger tips when he moved his hand. But the reason for his coming hither made no more sense than all his other adventures since he had left the Mirror of Thanth, that living Mirror so unlike those which walled him now. Still there was a kind of teasing in his mind, the feeling that there was an answer to all his questions, and it lay before him if he only had the wit to see it clearly. That teasing was, in truth, a gnawing irritation.

There was an end at last to the cavern or the chamber of the mirrors. The sword torch showed him a wall arching overhead, and here was another sealed door that Ayyar did not hesitate to burn free. He had no liking for where he was and would be elsewhere as soon as possible.

The corridor beyond was wider than any other he had found in these burrows, and there was undisturbed dust on its floor. Still the sword pointed him ahead. Then he came to another door and this was open, giving on one of the round terminals with a ladder climbing above. But the sword twisted down, tugging as it had under the tree, but with even more force, bringing him to his knees. Only, what had once been the continuation of the ladder stair there was sealed. Not by any door, but by a jammed mass

162

of twisted, half melted metal. Had it been done deliberately to close off that way? Ayyar thought so.

He tried the power of the sword, but the energy pouring through it could not free even the top layer of that fused mass. And at last, almost as if the power which energized that blade relinquished all hope of effecting an entry, it went loose in his hand. But he knew that below lay what he sought, the guiding brain and heart of all this place. By himself he could not force an entrance to face it, while it would seem that THAT'S power could easily operate beyond this place of its source, in the Waste, and farther, through servants and tools.

Had he come so far into the heart of the Enemy's territory just to know defeat as Hanfors and those others of the last days had met it? Ayyar sat back on his heels, the sword across his knees, studying that fused cork. He had a feeling that through him the power that had activated the Mirror of Thanth to bring him here was also considering the barrier and other matters. No one Ift could do this alone. There were tools, however, within THAT'S own territory that might be brought to bear—tools known to the off-worlders.

But could Iftin use them? The conditioning that separated them so sharply from those they had once been surely would not allow it—any more than they could approach the port itself through the confusion THAT had forced upon Janus. Yet they must reach what lay below.

There were machines, men with the knowledge to use them in the valley of the mounds. But those men were under THAT'S control.

Time—Ayyar got to his feet—this fretting over what he could not do in the here and now was only a waste of time.

Somewhere, somehow the Iftin must find the allies or the skill to dislodge this barrier, seek what lay below. None of them—Iftin, garthmen, off-worlders from the port—had any future here, save as mindless servants to THAT. And to meet death trying was better than just to accept defeat.

He sheathed his sword and turned to the ladder stair. He would have to find a way out, back across the Waste to Illylle and then to the others. Together they would decide. Perhaps all the changelings were from such varied backgrounds that they could put together their memories and so come to a plan. That which had looked through Ayyar's eyes moments earlier was gone, though he had not felt its passing until he was left empty.

Up he climbed, passing two more levels. Then there was more broken metal, some of it hanging in strips, the sharp edges of which threatened him as he squeezed between, to hack with sheathed sword at earth above. Dodging a shower of soil which poured around the ladder, he continued to push through until sun dazzled his eyes and the freshness of open air was in his face.

His efforts had brought him out on a height, and he wedged his body through with caution. A mound crest! Flattened to earth he crept along, shading his eyes to gaze down. The burrows under the earth must have confused his sense of direction, but he certainly now lay on the top of just such a mound as he had seen in that other valley. Or was he back in the same area? He tried to study the mounds about, seeking a landmark. Yes—there was the grubber from the port rumbling into view, no one in the operator's seat. He was again in the red valley. Now it only remained to cross that to the road beyond. But this was day, and he wore no disguising space suit.

XIII

WHERE WERE the men who had roamed here before? Ayyar peered between his fingers. Though the grubber trundled along, no one walked or lay prone on the sand. He could not be sure, but he believed that the road out of the valley lay on the other side of the mound. He brought out his leaf goggles, put them on. The glare became bearable. Ayyar looked down the shaded side of the mound.

It sloped steeply, with no fiber of any covering growth. To slide straight down might afford him the easiest and quickest descent—he could use the sheathed sword as a brake. The grubber had crawled on, veered away to his right. Now—!

He pushed over, the soil rising in ridges about him as he gathered speed, a small hillock growing ahead of his feet. The substance gave off a peculiar odor of old rottenness, which made him swallow convulsively. He loathed the greasy feel of it on his flesh. Twice he braked with the sword driven into that dank stuff—he no longer thought of it as earth. At last, with a cloud of it stirred up around him, Ayyar reached the sand and crouched there on one knee in the pile he had brought down with him, listening, smelling, looking for any guard.

This one mound he must set so deeply in mind he would have no hesitation over its position when he returned—if he returned. For this was the doorway to the Enemy, even if he did not now carry the key.

It stood close to the cliff wall at one end of the valley, the last in line, and it was circular in shape. He must count the number as he crossed the valley floor, set its place in relation to the other wall. Ayyar brushed the unwholesome dark soil from him as he arose, every hunter's sense alert.

He kept in the shadow of the mound as he shuffled through the thick sand which puffed up ankle-high about his feet as he went.

Ayyar had passed two more mounds without seeing either men or the machine which had crawled away, when without warning, attack came. A numbing shock struck him thigh-high, hurling him off balance against the earth wall. He looked down to see a feathered shaft protruding from his flesh. Ift! Where?

With shoulders braced to the dank substance of the mound he managed to keep his feet. But for how long? Ayyar could not see the bowman. Doubtless the other could pin him without effort. He tried to catch the false Iftin scent. There was no breeze here to bring it helpfully to his nostrils. And the blood was running too freely from his wound.

False Ift—sword— What had Illylle done back there when one of the robot monsters had stood in ambush waiting for them? Ayyar tried to calculate from where that shaft had been loosed. In his hand the sword swung slowly as he poured his will into it, for that was the only word he found to describe what he now did. Back—forth—

There had come no second shot. Was the Enemy so confident of his disablement to wish to take him alive?

Out—by what lies within me—come from Thanth—out and show yourself!

166

He had not quite believed it would work, but he was answered. The shadow of a bow stretching across the sand, then that of him who held it. And the shadow's head moved back and forth in time to the swing of Ayyar's weapon.

Out! He strove to make that thought an order, a cord to pull his attacker to him. Out—here!

Ift, yes, to the outward appearance. But no Ift to Ayyar's nose, his mind. The other came with jerky steps, feet lifted oddly high as if the sand were some flood it must breast to reach Ayyar. Always the green head wavered from side to side, echoing the swing of the blade that shimmered silver in his hand. While through his body he felt the ebb of that strength which was the alien power.

The blank face, its Iftin features expressionless—from what mirror had it been born?

"Come," he called softly, hardly daring to believe that he could draw it within striking distance. Every jerky step spelled its unwillingness to obey.

"Come—"

It had stopped, was teetering back and forth as if caught between two strong compulsions. The hands raised the bow, slowly, so slowly. Was his power over it failing?

He dared not wait. There was a trick once known to Ayyar for infighting. With his left hand he dug fingers deep into the foul dust of the mound, swung his weight for a moment onto his wounded leg, and then hurled himself at the false Ift. The black dust went before him to blind the other. And though he crashed short of the leap he had intended, his out-thrust blade touched the green body, scored along it, if only lightly, as Ayyar went down.

The false Ift shuddered, its bow dropping from its hands

as it went into a weird, stamping dance. Grimacing with pain, hardly sure he could make it, Ayyar got to his feet. His fall had broken the arrow shaft, driven the head deeper into his flesh. But he had no time for his wound now. He lurched on, swung once more at the twitching head of the false Ift. There was a shrill sound which hurt his ears, though he was sure it had not issued from between the thing's twisting lips.

It leaped forward, past him, running full face into the mound where it dug its hands deep into the earth. Then it was still, began to slide down, taking with it a fall of soil to partly cover its body when it hit the sand.

Ayyar watched, but it did not move again. Then he turned to examine his own hurt. He could force out the arrow head in spite of the keen pain. And he hoped it would not disable him past walking though he must go slow. He used a strip of his tunic to bind it and picked up the Ift's bow as a support.

How many more of the monsters lurked in the mound valley? He searched the shadows, to be startled by a clanking behind. The loader he had seen cross the river —how many days ago—rounded the mound, came straight toward him, almost as if intelligently guided to run him down. Ayyar limped as best he could around the end of the embankment.

The loader ground ahead, came to where the broken robot Ift lay. Almost Ayyar expected it to hesitate. It was difficult to believe that the machine was not under control from the driver's seat. But it trundled on, driving the crushed robot deep into the sand. Ayyar lifted his sword, though what good that would be against tons of mindless, moving metal—

If it turned left at the end of the mound, there was no

escape; he could not scramble away. He had to wait, and that waiting was an endless horror out of sane time.

As the nose of the loader appeared, Ayyar could shrink no farther away. He waited. But the turn he feared did not come; the loader proceeded on a straight course. And Ayyar, using the bow as a cane, limped as quickly as he could farther left, putting the next mound in line between them.

He went as a hunted man, watching. His shoulders were a little hunched, as if he feared the bite of another arrow. The pain of his wound was nothing to that apprehension.

But save for the loader clanking along at a course parallel to his, he saw no other moving thing. In spite of the need for speed his hurt kept him to a hobble, with pauses for rest. But finally he saw the road down the cliff wall. Did the patrolling suits still come this way?

Movement at the crest of the road. Ayyar again sought cover—but there was only open space between the last mound and the road. The need for reaching the only exit sent him limping to the valley wall. And there he crouched, knowing his choice had been impulsive and bad. There was a company coming down the slanting path. Not the suits of the patrol as he had feared but —women!

He stared unbelievingly. Some of them still wore the face masks forced on all of the garthwomen when they went abroad—the strips of cloth with eye holes and thin slits for mouths making them seem even more robot-like. Others had lost or tossed away the coverings, demanded by the standards of modesty among the garths, and went bare of face. The blankness, the lack of expression on their faces were as much of a mask as the cloths they had lost.

Women from the garths, who never walked abroad by

any chance. And with them children! Ayyar drew a deep breath. It would seem that THAT was making a clean sweep, bringing to IT all the Settlers on Janus.

They walked with the same staring eyes in the same unheeding march that the men had earlier shown. Some carried the smaller children; others led little ones by the hand. Yet they never looked nor spoke to their charges, and the children too, were caught in the spell. It was awesome, terrible, far worse to watch than the first parade of men. Ayyar kept firm his self-control to prevent his staggering out to meet them, seize the nearest woman by the arm, strive to awaken her.

He counted twenty in the party, and they did not pause upon reaching the floor of the valley but continued steadily out over the sand, taking the same path between the mounds as he had followed. He watched them go despairingly. They were no longer his species, and his aversion to them operated as they passed. Still Naill-memory pricked at him, urged him to some action that might restrain them from whatever fate they now faced. Only there was nothing he could do, save try to find his way to THAT, for the control of all this was THAT'S alone.

And to do such a thing he must have help, not of those who could be so ensnared but of his own kind. He began to climb the road resolutely, refusing to look back at that small company shuffling through the sand below.

This had not seemed so hard a road when he had descended it, but now he must favor his wound and the progress was a struggle. Ayyar did not know how much of the energy he had exhausted in his knock-out of the false Ift, but he was aware that his strength was steadily ebbing.

Up and up—then he could not stifle a cry as the glare

from the shattered bits of the White Forest blinded him. Even wearing the goggles he was afraid to try to look far ahead for any length of time. The sun was hot on his body as he crept along, dragging his wounded leg, unable to lean too heavily on the bow staff lest it break under his weight.

The crushed and rutted way was a guide. And he listened, tested the wind for any hint that there were others ahead. One of the outcrops of crystal was close. He put out his hand to steady himself and snatched back his fingers from its heat. But it was the only shelter nearby. He drew into that pocket, willing himself to bear the heat reflected from it, listening to a crunching that came closer.

He did not dare to look too long, but his sword was out and ready to thrust. Whatever came was heavy footed —one of the suits—or was a machine about to pass?

The black snout that now pushed into view was vaguely familiar. Ayyar tensed. Moving on its own treads was no machine intended for the subduing of land or forest, but one for the destruction of men. This was a vibrator from the defenses of the port, designed to ray human or humanoid bodies, to break the normal control of muscles, to render the victim for a matter of hours, even days, a helpless jelly! He had not known that Janus mounted one, but apparently the port defenses had been so equipped. And now, like the blank-eyed garthwomen before it, the vibrator ground steadily ahead, answering some summons from the valley which made it more mobile than its human masters had ever intended it to be.

This insweep of people and machines alike meant only one thing to Ayyar, the building of an army. Against what? The pitiful handful the Iftin changelings could mus-

ter? Even if they brought the rest of their company overseas, they could not hope to match THAT in open field.

Ayyar waited until the vibrator crawled well down the
road before he renewed his painful, half blind struggle in
the opposite direction. Suddenly a speculation that made
sense came into his mind. Did THAT feel IT was in
danger? In some way, could his own penetration of ITS
burrows have triggered a deep alarm? But no, this ingathering had started earlier—

How much earlier? He frowned, fitting one memory to
another. They had awakened to the warning of Iftsiga. The
port men had already attacked the Forest. But those men
had not been under open and complete control then. The
men he had seen at the camp had been normal enough.
And the raid of the false Iftin which they had witnessed
—then there had been no attempt to capture the garthmen
as allies. No, they had not seen this type of control in
action until they had called the flitter from the port, tried to
establish contact with a mutual understanding against
THAT.

This began to spell out the truth, Ayyar thought. THAT
had learned of their attempt, and such an alliance was a
danger to IT.

They had gone on to Thanth and wrought there after the
immemorial Iftin fashion. And THAT'S answer must be
this sweep of off-worlders, this ingathering of each and
every person or thing with which the Iftin might make
common cause. But again and again his logic struck
head-on against the one question he could not answer
—what did the Iftin possess which was so feared by
THAT?

Once a hero of the Iftin blood had gone to THAT and forced a restraining Oath upon IT, an Oath that was repeated again at a later date and that held IT impotent in ITS own place. Then IT broke the Oath, and the Iftin of the latter day could not stand against ITS might. So Iftcan fell before the Larsh. But could IT still fear that Oath; was IT now preparing an army of "Larsh" to make an end to all opposition?

The Oath! If there had ever been a history of what it was and how Kymon had administered it to the Enemy that secret had been so enfolded in legend that Iftin of a later day could not learn it. Ayyar had entered the burrows, he had found the plugged stairway, he suspected that below that lay the lair of THAT. This much he could offer those he sought now but no more.

Illylle—he must find Illylle. Then they would cross the Waste, reach the sea and the others. If would be hard to speak of failure, but that was all he could carry them, save a true account of all he had seen. And the others one of them might have knowledge from the days before he became a changeling that would enable them to make a plan—

Ayyar was very tired. It seemed that with every limping step more of his energy drained from him. Perhaps that power of strength had been given him for only one purpose. And since he had not achieved that, it seeped from him as did the blood stiffening his improvised bandage.

He had to depend mostly on his hearing or sense of smell for a warning, keeping his eyes closed to the glare, though he believed it was now well into afternoon. Night—how he longed for the coolness, the dim comfort of night. How long it had been since he slept through the heat of day he could not remember.

Watch now—he must watch lest he miss the turn to the valley where the true trees grew.

"Illylle?" He tried to call with his mind, as he shaped her name with dry, cracked lips. Hunger and thirst grew in proportion to his waning power. There was no answer, no stir deep within his brain.

He searched for the place where he had set a forked spike of crystal as a mark. Almost he was afraid he had missed it, gone too far, when he sighted it. He staggered out of the road, zigzagged painfully among the shards. The scent of the wood drew him, promising shelter, comfort.

Then he lost his footing on the slope, fell and rolled, and the pain of his wrenched wound sent a sharp red thrust of agony through him, whirling him into the dark.

"Illylle?" Was it his own voice, hoarse and husky?

Dazedly, Ayyar opened his eyes, grateful for a sweet shadow across his face. It was good to lie there with that green screen between him and the punishing light. Tired—he was so very tired. And there was pain— He tried to lift his hand to his body to seek that source of pain.

Dark—the good dark—he would plunge into the dark as one plunged into the sea—

Sea!

He must get to the sea—with Illylle. The shell about him broke—Illylle—the sea—the others—

It was hard to struggle up. His injured leg was stiff and too weak the first time he tried to rest any weight upon it. Ayyar clutched at a tree trunk and drew himself up along it as a man might cling to life itself.

"Great the tree, green the leaf,
  Iftin need beyond belief!
  Strong the tree, stout the branch—"

The old invocation spilled from his lips. Not that it held much meaning now. He did not have the bark of one of the Great Crowns rough under his hands. Yet the words and the prayer behind them came to him, and he clung to this sapling as he would have to Iftsiga.

Perhaps his will, his need, aroused in him the dregs of that energy with which Thanth had filled his body. He was able to push away, to stagger to another tree and another, making his way in such haphazard fashion to that portion of rock and wall where he had left Illylle lying in something deeper than any sleep he had known.

He fell to one knee, straightening out his wounded leg, began to work loose the stones he had left to shelter her. His hands shook, and he had to think of each move, impress his will upon his fingers, wrists, arms. But it was twilight, and that growth of shadow was comforting, just as the scents of his oasis of green refreshed his lungs, starved for Forest air. Four more stones and he could look upon her.

She lay just as he had seen her last, her face wan, sharper of feature, an odd kind of sorrow upon it.

"Illylle—" he called softly, coaxingly.

But those heavy lids did not rise. He could not even see she breathed.

"Illylle!" He spoke sharply, with a demand born of fear.

His hand on her shoulder shook her, and in his grip she turned a little, her right arm falling limply out, so that her hand rested palm up on his stiff leg.

"Illylle!"

Awkwardly he drew her into the open. She was a soft, limp weight, her flesh cold to his touch. He sat there, her head resting against his shoulder, her legs trailing back into the crevice.

Remembering how they had parted he caught both her hands in his, pressing them tight, willing that that force she had passed to him would now flow back to arouse her. But there was no answer. Had he drawn so heavily on that store that he could never wake her again?

This was a new kind of fear, different from that which had been his constant companion since they had left the Mirror. He had feared for their safety and then, after leaving her, for his own, and now—for hers, but to an extent that blotted out all else.

Jarvas—the Mirror of Thanth—a man, a place, either might hold the answer to her revival, and neither were close at hand. To reach the Mirror's aid Ayyar would have to take her there, and he could not bear her across the Waste with his injury. The answer was bitter. He must leave her here again and get to Jarvas, not with just news of THAT'S domain, but for Illylle!

Moving painfully and slowly, but with as much care of her as he could, Ayyar placed her slight young body back in the crevice, began wearily to replace the stones. He fitted them with the best care he could summon, using all his skill to hide any trace that would suggest they concealed something. He did not know whether the servants of THAT might penetrate here, but it was possible.

When he was done, Ayyar sat where he was for a long moment, unsure now if he *could* move away. Food —drink—where was that to be found? And without either he dared not leave. The green about him made him wonder dully if some food and water could not be found. Ayyar forced himself back to his feet, staggering along, pushing through bushes, under trees in an almost aimless search. He clutched at a bush for support before he was aware of the pods ripening there. Winter it might be in the outer world, but here was a more kindly season. Fussan seed! He pawed at the cluster of pods, managed to break one free, opened it and chewed at the seeds within. They were still tart, not sweet, but even their tartness revived him.

He ate and then set about picking the rest of the pods, tying them into a corner of the cloak he had brought from Illylle's crypt.

Water? Head up, he tested the air—the scent of water—? Yes! Faint—in that direction.

He limped heavily on to a place where a spring bubbled through the earth to feed a trickle of brook. There Ayyar buried his face in its coolness, drank, felt it wash from his skin the stain of the burrows and the mound valley. He had no way to carry water. What he drank now must last him through the Waste. Clutching the bag of fussan seed to him with his left hand, his right ever close to his sword hilt, he struggled for the valley wall. East and south now, the stars to guide him.

Ayyar did not pause as he passed where Illylle lay. If he did, he thought, he might not have the courage to go on. So small a hope, yet it was all he had. It was necessary to go on all fours to win the top of the slope, emerge into the Crystal Forest. But the night was a second cloak, comforting and encouraging him.

South—east—under the stars at a crippled crawl that not only slowed him but also would act against him if he were charged by wyte, false Ift, or any other servant of THAT which might roam the night. He limped on, tightening his lips against the pain of movement. Now and again he chewed upon a fussan seed, making it last as long as he could.

Time passed; he was out of the crystal shards and into the desert beyond. And he was crossing this, watching for every bit of cover to aid him, when a light flashed up into the sky from some point in the east—a beam that might be a beacon—for what?

XIV

STEADYING HIMSELF against a pillar of rock, Ayyar watched that light. It came from somewhere on the boundary between the Waste and the clean lands beyond. Now it pointed a finger straight into the sky, but at intervals a ripple surged along it. And when that happened, deep inside him, Ayyar felt an answering, an impulse to go to it, though that urge was well within his power to control.

However, as he watched, that pointing finger suddenly swung down, aimed no longer into the sky, but rather across the river at the land where the garths had been carved out of the wilderness. It appeared to hover for a moment before it settled, stark and still, while along the beam pulsations built up faster and faster. The light became so bright that Ayyar dared no longer look. But he guessed it was aimed at some garth, perhaps to summon the inhabitants into the hold of THAT.

Yet the Enemy could not control the Iftin so, and thus they had this small advantage, though who knew what else was abroad in this blasted land, serving THAT, able to influence or capture his own kind? Lurching away from the stone, Ayyar continued his journey at as fast a pace as his wound would allow.

The ground was rough and well provided with lurking places for trouble, so he went warily, sniffing, listening, alert to any sign that sentries or scouts were abroad. Once he heard the cry of a wyte afar off and stood to harken for any near reply. But that was the only sound save for the soughing of a wind.

Clouds scudded across the sky, veiling the moon. It was chill. He had come out of the valley wherein summer abode, and here that season was yet well ahead. Ayyar stumbled on a stone, leaned too heavily on his bow shaft cane and it broke.

Dawn was close, and he knew that he must hole up for a rest. He could drive himself no farther. There was a patch of leafless brush, and with the Ift's instinctive turn toward growing things, he managed to force a way into the center of this, breaking out a small nest, bending branches to close the opening he had made. The need for sleep was heavy on him, as it had not been since he left the Mirror. He chewed upon some seeds, settled his injured leg as best he could, and yielded to that need.

Once more he was in that misty place facing the game board. It seemed to him that the Iftin and the tree pieces had drawn together in a closer setting on his side, as if massing for a last stand, while on the side of his unseen opponent there marched an army in depth. Off-worlders, Larsh, false Iftin, garthmen—some of them pushed forward in moves meant, Ayyar believed, to tempt him into some rash sally. But he did not move; instead he studied the oddly constituted army of the Enemy, fixing each in his mind.

Of them all two held his attention the longest—the false Ift and the Larsh. Iftin and the mirrors— Who had made the mirror patterns from which these robots had been constructed? Were the patterns reflected from true Iftin, captives from that older time? If so, were those captives still preserved within the burrows, to be perhaps aroused and freed?

And the Larsh, who had risen from shambling beast-men to the space-suited one he had seen in that line under the counterfeit tree. It appeared to Ayyar now, as he stared at one of those, that the piece changed in outline as if one image for an instant or so fitted over another, that the core of the beast was the man— That puzzled him, was disturbing, for it reversed the logical process. Once more thought teased him. By the thinness of a dried leaf was he separated from an explanation, yet it eluded him.

He waited for that invisible player to move, to threaten his small defensive army. And then he knew that, though he sat by that board, waiting, the other was not here. Yet he felt no elation; it was rather that the other had set aside the board and his pieces, to pass on to a bigger and bolder game that Ayyar dared not essay.

Larsh—Iftin—

Ayyar awoke—if it was awakening, not a return from a place outside life as he knew it. Iftin—false! The stink of them was on the wind. He did not move, using his ears, his eyes to serve him.

His sight was limited by the brush walls of his hideout,

but he could hear. The Enemy did not attempt to hide their coming: a ring of boot heel against stone, the brush of a cape edge or leg against bush, were clear to the ear. Stealthily, moving by inches, Ayyar brought up his sword; he had gone to sleep with its hilt in hand. He feared that all the energy that had charged it had gone out of him. And without that additional safeguard how could he stand against these robots?

Now—he saw a figure in the gray dawn light. It turned its head, and Ayyar's eyes went wide. Almost he shouted a name aloud?

"Amper—"

Time whirled about him in a dizzy dance. This friend who had once been as close as blood kin, who had stood with him at the last battle for Iftcan— Amper! First Vallylle and now Amper, who had been far more a part of his life. Even seeing his face unlocked more of the Ayyar memory, flooded his mind with an array of pictures, all warm, glowing, drawing him—

The false Amper stood there, but he did not face the bushes where Ayyar crouched. And that fact saved Ayyar, giving him needed time to remember who and what this semblance of Amper was. The false Ift bent his head a little to his right, his attitude that of one intently listening.

Ayyar bit hard upon his lower lip. Let that one turn ever so little and, if his Ift sight was like unto the body he now wore, surely he could pierce the leafless covering behind which his prey crouched, to cut Ayyar down without hesitation.

Far off—a whistling, thin, shrill, like unto a true Iftin scout cry, yet also was different. Now this thing that wore the guise of Amper raised its head and echoed that cry, sending it on, to be picked up in the Waste behind by yet another. A net of the Iftin—hunting him? Or were they merely on patrol, ready to pick up any wanderers the beam drew into their master's service?

Steeling himself against any move, hardly daring to breathe, Ayyar watched as the other lingered. It seemed to him as if Amper might be playing a ghastly game, that the false Ift was well aware Ayyar lay there, was waiting for him to reveal himself when the tension built too high to control any longer. Still that other did not turn its head and look to him.

Ayyar could not believe he had escaped, for the moment at least, when Amper, drawing his cloak more closely about him, darted away, at a loping run. He waited, listening, testing the breeze for any warning of another one of the monster band being close at hand. It was hard when his nerves urged him away, to put more distance between him and that replica of his one-time comrade.

By so much had he learned another scrap of THAT'S secrets—the false Iftin must be mirror-made, copies of those who had once walked Iftcan. Shells, undead, evil shadows now of those who had once been loved, honored, had lived and breathed as did he. It would seem that the Iftin had not vanished from Janus. In one way they came as changelings, in another as the soulless slaves of THAT.

Ayyar crawled from his brush hole and stopped to uproot a stout piece of it, which, stripped of its small branches, made for him another cane. Day, with the sun coming. But he dared not wait for the night now. The false Iftin and those who traveled the Waste were not dependent upon the dark, and he could not allow their advantage to limit him when it came to the matter of time.

Still, as Ayyar hobbled on, he tried to make the land work for him. There was cover enough, the many eroded gullies, the outcrops of rock and brush and other ragged growth, though some of the latter looked so odd and evil he avoided any contact with them.

He huddled in the shadow of a stone at high noon, chewing the last of his seeds, trying to find in their tiny portion of moisture relief for his dry mouth. It was hard not to think of water. Memories of cool Forest pools, of the tumbling, rushing river, haunted him. The wind was growing stronger, and in it was another scent, the salt of sea. He could not be too far from his goal, though where along the shore he would find those he sought, he had no idea.

The glare of the sun was too much for him now. He had to remain under cover during its height. However, there was no cover from his thoughts.

Amper—how many more of those Ayyar had known, liked, loved, were now weapons and tools of THAT? The hall filled with mirrors, all picturing those strangers whose like he had never seen on Janus—had there once been here another race? Older than the Iftin, the Larsh, these late come off-worlders? How old *was* THAT? Had IT any age as mankind conceived of age? Had IT swallowed up, to hold in such bondage, whole nations of others?

The wind filled with the sea's breath curled about him, promised freedom from the stench of THAT'S Waste and the things that prowled there. It was not Forest-sweetened air, but the Iftin had once also known the sea and found it good. What did lie beyond the shallow finger of the ocean toward which he traveled now? The changeling Iftin withdrew there each cold season. With the return of spring a handful of them ventured to this shore to set out those "treasures" that would in time add to their company. So slow a way to reseed the Forest race, yet the only one they knew.

Would they ever be able to do that again—with the garths emptied of the Settlers, the port men all drawn into THAT'S net? But suppose it would be possible to revive and bring forth the captives of the mirror patterns? So might the seeding grow amain! Could one ever seize THAT'S meat from within ITS jaws?

Ayyar waited out the afternoon impatiently. Then, as the shadows grew longer and thicker, he ventured on once more, his face to that wind with its promise of soon reaching his goal. The land was changing, showing more and more patches of sand. Then, before him, were the dunes. He recalled that bay from which he had seen the log ship of the Iftin depart months earlier, having reached that spot just too late to join the brethren he knew existed but whom he had not then seen. But whether that lay east or west from here he could not tell.

The closer the sea, the colder the wind. He pulled his cloak tightly about him and kept to cover where he could. But that cover was very sparse now.

He threaded between the dunes to the flat outer beach. In spite of the brilliance of the sunset, the sky over the rolling waves was darkly sullen, and for the first time since his change Ayyar found himself preferring light to dark. There was loneliness and foreboding in that sky and the dusky, leaden-hued ocean.

Wave marks laced the edge of the sand, scudding around tangles of drift flung up in past storms. And above, flying things cried desolately as they soared and swooped. A long scaled creature crawled slowly from the pull of the surf, lay as if exhausted on the damp sand, then scuttled with an amazing burst of speed to hide in a pile of drift. Here Ayyar memory could not supply much in the way of identification, for Ayyar of Ky-Kyc had been Forest hunter, not seafarer.

He did not venture out too far on the beach. It was barrenly open there, which made him feel naked and vulnerable. Rather did he skulk among the dunes, searching ahead for those cliffs that had walled in the bay he remembered. A shadow to the left looked promising. With no better guide than that, he turned east, limping slowly, his cane slipping in the loose sand.

Cliffs began to rise ahead of him, stretching into the sand like extended arms, the hands of which were buried in the wash of ocean waves. And from one of those rugged heights Ayyar caught a whistle that was no cry of bird.

That sound drained the remainder of his strength, as if, having managed at last to come into communication with his fellows, the will and determination that had kept him going seeped away and he could not take another step. He swayed, leaning heavily on the cane, his weight driving it so deeply into the loose sand that he lost balance, tumbled forward, and lay unable to regain his feet.

The whistle sounded again, this time from a different direction. Ayyar waited, almost past caring, for their coming.

Lokatath was the first beside him, to be followed by Jarvas, and then another, strange to him. So, he thought dully as Lokatath raised his head and the Mirrormaster knelt to look at his bound leg, those overseas had come, ahead of time, and into danger.

Ayyar wanted to spill out all he knew, to set action going—Illylle—the blocked door to THAT—the scraps of knowledge he had learned so painfully in the burrows. But now that the time had come for speech, his dry mouth and his cracked lips could not shape the words.

They brought him around the cliff, half carrying, half supporting the body that refused to obey his will. There in the bay rode the huge log that might have been one of the Great Crowns tossed so to be the sport of wind and wave but that he knew was a ship of Iftin. Safe in the small skiff at the water's edge they settled him and paddled out to the opening in that log. He could not climb; they had to use a sling to bring him in.

He tried to whisper, but they would not pause to listen. Instead they carried him down a wood-walled passage and into a cabin, which was like unto one of Iftsiga's chambers. Its comfort closed about him as a cloak might shelter one against the bitterness of a storm wind. So he sighed with relief as they laid him on a bunk.

Then Kelemark bent over him, and there was a time of darkness, which was good, which he welcomed, pushing aside thought—

Illylle? Into that warm dark came first the saying of a name, and Ayyar stirred unhappily, reluctant to acknowledge the need to answer. He tasted sweet warmth, healing his dry mouth, his aching throat as he swallowed. Through his body spread new energy and well-being. It was as if he again quaffed Iftsiga's blood.

"What of Illylle?"

Ayyar opened his eyes. Jarvas stood by his side, his eyes intent and searching, as if he could see into Ayyar's skull, bring out the answer to his question.

"She lies in hiding—I could not wake her," he replied. "It was thus—"

Once launched into his story, the words came easily. Ayyar discovered that he could build pictures for the others' seeing, beginning with the journey from the Mirror into the Waste. He told of their finding the true wood within the Enemy's territory and how they sheltered there. Of Illylle's giving to him that which had been set in her by the power of the Mirror, of his journey in the suit, and of what else he had learned in the burrows.

He was aware as he spoke that others gathered behind Jarvas, listening to his words. But it was to the Mirrormaster that he told this tale, for to him in that company Jarvas was the leader.

When he described the mirror patterns and their use, the evil wood illusion, the false tree and the company under its roots, Ayyar heard their quickened breathing. Then he was interrupted for the first time. One who was behind Jarvas spoke, and his tone carried authority.

"This company of Larsh—tell us again of them—"

Ayyar was impatient, eager to finish his report. But he reacted to the note of command and once again described the silent line of the Enemy's servants, beginning with the bestial Larsh, ending with the space-suited figure of one who was wholly man.

"And these, you say, stood in reverse order to the company of the Iftin, beginning with the Larsh, ending with true man, while an Ift of the final days faced the Larsh?"

Ayyar nodded. Jarvas turned his head to ask of the questioner:

"You believe that this has some special meaning, Olyron?"

"It might. And what was beyond that, Ayyar?"

He continued with the room of the machines, of how his sword had unlocked the lower passage, of the place of stored mirrors. Again he heard the quickened breathing of those who listened.

On he continued to the stairwell, which was closed past his power to open. And now Jarvas asked:

"Are you sure that what you were sent to seek lay below?"

Ayyar did not doubt that in the least or that skill beyond his must be applied to draw that cork of slagged metal. He told them the rest—his fight with the false Ift, the coming of the garthwomen and children, his return to Illylle, and finally his sight of Amper in the Waste. When he spoke of that, he heard them stir uneasily.

Once his story was told, weariness again descended upon him. Kelemark must have sensed that, for he offered a wooden cup, and what it contained was tree sap, spring sweet, to clear his mind and wash away his fatigue.

"So—" Some of the company had gone, but Kelemark, Jarvas, and the man called Olyron remained. It was the latter who spoke. "So, it would seem that the task yet remains to be done." His tone was bleak, and Ayyar read into it criticism of the tool that had been chosen by the Mirror and then failed in action. And he regarded Olyron with answering coolness. But Jarvas smiled, if fleetingly, with a warmth for Ayyar.

"We know much more. And we cannot hope to win a war with a single small skirmish. Tell me, Olyron, who of those with us now holds in his other memory a knowledge of tools or procedure such as would clear that plug for us?''

Ayyar sat up and cautiously swung his wounded leg around. He found it stiff, but only a small ache remained, and there was already a scab formed, no need for bandage.

''To use off-world memory there,'' he pointed out, ''is to come under THAT'S control.''

''Then a memory of a memory, perhaps,'' Jarvas returned. ''A memory recalled, given to another who will use it second-hand and not be caught in the web of his own pre-Ift self. Possible, Olyron?''

The other nodded. ''It might be. This—this has such tangled roots that it is hard to trace any one stem from their supporting. I feel deeply that the line of Larsh has meaning for us—if we could only read it! And these mirrors that can pattern a man, then build a robot from his image—store it as you saw in the cavern— An Ift you once knew— So do they remain or only the mirrors? We follow a force that reaches us through a Mirror—yet that is a Mirror of water that lives and even wars upon occasion, while these reflectors slay or imprison.''

Jarvas looked beyond them—to the wood wall of the cabin. ''Tolhron,'' he said softly.

''Place of sorrow and of fasting,
 Of evil everlasting.
 Chained are they who lie on Tolhron
 By the blood and by the bone
 Of those who set the spell
 Delving deep into the well
 Wherein all nothingness doth dwell—''

Ayyar saw that Kelemark and Olyron were as much at a loss as he to interpret Jarvas' chant.

Then Jarvas laughed shortly. "Memory again. That is an old tale, one for children, concerning a master of wayward arts who set up a place wherein he kept captives. And they could not be freed because the floor of his prison was mixed with blood and bone over which he had evil control, so that only when similar blood and bone were brought there might the prisoners be freed. I do not know why this rises to mind now."

"There was in this story some connection between this Tolhron and THAT?" asked Kelemark.

"Not that I can remember."

"In many legends there lies a grain of true history," Olyron commented. "And the fact that it comes to your mind now— If only we knew more of the Oath of Kymon! But your idea of shared memory has merit. You are sure you can find the right mound again?" he demanded of Ayyar.

"I made as sure of that as I could. And Illylle?" He turned to Jarvas.

"She can be brought here. Then, I believe, we can restore her. Two parties, one to rescue her, one to go to the mound—"

"Why not one, picking her up on their return?" Olyron wanted to know.

"Because that one might not return!" Ayyar slipped from the bunk, stood up, one hand braced on the wall. They did not try to hinder him.

Olyron went to the door. "I will ask for any memory that can aid us."

"And what if he cannot find such?" Ayyar perversely saw all the stumbling blocks in their path.

"Then we shall have to do the best we can without—" Jarvas began when Kelemark interrupted him.

"There are tools, all we might need—at the port—"

"A second choice, though whether we could use them is another matter," Jarvas pointed out. Would their revulsion hinder that?

"Illylle had me rub the interior of the suit with leaves. I could bear to wear it then," Ayyar said.

"A good thing to keep in mind. We have substances here that might serve as well," Kelemark replied briskly. "Suppose I collect a few. We have not tried that before." He, too, left them.

Jarvas was staring at the wall again, past Ayyar as if he were now invisible. Tolhron or some kindred half memory again? If they did not have to depend upon such broken patches of Iftin history, they would be better armed.

"It is there—or here—" Jarvas held out his hand palm up and curled the fingers slowly inward as if he would clasp something tight and hold it so. "There is an answer before us in what you have seen, but I cannot discover it! If and if and if—! Are we always to be haunted by ifs?"

XV

THERE WAS a pooling of memories, both Iftin and human, among those gathered in the ship. As Ift after Ift was eliminated from that council, Olyron spoke to those left.

"Does it not strike you as strange, brothers, that while we seem in memory to be divided more or less equally between the age of the Green Leaf and the Gray, there are none among us from the Blue, which must have been the golden age of our nation? And that all we have in memory of the Oath between Kymon and THAT is legend only? If those who made changelings of us could draw from two ages, the vigorous Green, the fading Gray, why not from the third and, by their belief, the best—the Blue? Was that time so far back that they could not evoke the personalities of any living then to 'haunt' one of their treasure traps? Or is there an important reason why that age was barred to them?''

"Of what importance is that here and now?'' one of the brothers asked.

"I do not know. Save that a memory of Kymon's time could guide us so well. To go blindly into this struggle is to be chain-bound from the start.''

"If we lack knowledge of Kymon,'' Jarvas reminded them, ''at least we have that of Jattu Nkoyo.'' He nodded to the Ift on his left. Out of all the men questioned only Jeyken, he who had once been Jattu Nkoyo, robot-service tech, had training that might aid them. His was the best off-world memory they could find, and now it must work secondhand into the bargain, lest Jeyken, turning to Nkoyo's recall, be swept up by THAT.

"You must not depend too much on what I can give you.'' Jeyken spread out his hands as if refusing some task beyond his strength. ''What you really need is an engineering tech and his tools.''

"Since we can summon neither out of thin air,'' Olyron commented dryly, ''we shall do our best with you. Give us what you have, let Drangar learn it from you, going over in detail Ayyar's observation of what may be needed.''

"I have been thinking of that pillar in the Waste and its beckoning beam," Jarvas cut in. "It may be near time for supply ships at the port. Do you suppose that signal could bring a ship? These animated space suits came from ships. We found one such planeted back in the Waste last season, an old one. There could well have been others."

"So you propose making plans for an assault on the beacon? Just on the chance that it may be of some disservice to us?" inquired Olyron.

"If it is now being used, as Ayyar believes, to pull the rest of the Settlers into the Waste, then it is already a menace," Jarvas replied. "Yes, I believe that we must make that also an objective—for a third party."

Olyron looked skeptical, as if he wondered just how Iftin without machines or tools were going to accomplish such a program. And Ayyar could agree with him. Jattu Nkoyo might be a master robot-tech, but more engineering knowledge than he ever possessed could well be needed to unseal that stairway—let alone down the beacon pillar.

But he detailed for them again his best observations of the plug. At last the one-time robot-tech leaned back and looked to the Ift who would carry what technical assistance he could supply.

"It may be impossible. If you had a cutter set on high beam, you could go for the edge around the plug. Or if the passage below paralleled those above, you could cut through some feet back and drop down. But without a cutter—" He shook his head doubtfully. "You say these space suits still wear their equipment belts, with tools in them?" he asked Ayyar. At the other's nod, he continued.

"Any plug put in that way would be too well set to burn out with hand tools—the way the sword energy handled the doors. Doors—" he repeated thoughtfully.

"What about them?" Jarvas wanted to know when Jeyken did not continue.

"This place, these burrows, as you call them, they must have been set up by space men. You had that impression, did you not—I mean, they seemed familiar?"

"Yes, they did!"

"And you came up a ladder, past how many levels?"

"Two."

"Did the corridors on each radiate in the same pattern? And how far apart were the levels, how many steps between?"

Ayyar closed his eyes and tried to visualize the mound stairs. Could he be sure that the pattern had been the same on each level? Never had he flogged his memory harder.

"I think that the next level up had a like number of passages running in the same direction. Of the other I am not sure. There were—no, I cannot tell the number of steps—" Another failure to report, and this one he could have avoided. Why had he not taken greater care to be sure of such details?

"Then—I would advocate a break downward from one of the passages."

"Through this metal lining and rock—using what—our fingernails?" Drangar snorted. "I have dug fields in my time, but that was earth and I had a plow—"

Jeyken did not answer him directly. He spread out his hands on the table top, framing the rude sketch Ayyar had made there of the passages and the stoppered stairway as he had seen them.

"Here is your weak point." The former tech pointed to the door of the passage. "If it is to spacer design, then these doors on all levels will be hung on a column straight down, each above the other. And around here in the wall somewhere will be an opening to repair any jammed control. On a ship a servo-robot is generalized, which means it is bulky and well armored, to work inside or out in space. So it needs plenty of room. Thus a repair space must allow for that and so would be large enough for man to enter.

"You burn out the lock there, just as Ayyar burnt the doors, giving you access to any control cable. This will be strung in a well, and that will be your passage down to the sealed-off level."

"If and if and if again," commented Jarvas. "Always supposing that this is all made to a spacer design."

"Short of bringing in a large-size cutter, brothers," Jeyken answered, "I do not see any other way."

"But I no longer have the sword energy," Ayyar pointed out.

"Then you will have to capture a suit and get a blaster from it," was Jeyken's reply. "At a high voltage that will cut you in. Now, Drangar, this is what you are to look for—" He went into detail concerning the service doors and the machinery to be found within.

Ayyar slumped on the bench and stared at his hands resting limply on the table before him. He did not believe that they would have much profit from plans that left so much to chance, and guess work. Better accept defeat in this, rescue Illylle, retreat overseas, and leave the destroyed Forest, the Waste, and the off-worlders to THAT.

"We cannot—"

Ayyar raised his eyes to meet those of Jarvas.

"We cannot, or we would! Think you, are you able to set aside the thought that the seeding will fail, that our nation, now only a weak handful, will not have another springtime?"

Within Ayyar was a stirring. The sap drink had awakened and strengthened his body, not his weary mind. Now he knew Jarvas was right, that there had been planted in the changelings the need to perpetuate their kind, to set the treasure traps, to thus produce more and more Iftin. They could no more turn their backs upon that urge than the off-worlders he had seen could escape the call of THAT.

Perhaps if this was to be the end of the seeding, it was better that it came in battle with THAT than in slow decay. He got to his feet. That sense of purpose that had wrapped him, given him confidence when he had left the Mirror with Illylle, had ebbed. He had left in him now only a kind of weary determination to see this to the end.

"Illylle?"

"Kelemark and Lokatath will bring her back after we find her."

They waited upon the night. Two parties left the bay where the ship was already making ready to return overseas, after disembarking a third small force to remain at shore line concealment. One of the parties would go upriver, to deal with the beacon as well as they might. If any of them really believed that could be done, thought Ayyar, watching them disappear among the dunes.

The larger group, with him as guide, headed straight into the same trap from which he had come. His wound made him walk a little stiffly, but without the pain that had made his flight a torturous ordeal. Each of them carried at his belt a flask of oily spicy-smelling mixture that Kelemark and some of the other Iftin believed would overcome their repugnance to any off-world tool they used.

Undoubtedly they made better time than Ayyar had on his way out, covering the ground with their usual agile speed. Always they listened, sniffed, scouted for the enemy. It would seem that THAT'S servants did not patrol so far south. At least they crossed the trail of no prowlers.

"IT does not seem to care." Ayyar spoke his thoughts aloud as they finally halted, to drink from their sap bottles and eat sparingly of nut meal wafers.

"So it appears," Jarvas agreed, and then he added, "or else IT is so occupied elsewhere and believes us so weak as opponents that IT can grind us into nothingness under ITS boot sole when more important tasks are behind IT—"

"But IT began the attack against the Forest." Ayyar blinked. Had there been a shift of purpose as Jarvas suggested, THAT turning from the eradication of the remains of Iftcan to more pressing matters?

"Suppose that the struggle against a dying Forest is no longer important," Jarvas continued. "Suppose THAT discovered the off-worlders and Settlers, set in motion against us, made such excellent servants for ITS purposes that IT could easily forget Iftin and use these to build what lies in ITS mind. Suppose the Larsh were a tool which failed, that IT has slumbered through the ages, waiting the coming of stronger metal—"

"But IT is the ancient Enemy against Iftcan, against Ift—" protested Drangar, almost as if he resented the thought that they were as grains of dust, to be brushed contemptuously away to free a site for the building of another plan.

"To Ift, THAT is the great Enemy, yes. We know that we held IT static or powerless for generations, until IT fought us on our own plane with the Larsh. But perhaps THAT has another purpose, and our long struggle merely postponed it. Now IT has found material with which to carry out such plans."

"But the garthmen, the port crew, have been here for years. Why wait until now to use them?"

Jarvas shrugged. "Perhaps IT was not aware of them, not until the Iftin arose once more to disturb ITS quiescence. Then, triggered by old memories, IT moved against us. IT may not even know how few we are. Needing servants to take the place of the Larsh, IT found them. It may be experimenting. I believe that the false Iftin are an experiment, perhaps not a fully successful one. Remember the robot woman used to open the garth defenses? So THAT needs raw material for further experiments, summons it, molds it—"

"And, becoming so entranced with such a quest for knowledge, may not concentrate upon us?" Kelemark asked. "A welcome thought, but not one we dare to build too much upon."

"Look!" Rizak pointed to the northeast. The beacon was on, but this time it did not beckon from the garthland but turned in the direction of the port.

"Still gathering in," Jarvas said softly. "First the garths, now the port, or maybe from a ship there—"

Watching that beam, Ayyar wondered at their own rashness in believing that they could dispose of that, put down even so small a portion of the Enemy's works. And he could not see any success for the party pledged to try it.

They trotted on, glancing now and then at the distant beacon, which showed no change. There was no other sign that THAT was awake and aware. The Waste appeared deserted. At daybreak they sighted the glitter of the White Forest's ruin, and Ayyar picked up one landmark after another. The green valley could not be too far ahead.

"Scout first." He drew level with Jarvas. "I have been thinking if THAT does look for true Ift within its country, IT could use the valley for a trap."

"True. Take the point then, Ayyar. I will come in from the north. The rest of you, move with caution."

There were five others. Kelemark, his small bundle of healing supplies humping one hip under his cloak; Lokatath; Rizak—of their original company; Drangar and Myrik, another Ift volunteer, from the overseas party. Now they all faded into obscurity, using shadows and the rough ground to cover their passing.

Ayyar moved out, intent on reaching the valley, not from the direction of the road but from the south. The shattered spires and stumps of crystal rose about him, and he had to pick a careful way, not as concealed a one as he could wish. He relied upon his nose, and so far none of the stench of the false Ift or THAT'S other servants had come to his nostrils. But an early morning breeze blew, now and then raising a weird sound in its path across the crystal needles, and those forces might be downwind.

On this side of the green valley the rim was wider. He saw none of the welcome, leafed branches showing above it. Then he reached the edge of the drop, staying as close to the earth as he could huddle, searching all that lay below with a probing eye. To his most suspicious examination there was nothing to signal danger. He found a place that could be descended and started down, these few moments when he would be open against the cliff the most perilous.

He landed, in a leap that brought pain shooting through his thigh, almost knee deep in green growth. Before him were bushes, and he believed he was near that spring with the small pool. Looking up to where Jarvas must come in, he saw a hand raised and lowered and signaled back.

Ayyar moved on under the canopy of the trees. He had rounded one trunk when he came across a trail, and the sight of the crushed and broken vegetation stopped him short. Whoever had passed that way had paid no attention to any obstruction less than a tree, plowing ahead to beat and break a road. And Ayyar did not need to sight those footprints deep in the moss to enlighten him as to the identity of the invader.

One of the space suits, probably of the humanoid type since it left clear footprints, had stamped that path down the valley, one set going and then returning, or so the overtrodden prints spelled out—and some time ago, for growth not quite crushed was rising slowly.

Along that trail Ayyar ran, heading for the narrowed point of the valley, already knowing in his heart what he was destined to find. Those stones he had worked with such care to pile had been scattered in all directions. And the hollow wherein Illylle had been left was empty.

Ayyar stood there, not wanting to believe the evidence of his eyes. His the blame! If he had not left her—Perhaps he could have devised some way of getting her out. But, no, he had gone, leaving her to be found by some servant of THAT, taken off in bondage. If indeed she was still alive—

"She was there?" Jarvas joined him.

Ayyar nodded dumbly. How long had it been since they had taken her? Perhaps if the Iftin force had left the bay before nightfall—had he done so—it would have been in time.

Jarvas' hand on his arm tightened, anchoring him solidly to this spot where the earth was scarred by those ponderous beating feet of the space suit.

"Steady!" That was an order, delivered so sharply that the word pierced Ayyar's turmoil. "What is done" —Jarvis' words were slowly spaced, as emphatic as that "steady"—"is done. We go on from here—"

"To the mirrors in the burrows." Ayyar, remembering what he had seen there, twisted in an effort to throw off Jarvas' grip.

"Perhaps. But what good will it do us—or her—Ayyar, if you run headlong without thought? I do not believe that they can do aught with her while she lies in that sleep—"

Ayyar rounded on the other. "What do you know about it!"

"She fell asleep when she gave unto you what the Mirror had placed within her," Jarvas replied quietly. "I may not remember all that Jarvas who was once Mirrormaster knew, but I know this much, one who has been a vessel of that kind of power and emptied herself of it for the use of another is still under the protection of Thanth. Remember, you once saw the force of Thanth in action. And around you now, above this valley, lies the evidence of how it wrought here. The nature of THAT is a mystery. So also is the nature of Thanth, save that we of the Forest know that to call upon it wholeheartedly in peril brings an answer—"

"I am no Mirrormaster," Ayyar flung at him. "And the

memories I hold from the mists of time long past are of death and defeat. Where was Thanth then?''

''Who knows? But dare you, having stood and watched the Mirror rise to our call for aid, say that there is not power to challenge THAT? You carried that power within your body, did you not? And could you deny it then? I say to you, there are paths ordained for us, each with a purpose beyond our reckoning. If it is possible, then we shall bring Illylle forth again. Do you want my formal oath on that?''

Ayyar's eyes blinked, but they did not drop. He nursed this new rage in him, drawing from it a kind of strength that cast out all but the shadow of fear.

''At least this thing has left a fresh trail to follow—''

''Which we cannot take now.''

It needed an instant or two for those words to register. When they did, Ayyar jerked free from Jarvas' hold.

''*You* may not take it,'' he cried, ''but I shall!''

''No!''

Again so full of authority was that word that Ayyar paused.

''First the door and then—''

''No!'' It was Ayyar's turn to cry out in denial.

''Yes!'' Overriding his refusal, somehow by its very tone holding him there when he would be gone, came Jarvas' command.

''Show Drangar and the others the rightful door. Then we shall go for Illylle. Do you doubt me?'' There was an undercurrent of emotion in the other's voice, enough to hold Ayyar.

In the end Jarvas won. The sun was rising, and its glare had long since deadened their sight of the beacon, so that they could not know whether that other party had had any success against the sinister rod of light.

Every nerve in Ayyar's body urged him on, but in the broad day, with goggles for only four of their number, such a journey was impossible. They must wait for night or be fatally handicapped from the start.

He tried to work out some of his restlessness on sentry-go at the rim of the valley, keeping a wary eye on the crushed road that led through the ruined wood. This time no spacesuit sentries rewarded his vigil, nothing stirred on the land or in the air. It might almost be that the forces of THAT were as bound by day as the Iftin. But there was an expectancy in the air, a tension such as a man might feel while waiting at a barrier for the rush of attack, as if the Enemy drew now upon all stored strength, marshaling forces, moving out ITS pieces on the game board that twice in his dreams Ayyar had faced.

The noontime glare was so great that he had to retreat into the valley and seek out green shade to rest his eyes. Lokatath came to him.

"Ayyar, you spoke of the women and children drawn out of the garths—"

Ayyar nodded absently. That was all far, very far back in time, separated from the here and now by the dragging hours since he had found that niche empty, the trail down the valley.

"Did you know—from which garth?"

Ayyar shrugged impatiently. What did it matter? The Settlers were less than nothing to him. Once he had been a labor slave, then a changeling Ift, and neither looked upon garthmen, with their cruel, harsh religion, their morose ways, with any liking. "I do not know—"

"I suppose not." Lokatath was studying the broken bushes beyond. "It has been many seasons now; I have not tried to keep count. But sometimes I remember that I was once Derek Vessters, and I see old, known faces dimly, hear voices I once knew. It was a harsh, hard life, so narrow that no sun or moon ever lit to the bottom of it, so that no man sang as we Iftin do who know the joys of the Forest, or would know them if we were left alone. Still —one remembers—and then one wonders how matters have chanced with those one knew—''

''You left close kin?'' Some note in the other's voice reached Ayyar. He had his own meaningful memories from off-world.

''A father who sent me to the Forest when the Green Sick struck, and a mother who wept. I remember her tears. Perchance both are long since dead. Garth toil does not make for long lives. I do not know if I would recognize their faces if I were to look upon them now. By their standards I was no fit and proper son. Such strangeness to my kin was what brought me to the treasure and set the Ift seal upon me, for it is true that only those who can be so influenced have any desire to take up the bait and change.''

''Listen!'' Ayyar swung around, facing the rise that led to the glitter of the shards. He had been right; that was no wind through the splinters. Something moved—along the crushed roadway.

He climbed, crept out into the ruins, aware that Lokatath came with him. Together they took cover in a tangle of fallen prisms, broken trunks and branches.

Men, true men, walked with a steady tramp back up from the valley. They were not garthmen but wore uniforms, work clothes of the port. There were ten of them, and they strode as if with no fear of what lay either behind or ahead of them, rather as if they were moved by a purpose demanding their full attention.

"Are they robots?" whispered Lokatath.

Ayyar could not be sure, but it was very probable. They were armed with stunners and blasters, but those weapons were holstered—THAT'S servants went on some unknown errand.

XVI

"IT MAY BE that THAT mans the port with ITS servants in order to welcome in a ship," Jarvas speculated when he was summoned to watch that squad march northeast.

"Has it occurred to you," Rizak asked, "that the Enemy may not be native to Janus at all? Suppose IT came here from space, has been in exile, and now would return. That IT has reached for ships before, to find such efforts fruitless, and now makes another attempt—?"

"Why then the garthmen?" questioned Lokatath.

"Servants to use on this planet. Or, merely, IT would immobilize a possible opposition to ITS desires for now. I cannot forget those racked image mirrors. Perhaps those were brought with IT—"

"But the Larsh," cut in Drangar, "the Larsh were ITS servants before. Why not use those on the mirrors if they were available?"

"IT might have had several kinds of servants," Jarvas cut in. "But this is a thought to hold in mind, Rizak. If tin memories are only of Janus, and of the nature of THAT we have no idea, nor did those whose personalities we now wear. If IT came out of space ages ago, then the burrows, like unto space-ship corridors, all the rest—fit! Do you not see how it is so? And being alien to Ift, IT could well have no common meeting from the beginning, no common thoughts, for the Iftin were always planet bound, they were rooted deep in this earth, even as the Great Crowns, and they did not wish it otherwise. *We* can understand such thoughts, for we were once men who knew the stars beyond the sky.''

''Are we then better fitted to deal with such an alien should we uncover him?'' asked Myrik, the other Ift from overseas, a quiet, steady-eyed companion.

''That also we should think upon. Utterly alien has THAT always been to the Iftin. A planet-bound race could well be subject to xenophobia. Perhaps our present revulsion to close company with off-worlders and their possessions is not altogether a device set in the Green Sick to keep us apart from our one-time kindred. Perhaps it is just a stronger strain of what the Iftin always felt toward that which was not of Janus. To them—to us now—THAT embodies all evil, but by other standards that judgment might be different.''

''But THAT has always been. The survivor of any ancient crash would not live so long. Kymon was of the Blue Leaf, and he knew IT. Ages have passed since then.''

''How long have you been Ift?'' Jarvas counter-questioned.

Myrik's lips moved. Ayyar thought he was counting.

''I was Rahuld Urswin, stat-comp reader for the Combine. I came here in the year 4570 ASF. It was the next season that I took the Green Sick while on a hunting party in the sea islands to the south.''

''And you''—Jarvas spoke now to Ayyar—''you are the latest come into Iftdom. What year was it when you landed on Janus?''

''The year 4635 ASF.''

''And I landed here in 4450 ASF, or thereabouts,'' Jarvis continued. ''Now, have I aged or have you, Myrik?''

Slowly the other shook his head.

''Therefore, we can assume that the Iftin have a life span far longer than the two hundred years granted those of our particular species. And the Zacathans live close to a thousand years. Among those of the galaxy that we know, they are the longest-lived race. But how much of the galaxy do we know even yet, with all our wanderings and exploring just begun as the stars measure time? There may be other species to whom the Zacathans' span would be a quickly passing day.''

''What if such a being could have no common meeting ground with another species?'' Rizak hazarded. ''What if to IT the first Iftin, and now these off-worlders, were as animals?''

''That could well follow. We shall not know until we meet IT. But the fact that we are each two and not one may give us greater power against whatever lies behind that sealed door, for we have memories reaching into the dim past here, and also memories fed with lore from beyond the moon and sky of Janus. And if THAT is not native to this world, we can accept that knowledge to build upon.''

All this could be true, but it brought them no closer to

Illylle. Ayyar watched the squad of off-worlders march out of sight. There might be others sent out by THAT. And what stand could the Iftin make against the weapons they carried? He said as much.

Rizak nodded. "I guess four hours more of sun. If we try to move during that, we are handicapped. We must wait—"

Ayyar wanted to hack the earth before him with his sword— Wait, and continue to wait! But for Illylle there might be no waiting. He put little faith in Jarvas' suggestion that she might be safe because of the sleep in which he had left her. How did they know anything about it? That might have merely plunged her more quickly into the fate of the mirror reflections. Ift hatred and fear of THAT and all ITS powers haunted him. But side by side marched old terrors from his other life. Science, too, had its demons and dark powers. Almost it was easier to accept THAT as Ift saw IT, a vast, threatening force of evil without concrete form, than to reduce IT and make IT more tangible by fitting it with an alien "body."

Jarvas' hand on Ayyar's shoulder drew him back into the green shade of the valley while Rizak took his place on guard.

"Once more," the older Ift said, "tell us of the passages."

He had gone over this not once, but many times. Why again? Surely they knew it all well. But if it must be— Wearily, step by step, once more he marched through the burrows, retelling in detail all he could recall. Twice Jarvas stopped him, once during his description of the chamber wherein he had seen the port officer's body placed in the container, and the second time the area of the space below the false tree where the lines of Ift and Larsh faced each other.

"It would seem that the bodies of those reflected on the mirrors are preserved," Myrik commented. "Does that also mean that the process can be reversed? If so—what of those who made the patterns for the false Ift? Ayyar recognized one as a comrade of the last days. And the girl in the false wood, she was also one he could put name to."

"That line of Larsh," Jarvas mused. "I cannot think but in that lies the key, or perhaps one of the keys that, if we might turn them, would make us free of what we should know. But for the rest, are we now all sure of the ways?"

They gave assent. But still the sun was too high, keeping them prisoners in this valley. And time marched so slowly.

When Jarvas did give the signal to issue forth, in the early evening, Ayyar broke into a run along the rutted road, hardly aware of what he did until Rizak caught up with him and threw out an arm against his chest.

"Do you want to break your neck, brother, before you have a chance to break one of theirs? Give a thought to your footing here and to the saving of strength for what must lie before us."

Prudence was a hard dose, but he swallowed it. And they came at last into the valley of the mounds. Ayyar looked for some sign of the women and the children. But no one, nothing—not even the driverless machines —wandered here now, though they proceeded with caution along the rows of heaped-up earth. Kelemark paused by one, scraped off a little of that sour-smelling soil, and brought it closer to his nose. Then he flung it from him and stooped to scrub his fingers in the sand.

"That is not of Janus," he said, "or if it is, it has been changed by some process." He spoke with authority. As one-time medico from the port, he had first been drawn into the Forest of Iftcan in search of native herbs for experiment. Though his Iftin memories were different —those of a lord of growing land—yet in part his interests remained the same and had blended into a whole as a healer.

Drangar looked about with a shiver, drawing closer his cloak.

"All the Waste changed after the coming of THAT. There is naught here that is clean."

Resolutely, because he knew he now must, Ayyar passed the mound that had given him first entrance into the burrows. He made them pause there and pointed out the hold that opened the inner way. There were numerous scuffings and markings in the sand, but the powdery stuff held no clear prints. He guessed there had been much traffic through here recently.

They continued on to the other mound, climbed to its crest. Ayyar dug away the soil he had replaced to cover the entrance. And then they descended the ladder to the first level. Myrik swung off to investigate the other openings, and a moment later he was back.

"Slagged shut—and by more than just a blaster job. Melted tight."

The passages of the second level ran a little farther but ended abruptly in the same destruction. Then they came to the one where the stopper had been so firmly applied to the stairwell itself. Myrik knelt and ran his hands over the congealed mass.

"Same kind of job as that above," he commented. "And this was done a long time ago, I believe. Wonder why they did not close off the top of the stair as well."

"Who can understand any of THAT'S motives?" demanded Drangar. He, too, knelt by the stopper. "This cannot be stirred. You would need such a blast as would topple one of the Great Crowns."

"Or a ship torch," supplied Rizak. "Well"—he tossed back his cloak and set his hands on his hips—"what about this repair door Jeyken spoke of?"

Ayyar brought them into the passage that led to the hall of the stacked mirrors, and Drangar, Myrik, and Rizak began to search for the opening that might or might not be there, while Ayyar shifted unhappily from foot to foot, eager to be on his way in search of Illylle.

"Right in this much!" Drangar pressed his hands to the wall and outlined an oblong space. "Ayyar, has your sword power returned?"

He drew his sword, but no sparks flew from its tip; he felt none of the answering flow within him. "No."

"Then we try these. It will make a long job, if we can do it at all." Drangar took from his belt a roll of soft bark cloth. He opened this wide on the floor, revealing small tools fashioned of the same metal as the Iftin swords, intended for working in wood. Could any of them serve against metal?

"Do your best." Jarvas turned to Kelemark and Lokatath. "Do we go?"

Their answer was quick. With Ayyar well in the lead, they climbed the ladder and came out again on the top of the mound where the dusk of night had settled. Lokatath's head was up. He sniffed as might a hound.

"Smell that!"

Stink of false Iftin, strong enough to suggest the Enemy was close.

"There—!"

The flitting of a shadow from one mound to another. But that was not the only one out there. Some must be closer, or that warning would not reach their noses so strongly. Ayyar searched the sides of the mound by eye.

Lokatath shared his suspicion, crawling along the small level space on which they had come forth, heading in the opposite direction, while the rest waited, alert for what might come.

There Ayyar spotted a shape flattened on the wall of the mound, still escaping any eye from above. It was three-quarters of the way up to their perch. That climber would not attempt to use a bow. He must depend upon a sword, did he go armed with Iftin weapons. But the robot Illylle and he had killed in the Waste had been furnished with a hand arm of a new type.

The spidery figure was frozen on the slope, as if it were aware that its presence was known to those above. Ayyar dared to look away, along the rest of the mound wall. Another, he was sure, that was another just there—

"Around us"—Lokatath's whisper was soft—"and moving up—"

"Back"—that was Jarvas—"into the passages—"

Against his wishes Ayyar obeyed, but he was the last to seek the ladder and drop as far as the second level with its sealed-off exits.

"How many of them?"

212

"Six at least!" Lokatath made answer. "Doubtless more. What do we do?"

"The other way—" Ayyar's thoughts clung to Illylle and his own mission. "Back through the hall of mirrors, the false wood—" He had one foot on the ladder when Kelemark caught him.

"The others must have time to work—"

"Your cloaks," Jarvas ordered. "Off with them!"

Ayyar fumbled with the neck clasp and freed the length of cloth.

"Flat. This way." Jarvas threw his own cloak on the space about the ladder, to be followed by Lokatath, Kelemark, and Ayyar. Together they now covered the floor and encircled the ladder.

"Now, each of you, into a passage!"

Jarvas' plan remained a mystery, but Ayyar found himself obeying the order. The passage was a short one, the fused metal sharp at his back as he swung around to face the ladder area. He was just in time to see Jarvas toss onto the carpet formed by their cloaks what looked to be some common pebbles. Then he knew what surprise was intended for those who hunted them.

The Forest was not only the Iftin home. It also provided that race, born and bred in its shadow, nourished by its life, with many things. And there were oddities in the vegetable world of Janus that were as dangerous as some of the wild life that roamed the woodland's aisles and glades. Those gray pebbles were not the stones they resembled but seeds that could be used as a weapon. Would they work against false Iftin as they had at times against the true?

Jarvas was in no haste to trigger them. Ayyar watched

him across the space by the ladder, down on one knee, a flask of tree sap ready in his hand, his head up as he listened.

Waiting was always hard, but this was the kind that dried the mouth, set one to the need for moving, to break the tension. Ayyar must stay, sword ready, crouched in his small section of safety, listening for the sound of a boot on the ladder, glancing now and then at those small things lying innocently on the cloth, hardly to be seen in the gloom, save by Iftin eyes.

Sounds at last. Ayyar caught a small movement across from him. With one hand, Jarvas was worrying the stopper from the flask of sap.

Light, not as brilliant as a blaster ray yet deadly in promise, caught the cloak fabric, to be followed by a curl of smoke. Jarvis threw. The sap spattered over the pebble-seeds. There was an instant of anxious waiting, then soft plops, loud in the silence, steam rising where the sap touched the scorched cloth.

Wriggling things burst from the seeds, writhed reptile-like around the ladder, clinging to it. Water alone would have brought life from those seeds, but sap made the growth twice as rapid. It seemed as if those stems reached into nothingness, caught emptiness to them, wove substance of it. From finger size they swelled into lengths as thick as Ayyar's wrist, putting forth all the time more and more tribute vines. They seized upon the ladder as a trellis, leaping up its steps at a speed Ayyar could hardly believe, filling it in, winding about it to choke the opening.

From the vines came a thin orange light. This streamed

upward, revealing itself as a cloud of dancing motes. Each of the Iftin in the passages snapped up the edges of the cloaks, shielding their own bodies from that cloud. But the motes did not drift much laterally. Following their nature, they rose vertically, drawn by the promise of outer air in the roof opening.

The Iftin heard nothing as they huddled behind the cloaks. Whether the false Iftin had already been attacked by the motes as living flesh would have been, those in hiding could not tell. But they had put an efficient stopper in the passage to form a rear guard. Jarvas motioned. Ayyar saw Kelemark raise his portion of the cloak yet higher, slide under it, creep to the ladder hole and descend, the others holding steady as he moved.

Ayyar went next, finding that way of escape a stifling one, yet he dared not hurry. He tried to hold his breath, fearing some seepage of motes; inhaled, they would root and grow within a body. Then he was through the bolt hole, waiting for Lokatath, and last of all, Jarvas.

"No sound up there," their leader reported as he came. Above him the cloaks heaved, bulging downward under the weight of what grew there. They had made their escape just in time. Lokatath watched with satisfaction.

"It feeds, or it would cease to grow," he murmured.

"It closes the door, whether it does aught else," Jarvas commented. "Well, so now we must go hunting another way."

There was a ripping overhead. A white serpent of root wriggled free, swung in the air, then writhed and curled up to force its tip back through the same hole, seeking the air above rather than that of the burrows below.

Ayyar relaxed. He knew the nature of the thing they had loosed, but the small fear that it might follow them down had been with him after he had witnessed that frenzied growth. As Lokatath said, it must have fed enough to give its spread further impetus. Robot or not, the false Iftin had not been immune to balweed.

They went to where the others worked on the door. A hole now gaped in the wall, but Drangar looked at the mass of wiring so disclosed and shook his head.

"How goes it?" asked Jarvas, after a brief explanation of what had passed overhead.

"Thus—" Drangar displayed four broken tools. "We do not have what is needed here now."

"But elsewhere there is plenty!" Rizak broke in eagerly. "Those machines stored under the false tree. Among them should be maintenance tools."

"Worth trying." Drangar sat back on his heels. "Let us go—"

He would play guide so far, Ayyar decided, but once there, he would keep on, across that ill-omened wood, back to the place of the captives. And Lokatath, at least, might go with him.

They hurried down the passage into the place of racked mirrors. There they paused several times to wipe away the coating to look upon the reflections.

"How many—?" Kelemark looked about. "There must be hundreds!"

"Or a nation," returned Rizak soberly. "Maybe more." He had halted by one Ayyar had earlier uncovered and was looking at what was not humanoid but furred, with a narrow muzzle. "What was this, another species of intelligent being, a pet—?"

216

"On!" Ayyar urged, and they quickened pace after him.

They came below that opening in the floor of the place of machines. One standing on another's shoulders, a third using them both for ladder, then Ayyar was above, fitting together the lengths of sword baldrics to give them all a way up and out. They swept aside the dust with impatient hands, explored the vehicles, forcing open long closed spaces that might have been intended to hold cargo or passengers or both. The designs were alien to what their off-world memories could recall, and only dire need kept them at their search, since the revulsion operated here also.

But in the end Drangar had a selection of tools, oddly shaped, perhaps intended for work far different from the use they would be put to now, but better than those they had brought with them.

"These—but—" He glanced at Jarvas. "We could do better with one of the blasters the suits carry."

"Yes, if we can find them. Start with these. We shall do what we can."

At least the space suits and Illylle lay in the same direction, Ayyar thought. They would not put him off again!

Rizak, Jarvas, Kelemark, Lokatath, himself—five to face whatever concentration of power there might be in the burrows. Ayyar did not wait to watch the others take the back trail. He was already at the doorway into the place where Iftin and Larsh faced one another for endless time. Between those lines he sped. There was still the false wood and its pitfalls waiting.

He did not linger, if the others did, to look upon those

figures. Now he was in the narrow way down which he had fallen on his race to the false tree, hoping he could find again the spot where he had made that unplanned descent.

Lokatath caught up with him as he was forced to cut his pace to search the other rim for some landmark.

"Where now?"

"Up there. But I do not know just where—"

The other was looking back at the rise of the tree.

"That—that is one of the Crowns—" There was an odd note in his voice. Ayyar glanced from the ridge top to his companion.

Lokatath stood staring at the tree, a kind of hunger, even a shadow of rapture on his face. He began to walk back and down the cut toward it. Ayyar caught his arm and held him so as the other three joined them.

"Do not look at it," he ordered. "It is a lure to pull you!"

Involuntarily the others looked up. But Jarvas instantly turned his face away. Like Ayyar with Lokatath, he caught at Kelemark and Rizak.

"He is right. That is a deadly thing for us! Turn!" He pulled and shoved them along. "Do not look at it!"

Yet the temptation worked in them all and had to be fought. Ayyar no longer tried to locate the right place on the opposite earth wall. He merely wanted to get up, anywhere.

Again they stood one upon the shoulders of another and so reached the top. Each aiding the other—so they came into the wood. And there might be other pitfalls than those Ayyar had already encountered.

Single file they worked their way under the canopy of green that was false in its welcome, where they must look

218

upon all as suspect. Following Ayyar's example, when they reached the real trees, they climbed aloft, using every patch of shadow as cover in reaching the distant wall and the entrance to the burrows.

XVII

THERE WAS a difference in the wood. Those sounds that had lulled Ayyar's suspicions were now stilled. The Iftin moved in silence, save for the noise made by their passing. Yet it was not a waiting silence, as if a trap beckoned them. Rather it was as if that which had animated this place had been turned off or withdrawn. And Ayyar commented on that to the others.

Jarvas steadied himself on a wide branch before making another leap. "Withdrawn?" he repeated thoughtfully. "As if, perhaps, there were a need for concentration elsewhere. But where?"

"At the door Drangar seeks to force?" suggested Lokatath.

"Perhaps. Yet I am not sure. THAT makes a bid for power, all power now. IT is sending ITS servants out, rather than massing them here for defense."

"All the more reason for us to hurry." Ayyar led the way up the slope. Already they were skirting the place where the poison vines hung heavy in the trees. He found himself listening, watching, for the false Vallylle. But if she still walked this evil wood, she did not seek their company. And, somewhat to his surprise, they reached the wall below the burrow mouth with no challenge from any creature of the Enemy. The passage down the cliff was still missing. But they did not hesitate to hack at the trees, trimming their spoil to make a crude ladder.

As they entered the burrow above, they hesitated, nostrils wide, eyes alert. Disgusting odors in plenty, or so they seemed to Ift, came out of the corridor. It was hard to identify any one smell. Jarvas spoke:

"Machines—"

"Chemicals," added Kelemark, sniffing.

"No, false Iftin, I think," Lokatath began.

Rizak put his hand palm flat against the wall of the passage.

"Power flows here. This place is alive with energy."

Jarvas followed his example, then snatched back his hand as if the vibrations were a searing burn for his flesh.

"The crystal panels," Ayyar warned. "I think they are alarms; we must avoid them."

As far as he could see the passage ahead by the wan light, it was empty. He slipped past Jarvas to lead again, dropping to his knees to pass the first pair of crystals.

"This is the room where they store the bodies," he said a little later, pausing by that door. Kelemark pushed past him and stood staring at the lines of containers.

"More—there are many more of them now filled," Ayyar whispered. "When I was here before, only four in this line were occupied—now all are completed!"

"Where do they make the mirrors?" demanded Jarvas.

Kelemark had gone to the nearest cylinder. He put his face very close to its surface, his hands cupped about his eyes. He shook his head. "It cannot be seen—"

"The mirrors—" pressed Jarvas.

Illylle! That sent Ayyar racing down the corridor. He had to force a curb on his reckless need to get her out of this place—if he still could.

"Let me see the place where they grow the robots!" Kelemark ordered as if he were now in command of the party. But Jarvas held up his hand:

"First the mirrors!"

Ayyar was cautious enough to halt before he passed any of the doors, listening, sniffing for trouble. So far there had been nothing, no stir of any space suit in action. Save for the feeling of life in the walls about them, the Iftin invaders might have been walking through halls as deserted as those leading from the false Great Crown.

They came into the place where he had witnessed the making of the reflections. The table there was unoccupied, nor were there now any mirrors on the wall! But there were suits—two of them.

Ayyar signaled caution. The suits were humanoid, yet not of a type he knew. One had an arm twisted and snapped off short a little below the shoulder plate. The ends of that break slagged into a blob of battered metal. The other lacked a helmet.

When neither of the metal cripples moved, Ayyar decided they were harmless. Rizak crossed warily to examine them. Once an astro-navigator on a spacer, his acquaintance with such aids to stellar voyaging was far greater than Ayyar's. But now he shook his head.

"Nothing such as these have I seen before."

Ayyar went to the table, bent his head, and sniffed long and hard. There was odor of garthman, undisguised, and of the port men. But not Ift—at least not so lately that it had not been completely overlaid with the effluvia of the others.

Yet Illylle must have been brought here. From the deserted mirror room Ayyar sped to the laboratory, where he had witnessed the growth of the false creatures. The stench was a blow in the face, but the tables here were also empty. No jelly bubbled on a mirror bed.

Kelemark sniffed deeply, in spite of the torture to his Ift senses.

"Some form of plasta flesh—proto base—" he reported.

There was that third room Ayyar remembered in which he had seen the false Ift body being fitted with wires, up corridor. There he went now, to find it empty.

"Where—?" He knew that Jarvas, the rest, could give him no better answers than his own mind could supply. Maybe—Ayyar's head swung sharply around—maybe not his mind but his nose!

There were other doors along the corridor, and from one of them—it must be from one of them—came that scent, so faint in this place of ugly odors, yet to be traced. Illylle—surely Illylle!

Sniffing, rejecting, sniffing, Ayyar prowled along. Illylle or Ift—but there were other smells, strong, piercing as a pain when he breathed them in. Garthpeople —here—here— Ayyar's head swung from side to side at two closed doors facing one another across the hall.

Illylle—Ift—to the right! His hands went to the door, strove to push it, first inward, and then to either right or left. But it was as immobile under his hands as if it had been sealed by slagging. Lokatath joined him, then the others, all with their nostrils distended as they followed that same faint scent.

"Locked," Jarvas decided.

"Wait!"

As if they could do anything else, Ayyar thought impatiently. Rizak ran back toward the chamber of the mirrors. Ayyar continued to push at that stubborn portal, but it only wore out his strength uselessly. If only that which the Mirror of Thanth had planted in him had not been exhausted. Thanth!

He stopped his vain fight with the door and glanced at Jarvas. "You are Mirrormaster. What can be summoned now from Thanth to our aid?"

Jarvas stared back, almost as if that demand had come as a shock. Then he looked thoughtfully at the door. "If you no longer hold the power, there is naught Thanth can do—"

"No?" The Mirror had sent him here filled with the substance of its force. And Illylle had given him a double portion when she had sent him to fulfill their mission. He had failed at the fused stairway. Then the power had ebbed with every step of retreat from that failure. But now, cried Ayyar silently, I have returned. I am here to do whatever is needful to free Janus from this burden long laid upon her clean earth. I have not deserted the quest or fled battle. I have returned with fresh forces!

He closed his eyes, trying to visualize the ledge above the Mirror, the great sparkling tongue rising from its surface to touch upon Illylle and then him, choosing them as fit receptacles of whatever force did enter into Janus through Thanth. He did not know that he had drawn his sword, that its point rested on the floor of the corridor

223

between his firmly planted feet, that his two hands were clapsed on its hilt.

In those moments when he had stood before the Mirror and watched it in action, he had known awe, belief in something beyond his powers to understand or explain. How much of that was inherited from the Ayyar who had been he did not know, nor even if that belief itself was so strong in him once he was removed from the Mirror where the united worship of the others had been a part of what he had seen and felt.

The Mirror, that reaching finger or tongue of sparkling water that had risen from it—Ayyar tried to will to life that tingling which had coursed through him.

He was out—no longer in his body—but in a space like unto that where he had sat across the game table from that other presence he had never seen, save that this space was not the same, nor was the presence he sensed now—in any way.

> "Green the growth, deep the seed.
> Stand high a Tree, to Iftin need.
> Sweet the wind, soft the rain—
> Rich the soil, without bane—"

Green growing about his feet, up and up, he did not have to see those plants. They were a part of him, like his blood, his flesh, and the bones beneath them were a part. As if he, too, put roots into the soil, drew life and nourishment from it? Around him blew a wind as caressing as the dawn winds of summer, and on his cheeks, his lips, was the soft, refreshing touch of gentle rain, satisfying all thirst, all hunger.

"Straight the sword, sharp the blade.
Bright the leaf that does not fade.
Still the Mirror, wide and deep,
High the Moon that doth keep
Silver caught within the Mirror.
Stand here, Ift, without fear.

He could not see Thanth with the eyes of his body. But it was there—deep, dark, yet silver where it caught and held the moon. That moon's reflection shivered and broke into a thousand silver motes, free and floating. They arose and were one with the wind, the soft rain. So were they borne to him, gathering about his body—entering—

"Iftin sword, Iftin hand,
Iftin heart, Iftin kind!
Forged in the dark,
Cooled by the moon—"

That was the Lay of Kymon, Kymon who had walked the blazing white, searing paths of the Enemy, and returned therefrom with the Oath for the safety of his people. Ayyar did not sing that, the chant came from without and beyond.

"Borne by warrior who will stand—
When tree grows and THAT will fall.
Iftin swords, Iftin hands—
Come to save and cleanse a land!"

The sparkling silver touch of Thanth was once more within him. As he had before, he felt that strange life allied

with his own, and he exalted in it. Ayyar opened his eyes
to face Jarvas. And the Ift who had once been Mirrormaster and so able to call upon the power looked back with a
depth of concentration, a willing. His lips moved as if he
would speak, but at first he did not utter a sound. Then he
said:

"Power has returned to you, brother."

"It has returned." Ayyar raised his sword with confidence and traced the outline of the door. A bright line
followed the touch of that point, easing away the substance. Ayyar put out his hand, and the door fell away,
back into the locked chamber, just as Rizak came up with a
blaster from one of the suit belts in his hand. Jarvas waved
him back, and they stepped into the room.

The occupants lay on the floor as if they had been struck
down without warning—women, children, perhaps those
Ayyar had seen enter the valley of the mounds—
garthpeople all of them, yet his nose told him that
among them was an Ift. They found her in a far corner, as
if she had been flung there in haste, some broken machine
for which THAT no longer had any use.

Jarvas gathered her up and carried her into the corridor,
held her while Ayyar took her two limp hands into his. As
she had willed her Mirror-born strength into him, so did he
now return that with which he had been newly filled to her.
And he heard them chanting softly:

"First the seed, then the seedling.
From the rooting to the growing.
Sap of trunk, stir of leaf,
Ift to Tree, Tree to Ift!"

226

Kelemark held a flask to her lips, dripping sap drops between them. Then Illylle opened her eyes and looked at them, at first in an unfocused stare, as if she still saw, not them and the burrows, but another place in which she had been long lost and wandering.

"Illylle!" Ayyar called gently, but yet as one arousing a comrade at the first alarm of battle.

Now she saw him, knew him, moved in Jarvas' hold. And her eyes were anxious.

"Do you not feel it?" Her voice was strained and hoarse. "THAT knows!"

They glanced about them as if they were suddenly beleaguered by Enemy forces, for she was right. That silence, that lack of watchfulness, that emptiness through which they had come had vanished. They were now discovered.

"Come." Jarvas, his arm about Illylle in support, led them past all the other chambers. Ayyar saw Rizak and Lokatath drop behind, dart into the doors they passed. When they returned, they bore not only the blaster Rizak had already found, but also two more strange weapons, but clearly designed as arms.

All that time they listened for what might march upon them, watched for any sign of movement ahead or behind. But they reached the false wood aware only that THAT was conscious of them in the midst of ITS own place. Ayyar wondered uneasily why the ruler of these burrows held off from attack, why IT had not overwhelmed and crushed them as IT might have so easily done, for, Mirror power or not, they could not stand up to the off-world weapons in ITS arsenal.

There was a change in the place of the wood. That unaltering moon that had been such a relief to Ayyar's eyes on his first journey across that sinister jungle was gone. The dark was that of a stormy night. But in the dusk his bared sword gave forth a steady glow, and as they descended into the wood, the growth drew back and away from the brand, which it had not done before.

Illylle put forth her left hand and laid it on Ayyar's shoulder, saying:

"Link, brothers, link. I do not know why it may be, but in this hour that which speaks through the Mirror rises in all of us. Perhaps it may in turn draw upon the very forces here to feed. Link, one to the other, so that it may flow equally through us all!"

Her touch drew nothing out of Ayyar as he had thought that it might. Rather did there follow a new warmth and confidence. They did not take to the trees but went steadily ahead by the shortest path to that tree which aped the Great Ones with such evil travesty.

Things fled from their path or perhaps from the light of the brand, and once they heard a moaning call, like unto an Iftin voice, but with no words they could understand. Then did Illylle turn her head to that portion of the underbrush whence came the sound. And she chanted what could be an answer, a counterspell, or a warning. The words were not of the common speech, and Ayyar knew that they came to her out of the far past when Illylle had been a Sower of the Seed, thus one who dealt with the beginning of life and not its ending, while this place in which they walked negated life with counterfeit shadow and so was to be faced only by the real.

They continued without hindrance, though a part of

Ayyar's mind continued to wander and be alert for any sign of trouble, to the tree and into that place where stood the lines of Iftin and Larsh, frozen so for eternity.

As they passed between, Illylle and Jarvas, inspired by something Ayyar did not share, out of the old mysteries of which they had once been a part, turned their heads to certain of the Iftin and greeted them by name in such tones that Ayyar half expected those statues (if statues they were in truth) to step from that company and join theirs.

Next they went through the place of machines and down into the corridor that brought them to the vast room of mirrors. There for the first time Illylle faltered. She dropped her hold upon Ayyar and Jarvis, breaking their linkage, holding up her hands before her eyes as if she dared not look upon the racks, crying out:

"These are the children of THAT! Let them be shattered, and it will come to an end!"

Then, once more, her trembling hands came out to Jarvas and Ayyar, but she would not look upon the mirrors, shutting her eyes tightly, letting them guide her. And she did not cease trembling until they were out of the chamber.

For the first time they heard sounds—from behind and also ahead. They began to run to the place where they had left Drangar and Myrik. What came from there, Ayyar was sure, was the sound of battle. Of a sudden his sword blazed, yet the brightness did not hurt his eyes.

A tangle of wiring twisted and broken had been dragged from the service door into the corridor. And in the midst of that lay Drangar, dead, while, flattened to the floor, among the coils, was Myrik, pinned by beams that laced back and forth. As one, the others threw themselves down behind that tangle that was so poor a shield. Rizak and Jarvas had blasters and began a counter sweep.

Myrik raised his head. "The door—if we can get through—"

They had done well with the tools from the storage place. Ripped out were all the cables and fittings that had once filled the shaft. Ayyar hesitated to descend without knowing what might wait below—yet to remain here, pinned by those ahead, hunted by what moved from behind—

"I go!" Lokatath crawled to the opening, entered feet first, then sank from sight, but slowly, as if there was something in the way of hand and footholds within.

"You—" Ayyar pushed Illylle to that only promise of safety.

She did not protest, but went. And after her, Myrik, and Kelemark followed. Jarvas spoke to Ayyar—

"You!"

He and Rizak still replied to the beams of destruction with the counter rays from their weapons. And now there were lulls in that exchange of fire.

Sheathing his sword, Ayyar wriggled through the opening. The shaft was not as confining as he had expected, and torn-off projections of metal and wire gave him foot and hand supports. Then his feet touched more wires, and he had to work a passage through this obstruction, crawling on hands and knees into a corridor twin to that above. Those who had preceded him were alert and waiting. That force which enlivened the walls of the other portions of the burrows was here much greater. The whole of the space around them throbbed with it. When Ayyar ventured to touch the wall, energy ran painfully up his arm, so that he cried out. Instinctively his other hand had gone to his sword hilt. Now the scabbard that held the blade smoked until he snatched it forth from that covering.

The length of well-forged metal was blue and green, then both colors together, rippling, dripping sparks that vanished as they hit the floor. Ayyar was no longer sure that it was fed by the energy stored in his body or whether it now fed him. But he was not its master. No, now it was the wielder and he the weapon. Under the compulsion it wrought, he turned away from the rest of them and marched back down the corridor.

He expected to confront danger. He was not surprised nor, oddly enough, alarmed when things moved out of the gloom to intercept him. They came with a steady purpose to match his. And, without his willing it, his sword raised waist high, point outward. The force in it grew so strong that it jerked and quivered, so that the only way Ayyar could continue to hold it was to turn that movement into a swing, right and left.

They were armed, those thundering, stalking machines. There were rays that bit into the walls where they chanced to touch; there were other energies. But that waving, dancing sword set up a barrier of its own force to stop, to suck, to feed—for feed it did, and the backlash of that feeding was in Ayyar. Once he had been man, then Ift; now, thought a small part of him, he was a vessel of energy, alien to the place in which he walked in that he could draw upon the Enemy's strength to give fuel to his own.

The machines continued to attack until the light from

the sword touched them. There were blazes of shorting wires, the acrid smell of destruction. He pushed past them, stepped over them, to advance.

How many did he meet in that corridor? Ayyar did not count; there was no need. In him was only the compulsion to move ahead, seek that will which lay behind the machines, behind this plague spot that sickened Janus.

The passage ended, and he stood in a great chamber, near its roof, he thought, with dark below. He was on a platform from which descended a curling stairway. Down that the sword pointed, and he must go. This whole place was charged with force, and Ayyar wondered dimly if he would end as Man or Ift, burned out by the weapon he bore, which yet had not been used as it must be. Round and round the steps he went, down and down. Now his eyes were no longer dazzled by the raying, and he could see what lay below, built up against the walls, clicking, flickering with small lights, filling all the vast place with a moaning hum. Sections of it were dark, dead, perhaps long dead. But others were very much alive, with something inimical to all living flesh and blood. Naill-memory supplied an answer, for Ayyar-memory had never seen machines mankind had built to supplement brain power. He was descending into the heart of the largest computer he had ever seen or dreamed might exist.

XVIII

"COMPUTER!" Myrik's voice rose above the hum that filled the place as the murmur of wind in leaves filled the Forest.

Ayyar faced the great banks of flashing lights. The sword and the power had led him here. But what weapon was it against this, no thing which could be put to rout by any attack that he knew. Unless—who had set this giant brain to running? He was the Enemy!

He began to run along the towering wall of machine, came to a corner to front another section at right angles, turned along that to face another, and eventually returned about the square to join the others by the stairway. There was no other exit from this chamber, nothing here but the machine—part of it running, part dark and dead. Baffled, Ayyar came to a halt, still unable to believe there was no Enemy to front.

"Computer"—Jarvis studied the walls—"and programmed."

Myrik walked, not ran, along the same path Ayyar had taken, surveying closely each bank as he passed it.

"It is a computer, yes. But of no type I have ever seen—and it has been programmed, is in operation, part of it. Also, I think that it has once before been interrupted in the task set it. Come here—"

He motioned and they followed, almost timidly, to one of the dark sections. There he pointed to lines burned into the fabric of the machine. There was fusing, signs that repairs had been made—perhaps more successfully—in a neighboring section now working.

"Those machines Ayyar knocked out in the passages," Myrik said, "were servos—for computer repairs. I would say they have been on duty here perhaps longer than we can guess."

"Kymon!" Illylle's voice shrilled. "Kymon was here! But a machine—why—?"

"It was intended"—Jarvas moved out into the open area in the center—"for some great and important task. And it is not Iftin. Once it was half destroyed; now it is partially at work again. And we have seen the results of that work. It was set a task, which it strives to carry out—"

"But who set it?" queried Illylle. "Who or what is THAT?"

Rizak had gone to the nearest wall and was watching the lights in motion there. "I think," he said slowly, "that this is what we seek."

"This is what I was sent to find!" Ayyar broke in, as sure of that now as if someone had spoken in his ear.

"I do not think it was ever programmed on Janus at all!" Jarvas added. "It is not Iftin in any part. And we cannot but believe that Ifts are truly native to this world; they are so one with its nature. Therefore, this is alien—"

Rizak laughed a little wildly. "Did it ever occur to you, brothers, that what we stand in now might be a part of a ship—a long planeted ship?"

"Ship?" echoed Kelemark. "This—this *big*? What kind of ship could be so large?"

It was Lokatath, perhaps because he had once been a garthman, who ventured to answer that.

"A colony ship?"

Jarvas turned sharply, but Rizak spoke first:

"Could just be! A ship, with a computer programmed for colonization duties, perhaps never meant for Janus at all, making a crack-up landing here. Then the computer taking up its duties—not properly, under the circumstances."

Jarvas caught him up, speaking out of the knowledge of Pate Sissions, First-in Scout, one who had been the forerunner of such flights for those of his own species.

"Trying to alter the country to fit the needs of alien colonists. Ready to put down whatever would be inimical to settlement—"

"Such as the Iftin!" broke in Lokatath.

"And Kymon," Illylle added quickly, "coming here, armed with power, perhaps doing this—" She pointed to the bands of ancient destruction. "Then it was repaired after a long time. But why would it come to life again now?"

"Perhaps it had been alive all the time," Ayyar said, "but crippled, and it did not sense an enemy until the Ift changelings went abroad in the land. Why did it not rouse the colonists—or were they all killed in the crash?"

"The mirrors!" Illylle's eyes widened. "The colonists are the people on the mirrors."

"A reasonable assumption," Kelemark agreed. "And now it will be my turn to guess. You were right, Jarvas, when you claimed there was much to be read in those companies at the foot of the false tree. I do not know why the Iftin were set up there—but the Larsh—they were not the beginning but the end!"

It would seem that Jarvas understood, for the one-time

Scout nodded. "De-evolution, not evolution. The computer aroused some of the passengers, found that there was that on Janus it could not change, could not alter. Though I imagine that all the resources left it have been turned to that task ever since—"

"What are you talking about?" Lokatath demanded.

"The ones it aroused did not remain the same," Jarvas explained. "They must have slipped back, generation by generation, from men—or what we may term 'men'—into the less-than-men we remember as the Larsh. And finally the Larsh were thrown against us to free Janus from any interference while this machine labored to fashion a new world, one that would safely accommodate its burden. But it was crippled—perhaps actually by Kymon of the legend."

He looked at the ancient sear marks. "We may never know whether those represent the coming of our folk hero or not. But the destruction was certainly deliberate, and it must have taken a long time to repair, even in part."

"But it failed—that destruction—" Myrik mused.

"Because," Rizak broke in, "it was wrought by an Ift, not one who knew the real meaning of this. He may have sprayed some energy back and forth, wrecking widely, but not to the roots—the heart of the machine."

"But the Oath, what then was the Oath?" asked Illylle.

Jarvas shrugged. "What history does not take on embroidery when it becomes heroic legend? I do not think that Kymon, the Ift, could explain, even to himself, what he found here—if this *is* where he fronted THAT in all ITS might. Now we must have an answer to something else—what do we do? Myrik, Rizak, what do we do?"

"We can cripple it as was done before. But again that

might prove to be but temporary, if you reckon centuries as temporary. If this was programmed to do what we guess it was, then it has also been provided with safeguards and repairs. And we do not know what lies in all these burrows. No, we have to find the heart control, wherever that lies, and burn it out for all time!"

"Jarvas." Illylle took a step forward and laid her hand on his arm. "What of those it controls, made into mirror patterns and then robots? Can they be restored—saved?"

He did not meet her eyes. "Perhaps no, perhaps yes. But for that we must have both time and knowledge. And with this running, ruling the burrows and the Waste, able to muster an army against us—time we do not have. The machine first—"

They were all agreed upon that. Ayyar lifted the sword. Should he use the energy in that weapon to blast the banks around him? He had taken a step toward the nearest when Rizak thrust out an arm as a barrier before him.

"Not there!" He looked not at Ayyar but at the banks of lighted, clicking relays on the nearest wall.

"Where then?" Ayyar demanded. All he knew of computers was their servicing, not their innermost workings.

"We do not know," Myrik returned. "This thing runs the burrows—it controls ventilation, everything else. Smash it and it could close doors, stop air, bury us—and still we might not finish it off. We cannot move until we are more sure—"

"Look!" Illylle called sharply. She pointed to one of the banks they had thought dead, as it had been dark since they had entered.

Now a zigzag of lights streaked down it, to be as quickly gone. A second pattern flickered into life and vanished

237

while they watched it. So small a thing, sparks of light coming and going swiftly. Yet somehow it was ominous, an alert they did not understand.

"Back—" Jarvas' voice was a whisper, as if he feared words could be picked up, read, understood by the machine that boxed them in. And Ayyar shared that feeling for the moment. An enemy one might see, that came openly, a kalcrok, one of the false Ift or an animated space suit, could be faced with firmness of purpose. But lights on a computer board, meant to awaken some menace, they were certain—that was another matter.

Three times those lights drew a design on the board, and each time the sequence was different, as was the color. For the first time they had been a light blue, the second a darker hue, and the third time purple. Ayyar knew that the others were as tense, using all their senses for any intimation of present danger.

"Myrik—where do you place the master controls?" Jarvas whispered.

"They can be anyplace. I am not expert on alien computers."

"Ayyar, do you feel any pull from a source of power?" The Mirrormaster rounded on him.

He raised the sword and pointed it to the board that had just come to life. He could feel his own form of force surge through his body, as if it fretted at the bonds of flesh now containing it—would be free to meet, in some flare of incandescence, that other and alien power.

Closing his eyes, he tried to measure that ebb and flow of energy, turning slowly, blindly, using the sword as a pointer to hunt out the center of THAT. There was a slight change as he turned to the right, so slight that he could not actually be sure he had felt anything. He took another fraction of a turn, *was* aware of a difference, for now he was rent by a rising storm. He might have cried out; he was not sure, but still he turned. Ebb, to be followed again by flow, now ebb—complete quiet. Ayyar opened his eyes. Now he faced a dead portion of the banks, crisscrossed by the old scars, with no signs of repair.

Eyes closed once more—why that was needful he did not know—but self-blinded he was more inwardly aware of that other force. Turn—flow—to a lesser degree, turn, ebb, flow, sharp and strong, lessening—dead. Then, following so quickly on the dead that he swayed and nearly fell, strong, very strong, flow, flow, ebb, flow—

Yes, by so much could he chart the life of the banks, but that also the others could see and hear for themselves. He was about to say this when Illylle spoke.

"Try underfoot."

Why she suggested that Ayyar did not know. He took a step or so along, and the sword dipped in his hold, its tip not now pointing to the banks but to the floor. Again he made that slow swing to face each wall. Ebb and flow again, as above—

Then he was being pulled forward as if the sword were a rope, the end drawn by a port machine. This time Ayyar could not save himself against the urgency but went to his knees, and as the sword point dug into the flooring, Ayyar opened his eyes. He was at the foot of the ladder down which they had come. And from his sword point sparks arose higher and higher, while under the tip the floor began to glow red. He dared not watch; the glow hurt his lft eyes. The sword sank, as if the floor were soft sand, to engulf the blade and finally the arm of its bearer.

"Move it to cut!" Jarvas knelt beyond that fire of sparks. He put out a hand as if to lay it on the sword hilt, then flinched back.

Only half understanding, Ayyar tried to move the blade. It yielded a little so he was cutting through the substance of the floor, or was that merely melting away from any contact with the blade? Wider grew the hole. He thrust right, left, forward, back, enlarging it yet more. Now he must jerk back himself to escape a puff of heat coming from the red and glowing edges of that opening.

Out of him flowed the energy that had been pent in his body. He could almost watch it going into the sword, helping to open this door. Now the opening was large enough for a man, and the smell of molten metal a fog.

"On the stairs—watch out!" He did not know which of them shouted that warning. A ray beam cut down, struck across the edge of the hole, touched the sparks of the sword force, flashed up in a great burst of light.

Ayyar cried out, blinded. He could not drop the sword that moved, pulling him after it. Heat seared his body, pain such as he had not known could exist— He fell, blind, the sword a great weight he could not master or loose. He struck something below, close below, and lay there writhing in pain. Still the sword was heavy, inert; he could not even stir the hand that held it. And again energy flowed out of him. He could smell burning—acrid —choking—

He sat by the game board, and on that board shone brightly all those curious lines, squares, and dots he could not read. THAT, which had been his opponent there, which he had never seen, only sensed—yes, IT was there, but IT no longer heeded him. IT had—not retreated, no—IT had closed into ITSELF. When he looked down upon the board, all those figures—the space suits, the Larsh, the others—were overturned, rolling. Now and then one rose, only to topple.

On his side, though the trees—the thin line of Iftin —trembled and shook, they did not fall or roll.

And THAT which had played the unknown game so confidently—IT drew farther and farther in upon ITSELF. Yet IT was still to be feared, for now IT was mad—mad!

Arms about him, holding him—the board vanished. He must say it aloud—

"IT—is—mad—"

They were pulling at him, racking his body with pain. He could not see—

"Let—me—" But they did not listen to his pleas, and he was an empty thing, hollow of all the energy he had held, so that he could not beg or fight those hands.

"To the air—can you bring him? Look out! Blast that one—now move!"

Words without meaning uttered in high voices. Words did not matter—nothing mattered. He was lost and empty and knew only pain that was sometimes sharp, sometimes dull, but always a part of him. After a space it was in his chest, so he choked and coughed and choked again. And this added to the pain. He longed for the dark to shut it out.

"Look—IT has gone crazy— Oh—" Shrill that voice, so shrill and high as to pierce his dark. "The trees —Rizak, look out for the trees!"

Ayyar could breathe better now. There was a difference in the air. Hands still on him, holding him tight. Liquid dripped into his mouth, cool on his lips and chin as it dribbled out again. He swallowed. It was cool inside him, too.

Coolness on his eyes, soothing their burning. He drew a breath that was a little broken sigh, relaxed.

Around him was a sickening lurch of earth, a grinding—then a shrill screaming from farther off. He could not move, though in him worked a ferment to be up and running, away from this mad place. The arms that held him tightened, bringing stabbing pain to his chest and shoulder. Ayyar tried to cry out, but any sound he might make was lost in the surrounding tumult. Again the earth heaved, there were crashes—

He blinked, trying to clear his dim sight. Shadows moved against a lighter surface. Something large and black flew past—he heard another cracking—splintering—

"Out! Out of this trap!" That came at his ear. He was raised and carried between two others, his feet helplessly bumping against the ground.

They paused, holding him upright. The ground no longer swung sickeningly underfoot, yet still he waited for that to happen again. They were fumbling about his body, pulling a band tight under his arms. He was hauled aloft, the pressure of that band causing such agony that once more he plunged into a blackness of nothing at all save the blessed ceasing of torment.

"Ayyar—Ayyar—"

He lay in the hold of a ship, frozen, dead. He was Naill Renfro who had sold himself into labor on a distant world. But he had awakened before his time, and now he was dying deep in the emigrant capsule, his lungs denied air, his flesh freezing in the cold of space. He strove to fling out his hands, his arms, break open that coffin for a few moments of life—of—

Dark—but no longer cold. There was moisture in his mouth, soothing, more on his eyes, his face. They had heard him in the ship and had come to save him. Not death between the stars—but life!

He opened his eyes as that cooling substance was withdrawn. He could see—mistily—but still he could see!

No ship's officer, no medico bent over him. An oval face, green of skin, large eyes set slantingly in it. A delicate face, in its way fair. No eyebrows, no lashes, no hair above the wide brow—

"Ayyar—" Those lips shaped a word.

Ayyar? Greeting, inquiry, name? He wanted to ask which, but he could not find the energy to speak.

Another figure behind the one bending over him rose out of the ground. Like unto the first—still different—

"How is he?"

"Awake, I think—" Doubt from that first one, the nearest.

"Ayyar?" The newcomer dropped beside him, a green hand passed before his eyes, and he watched it move.

"He sees!" There was satisfaction in that as the tester straightened. "Ayyar?" More demanding now.

Ayyar? Who, what, was Ayyar? Ayyar of Iftcan! Triumphantly his memory supplied so much. He—was—Ayyar! He was pleased, excited at that discovery.

"He knows—he is Ayyar once again!" The first of the green people—Green People? Iftin! Again his mind sluggishly supplied a name and knew it to be the proper one.

"Ayyar, we must go!"

The taller of the two drew him up and let him lean against his shoulder to look out dizzily on what lay below. The ground swung wildly and then steadied. Red and black, churned earth, stirred together as one might mix the ground if one were a giant and set to work with a paddle or a sword of force—

Sword? His hand went out—seeking. "Sword?" He was not sure he asked that aloud, but perhaps he did, for she who faced him, concern in her eyes, made answer swiftly:

"It is gone—when it met THAT. Kymon's blade did not do as well in its time as that which Ayyar bore—"

"Later will come the weaving of legends," he who supported Ayyar said. "Now let us go, if still we can."

Another man came to aid him who held Ayyar. He looked from one to the other. Memory again gave Ayyar names.

"Jarvas—Kelemark—"

They smiled at him eagerly, as if that naming gave them pleasure. But the smiles did not last, for they must go down into the torn land and make their way through it.

Ayyar thought he dreamed sometimes as they made their slow and painful journey, for it seemed to him that once they hid in a cut in the ground as a hurtling thing, squeaking and groaning, rocketed by. And again they crouched among rocks as green people, like unto the Iftin, yet very different inwardly, struggled blindly, seizing upon one another with fierce tearing, or rushed headlong into rocks, making a wild, mad battlefield of a place where light hurt his eyes so he must close them tight. But none of this was real, nor did he fear what he saw.

The world began with a green covering. Thin was that

covering, a small lacing of budding leaves along stem and branch, and through that delicate pattern came the silver of the moon to rest on his face. He breathed in subtle scents, and in him Ayyar awakened fully, so that though his body did not have the strength when he strove to move, yet his mind was clear, and he could recall the past—some of it.

His struggle to sit up must have summoned her, for Illylle came to him and knelt, carrying in her hand a wooden bottle. She gave him to drink, holding it quickly to his lips a second time when he would have asked questions. Once more the sap revived, and he let it do its work, coursing through his body. Then he braced himself up with his hands. They were in a glade of a forest or wood, and spring was there. Was this a dream—?

"Where are we?" he asked, for somehow it was important to be sure they were free of the burrows.

Illylle sat back upon her heels, smiling at him, one hand tamping the stopper well into the bottle.

"In the wilderness to the north."

"Iftcan!"

"No. Iftcan is not and will not be again." There was a shadow on her face. "It cannot be again, for a new rooting is needed, not a graft upon the old—"

Ayyar did not try to puzzle out her answer. For the time he was content they were in the woods again, Iftcan or no. But that content did not hold long. When the others came through the aisles of budding trees, he wanted to know more.

"We have won the victory against THAT," Jarvas said. "Or rather the power granted by Thanth won it, for your sword—with its energy—ate to the center of the computer, burned it out. But THAT went mad when the controls were cut. And we do not yet know what remains. The false Iftin, the machines IT took as servants—they, too, went mad and destroyed themselves. How it fares with those it captured, we do not yet know. A party has gone to the port. If they find the false off-worlders there and also uncontrollable, they will do what they can to take over. What has happened, how far the curse set upon Janus has passed—'' He shook his head.

''This much is true. We have finished THAT for all time, for with ITS heart burnt out IT can never rebuild ITSELF again. The chaos IT has left is wide wreckage. If we cannot free those IT captured, and we may not be able to do so, then we have a second plan. We shall leave a tape at the port stating all that has happened and also beam an off-world distress signal. Our own secret, that we are changelings—we shall keep yet awhile. But we can treat with any who come as natives of Janus. Only, until such arrive, we shall retreat overseas—if nothing can be done for the prisoners.''

He looked beyond Ayyar as if he sought something, to find it missing, and regretted that, but was willing to put aside his regret.

''Iftcan is gone, not to rise again. We do not know how much of Iftin past lies in the wreckage of the Waste and THAT'S domain. Perhaps with off-world aid we can learn. We shall raise a new nation, and one that will not have the canker of THAT eating at it. But for one day, one task. Seeding, growing cannot be hurried—to try that is to fail.''

He fell silent, and Ayyar, who must forget that he was never Naill, lifted his head to the night wind. It was cool, sweet with all the promise of spring. They rested in the wreckage of a world, yet around them grew strong new life to which they were akin. And in him, just as that energy from the Mirror had risen, so did another renewing begin. Iftcan was dead to them, yes. But the Great Crowns would rise again, and there would be songs sung there of the remembrance of this time down a long, long trail of years, though legend might twist and turn the tale so that false would in time bury true.

> "Iftin sword, Iftin hand,
> Iftin heart, Iftin kind.
> Forged in the dark,
> Cooled by the moon,
> Bane of evil, final doom.
> Borne by a warrior who will stand
> Before the Enemy, blade in hand—"

Illylle was singing, gaily, almost tenderly, as if her thoughts marched side by side, sword comrade with his. Ayyar shook his head.

"I am not Kymon, and I was not alone. No hero song for me."

Jarvas laughed. "Leave judgment to the future. Now, shall we be about the needs of the present?"

He held out his hand, Ayyar grasped it, and the Mirrormaster's strength drew him to his feet. His other hand went out to Illylle. And they went from that glade singing the song of Kymon, as was fitting on a day of such victory.

247

ABOUT THE AUTHOR

Andre Norton, born Alice Mary Norton, has long been regarded as one of the best writers of science fiction and fantasy. She was born in Cleveland, Ohio, and began her literary career as editor of her high school paper. Before the age of twenty-one she had published her first book.

After attending Case Western Reserve University, she became a member of the staff of the Cleveland Public Library in the Children's Department. Failing health caused her resignation and she then became a full-time writer.

In 1979 she was awarded the BALROG for professional writers in the fantasy field. She has also been awarded the Phoenix, the Invisible Little Man award, and a plaque from the Netherlands government for her past work.

GREAT ROMANTIC NOVELS

SISTERS AND STRANGERS   PB 04445 $2.50
by Helen Van Slyke

    Three women—three sisters each grown into an independent lifestyle—now are three strangers who reunite to find that their intimate feelings and perilous fates are entwined.

THE SUMMER OF THE SPANISH WOMAN
CB 23809 $2.50

by Catherine Gaskin

    A young, fervent Irish beauty is alone. The only man she ever loved is lost as is the ancient family estate. She flees to Spain. There she unexpectedly discovers the simmering secrets of her wretched past . . . meets the Spanish Woman . . . and plots revenge.

THE CURSE OF THE KINGS   CB 23284 $1.95
by Victoria Holt

    This is Victoria Holt's most exotic novel! It is a story of romance when Judith marries Tybalt, the young archeologist, and they set out to explore the Pharaohs' tombs on their honeymoon. But the tombs are cursed . . . two archeologists have already died mysteriously.

8000

MASTER NOVELISTS

CHESAPEAKE CB 24163 $3.95
by James A. Michener

An enthralling historical saga. It gives the account of different generations and races of American families who struggled, invented, endured and triumphed on Maryland's Chesapeake Bay. It is the first work of fiction in ten years to be first on *The New York Times Best Seller List*.

THE BEST PLACE TO BE PB 04024 $2.50
by Helen Van Slyke

Sheila Callaghan's husband suddenly died, her children are grown, independent and troubled, the men she meets expect an easy kind of woman. Is there a place of comfort? a place for strength against an aching void? A novel for every woman who has ever loved.

ONE FEARFUL YELLOW EYE GB 14146 $1.95
by John D. MacDonald

Dr. Fortner Geis relinquishes $600,000 to someone that no one knows. Who knows his reasons? There is a history of threats which Travis McGee exposes. But why does the full explanation live behind the eerie yellow eye of a mutilated corpse?

8002